Blackthorn Grove

A Katie Bishop Novel

LUANNE BENNETT

For all the fabulous witches in my life.

RITA CAVANAGH, SATURDAY NIGHT

"Who wants another drink?" Rita Cavanagh raised her glass and smiled at her dinner guests seated around the long table. Prime rib, king salmon, three types of vegetables. There was enough food on the table to stock the local food bank for a week.

The party was coming along nicely. She'd invited just the right names that would practically guarantee a mention in Savannah's social circles, something her husband had encouraged despite her aversion to most of the people sitting at the table.

Bob O'Neil raised his own glass, taking her up on the offer. "I'll take a refill. I can use all the fortification I can get, sitting around a table with all you yappy women." Everyone laughed, the women with a smidge of *screw you, Bob,* in the backs of their minds, not one of them giving a shit about a man who sold used tractors for a living. There was nothing wrong with used tractors, but why waste time on a buffoon like Bob O'Neil when Harry Cavanagh was sitting at the table.

Harry, their co-host for the evening, was the CEO of Cavanagh Holdings, a property development company that had its name stamped on a number of high-profile projects in town.

Being an attractive man of wealth with a boatload of charm, there was bound to be competition. Not a woman in the room—married or otherwise—didn't have her eye on him. But the poachers at the table didn't bother Rita in the slightest. It was all just a game of masks and discretion, and she didn't care who he screwed as long as that blind eye went both ways.

"Bourbon? Or would you prefer wine?" she asked, reaching for his glass.

"Wine is for women," he replied with a cocky scoff. "I'll take a little more of that Jim Beam Black, if you wouldn't mind."

"I don't mind at all." She turned and headed for the bar, muttering under her breath, "You fat fuck."

She refilled the glass and walked back to the table to deliver his drink. After sitting back down, her eyes wandered past the faces as they shoveled food in their mouths and drank her expensive wine. She'd coordinated the party to include just the right mix of men and women to keep the conversation light and airy, with no offensive talk of politics or business. Just a good old Southern evening of folks trying to one-up one another and ride the coattails of the person sitting next to them, straight into Savannah society.

Out of the blue, Rita stood up with dramatic flair, a sly grin forming on one side of her perfectly painted mouth. She clanked her fork against her wine glass three times. "Okay, folks, it's showtime."

Everyone's eyes darted around the table, looking to see if they were the only one in the dark about what their host had in store for the evening. Rita took a long soothing breath through her nose, and with a mischievous smile she excused herself and stepped away from the table. Heading for the kitchen, her grin never broke.

"I guess we're in for some entertainment tonight," Harriet Davis said. "Anyone else as ignorant as I am?"

A moment later, Rita returned with her hands behind her back, that strange smile falling into a twisted grin as she brought her right hand back around to the front with a gun pointed at the table. The sound of the shot crippled their ears as it rang through the room. The bullet hit Harry Cavanagh in the center of his forehead, leaving a perfect little hole that immediately began to ooze a thick line of blood down the bridge of his nose.

The chatter in the room went eerily silent. A second later, a single high-pitched scream came out of Susan Morrison's mouth as Rita Cavanagh took her seat and reached for the bread basket in the center of the table.

"Who wants a roll?"

"ABEL, PLEASE DON'T ENCOURAGE HIM." I rolled my eyes at Tom Billford who was following me around the shop like a puppy.

"Come on, Katie. Just have one drink with me," he pleaded.

Mouse snorted as she worked on her client's skin, drawing the outline of a tarantula over his forearm. "Can't wait to see Jackson tear you a new one, Tom."

He scoffed. "I don't see no ring on her finger."

"Let me make this perfectly clear," I said, turning to look him in the eye when I delivered my firm rejection. "I don't want to hurt your feelings, Tom, but you're pushing my patience."

"As long as I'm pushing something." His cocky grin grew wider.

"I. Have. A. *Boyfriend.*"

Right on cue, Jackson walked through the door to join me for lunch. He took one look at Tom, and I knew what was going through his mind. He'd gotten used to that look on men's faces when they were after me. But jealousy wasn't something he both-

3

ered himself with, because he was smart enough to know it was a useless emotion, which was one of the reasons I was so crazy about him. Confidence was just plain sexy.

He gave Tom a look. Nothing malicious, just a look. Tom shrank back a bit. Jackson had a good seven or eight inches on him and tended to intimidate people with his long black hair and that perpetual brooding look in his eyes. And if he knew what Jackson was capable of doing to him—aside from the obvious—he would have been out the front door already.

Jackson grabbed a magazine off the chair before sitting down to wait for me. In the six weeks we'd been seeing each other, we'd had breakfast just about every morning but limited our lunch dates to twice during the week. I needed a little bit of space, and so did he. Not wanting to end up like those couples who lost their individual identities, we made a real effort to maintain some semblance of separate lives.

Sea Bass came through the back door carrying a bag of food from the Mexican place a few blocks down. He set it on the counter near the coffee machine and pulled out a burrito, biting off a third of it as his eyes caught sight of Jackson reading on the other side of the room. "Well, if it ain't the worse half of Jatie," he said around a mouthful of food, concatenating our names in a way that made my skin crawl.

With a pair of sharp scissors in my hand, I glared at him. "I will cut you if you call us that again." He swallowed his food and held his free hand up in surrender. Jackson had his face buried in the magazine when I glanced over at him, trying very hard to suppress the grin edging up his face. He didn't have as much of a need for independence as I did. In fact, I had a feeling he'd be just fine with having me tattoo my name across his chest, if I'd do it—which I damn sure wouldn't. No more than I'd tattoo his name on mine. People had a tendency to disappear, but ink was permanent.

I was about to grab my purse when the front door opened. My heart sank into my stomach when I turned around and saw Finley Cooper walking into the shop. The sun hit his profile as he stood in front of the window, illuminating the lines on his face that seemed deeper than the last time I saw him, which was only about a month earlier. The last time we met was the day he handed me the deed to the building we were standing in, as payment for helping the Crossroads Society recapture a demon god before he wreaked havoc on Savannah. That demon almost took me as his slave in the process.

Savannah is a crossroads, a place where the realms meet and the world becomes fluid and unpredictable. Anything is possible in this town, good or bad, which is why the society was formed—to steward the city. I'm a member of that society, now. I was hoping to remain a silent member, in status only, but the sight of Fin standing in my shop sent a jolt of dread straight through me.

"The bones," I muttered under my breath, wishing I hadn't said it aloud, because somehow speaking the words made it seem more likely I was right. That god we'd managed to recapture left behind some pretty powerful bones, buried at a crossroads somewhere between the boundaries of the city. Fin made it clear the last time I saw him that they'd be needing my services again to find those bones. I guessed the Crossroads Society was kind of like the Mafia—once you were in, you didn't just walk away.

"Fin," I said with a wary look.

"Now why is it I incite such an unpleasant response from you, Miss Bishop?" He looked at Jackson on his way over to me. "I see you've decided to stay in Savannah for a while."

Jackson tossed the magazine on the front counter and nodded once. "I think I'll be staying."

The two men locked eyes for a few seconds before Fin moved on to Sea Bass. "Your grandmother doing okay? Last time I saw Davina she was getting ready for her trip back to the mountain."

"Already back," he replied, referring to Gram's trip to the Ozarks where she was born. "She's doing just fine." Davina McCabe had walked off the "mountain" Fin was referring to at the age of fifteen, but with family still living there she took a trip to visit her people occasionally.

"I don't mean to be rude, Fin," I said, "but why are you here?"

"Can't I just drop by for a visit every now and then to check in on a fellow society member?"

Fin Cooper never did anything without a motive, and I called him on it. "Right. Who do you think you're talking to, Fin?"

"I'm afraid the society is going to be needing your help again."

I maintained my best poker face while my insides vibrated from all the adrenaline rushing through my bloodstream. Making it worse was the way my tattoo was beginning to stir on my back. My dragon had a real talent for sensing trouble, and right now it was itching to surface. The beast was becoming a downright pain in the ass to control, and if it wasn't for my regular trips to the beach at night to let it loose, there's no telling how dangerous and unpredictable it might become.

"Get to the point, Fin," I prompted, trying to move the conversation along before I was outed in the middle of the shop. Some of the people in the room weren't privy to my little secret. "Better yet, maybe we should take this conversation outside."

Fin finally caught on as I rolled my shoulder nervously, trying to ease the beast. "There's been a murder. The wife of a high-profile citizen of our town decided to blow her husband's head off the other night. In the middle of a dinner party."

I recalled seeing something on the news about it. "You mean that millionaire who owned some kind of property company?"

"Harry Cavanagh, Founder and CEO of Cavanagh Holdings. They were entertaining a house full of rich folks Saturday night when Rita Cavanagh got up from her seat to retrieve a gun from the kitchen. A minute later, she came back into the dining room and shot her husband point-blank in the head. Smoke was still coming off the barrel of the gun when she laid it on the table and continued with her dinner." He paused to let it all sink in, giving me time to conjure the surreal image in my mind. "Witnesses say she acted like she had no idea what she'd done, even after her husband's face came crashing down on the table and everyone jumped out of their chairs to scurry out of the room."

"Seems pretty open and shut to me, with all those witnesses." I could see the image of the dead man's face landing in a plateful of whatever rich folks dined on these days. I was afraid to ask the next question. "Tragic as it may be, what does this have to do with the Crossroads Society?"

Fin inhaled sharply, glancing at all the faces in the room. "A little discretion, Miss Bishop. Why don't we take a walk across the street." He was referring to Lou's Diner.

Jackson stood up, waiting for me to decide if he should stay put or tag along.

"Just the two of us," Fin said.

Jackson was well aware of what went on at the society, but I agreed to speak with Fin alone. "Give me a few minutes," I said to Jackson. "This shouldn't take long."

We walked across the street and stopped at the counter to grab some coffee. Having Fin walk back into my life had my adrenaline pumping, so caffeine was probably a bad idea. But you didn't just waltz into Lou's and take a seat without buying something.

Mae took our order and eyed Fin with an unfriendly glare.

"Mae," he said. "It's nice to see you again." She barely acknowledged him, other than the eat-shit-and-die look shooting from her eyes.

We took our coffee and headed for a booth. "What was that all about?" I asked.

"There are two things people tend to hold a lot of animosity for," he replied. "Their dentist, and their landlord. I can understand the dentist, but I'll never understand why people find it so unpleasant to pay for their goods." He glanced at the cup in his hand. "You don't see me coming in here looking for a free cup of coffee."

I was surprised. After forty years, I just assumed Lou and Mae owned the building. Then again, people had a tendency to mortgage themselves to the hilt and never get back out from under that mountain of debt. Maybe Mae was just transferring her anger to the most convenient target.

We slid into the booth and I waited for him to tell me why the death of a prominent Savannah citizen at the hands of his wife was a matter for the society—and what he needed from me.

"Mrs. Cavanagh has entered a plea of not guilty," he began. "She's insisting she doesn't remember shooting her husband in front of a room full of witnesses. Police walked into her house and found her sitting across from his body, eating a thick cut of prime rib with his blood seeping across the table right up to the edge of her plate. When the officers told her to stand up, she offered them dinner."

I shrugged. "Maybe she's nuts."

"Maybe she is. But it appears she had motive. Rita Cavanagh was having an affair."

And there it was, the oldest motive in the book for killing one's spouse. Rita Cavanagh was sleeping with another man. But it didn't explain why she would shoot him in front of a dozen witnesses, guaranteeing the end of her adulterous affair as she rotted in jail for the rest of her life.

"Well, that was stupid," I said. "For whatever reason she did it, no man is worth going to jail for the rest of your life."

"Or in this case, no woman. It seems that Rita Cavanagh has been living the picturesque life of a rich and pampered wife of a powerful man while satisfying her true needs with another woman."

I gaped at him. I didn't see that one coming, and God help me if I wasn't immune to the lure of juicy gossip. "Okay, I admit I'm shamefully intrigued, but what does any of this have to do with the Crossroads Society?"

Fin nudged his cup away. "I never did learn to like the stuff after breakfast. Gives me a headache." He sat back and exhaled the air from his lungs. "Mrs. Cavanagh wasn't just keeping a woman on the side—she was keeping a witch on the side."

I swallowed my sip of coffee and processed what he'd just said. A picture of Emmaline, the demure witch I'd met at Lillian Whitman's house the night of the Crossroads Society's annual ball, popped into my head. "Not Emmaline?" I doubted it, if for no other reason than she struck me as someone with a moral compass. I just couldn't quite picture her sneaking around with a married woman. Besides, there must have been hundreds, if not thousands, of witches in Savannah. But so far Emmaline was the only one I'd actually met.

Fin looked at me like I'd lost my marbles. "No, Miss Bishop. But unfortunately, Rita Cavanagh's lover is a priestess of Blackthorn Grove, and anything that threatens the grove threatens the society."

The Crossroads Society had connections to Blackthorn Grove, Emmaline being a member of both, for one. If the society was anything, it was loyal to its members, and I suspected there were many more witches who held membership cards.

"Her name is Esrial," he continued. "She's being accused of compelling Rita Cavanagh to murder her husband to collect their considerable estate."

"Compelling her? How do you compel someone to commit murder?"

"With a spell, Miss Bishop. A powerful one."

I shook my head. "That doesn't make sense. Why would this Esrial 'compel' Rita Cavanagh to kill her husband in front of witnesses? She goes to prison for life and gets nothing. Neither does Esrial."

"Well, that's the million-dollar question. People will speculate that the timing of the spell simply went wrong. They'll argue that Rita Cavanagh was supposed to pull the trigger without a room full of witnesses. It wouldn't be the first time a spell has gone haywire. Magic can be unpredictable."

"That's a pretty sloppy mistake, isn't it?"

"Sloppy indeed. But since we don't believe for a second that Esrial was involved in the murder, that sloppiness is not our concern." He leaned in and delivered his next statement with conviction. "I can assure you, If Esrial did cast that spell, it wouldn't have failed." He settled back into his seat and poured some sugar into the lukewarm coffee he'd given up on. Then he took a sip and continued. "The Chatham County District Attorney's Office is trying to build a case against her. They're trying to prove a conspiracy between the two women, but the society is confident that it will be quashed for lack of evidence. But we have a bigger problem."

The bigger problem, I assumed, was the part that involved me. I wasn't sure I wanted to hear it, but I'd agreed to work with the society. And seeing how Fin had helped save my life and then handed over the deed to my shop, I owed him. "All right, Fin. You have my attention."

"Miss Bishop, I'm afraid we have a witch war on our hands. Blackthorn Grove is being accused of using black magic to compel Rita Cavanagh to walk into that room and put a bullet in her husband's head. Against her free will. That would explain her claim of not remembering a thing about brutally murdering her husband in front of a room full of people."

"I'd like to see the police prove that. Witchcraft? Come on, Fin. The prosecutor will be laughed out of court."

"Not the police. We're looking at a tribunal. If that happens and Blackthorn Grove is found guilty of practicing the dark arts in order to harm someone, the convicted party will be dealt with in a much harsher way than a jail cell. We have our suspicions about who did this. If we're correct, we're going to need the help of that dragon of yours."

2

It's hard to commit to anything in the future when you don't even know if you're going to be here to honor that commitment. Of course there's no guarantee that any of us will be here tomorrow. I could walk out my front door in the morning and get hit by a truck. But it wasn't the fear of death that limited my future. It was the fear of what I'd become.

My birthday was approaching fast, and that meant a decision had to be made. Certain birthdays are markers of our time on the planet. Pivotal points in life that are meant to be celebrated. I always pictured my twenty-fifth birthday as one of those milestones. A rite of passage. And it would be, in an unorthodox way.

I'd only known for a few years that I was a dragon's child, and I'd accepted my life as a woman with a subservient beast living on my back. But my aunt had shown up out of the blue a month earlier and blown my whole world right out of the water. *No, Katie, you are not a woman with a dragon on her back; you are a dragon when the beast wakes, and a woman when it sleeps. But make no mistake, you are the dragon first.*

I was stunned. She'd informed me that on my twenty-fifth birthday I would transform into the dragon permanently and end up with my father—a full-blooded zmaj—in the Julian Alps where the first of our kind was born. She'd also explained that I had a choice. I could change the course of destiny and choose to live my life on my own terms. To avoid turning into a full-fledged dragon with a permanent set of wings and a new address in the Alps of Slovenia, all I had to do was die—by fire—on my twenty-fifth birthday.

At the time, I'd scoffed. But as she explained the bizarre reality of a zmaj dragon's demise, I began to understand why the timing was so critical. Apparently, the only way to kill one was by fire. But ironically, being a fire beast, the flames couldn't penetrate the fire-proof armor of a zmaj. Hence the conundrum for anyone trying to eradicate dragons. It also posed a real problem for me. I needed to be set on fire at the exact moment when I was between the girl and the beast, with my human skin just strong enough to ward off the flames and the dragon's just tender enough to be vulnerable to it. But the timing had to be perfect. If we started the ritual too soon, I would die and take the dragon to the grave with me. Too late, and the dragon would win, and I'd become a slave to its will.

The dilemma had been eating away at me for weeks. The dragon was part of me, and killing it would be like cutting off a limb. I just wanted things to stay as they were, with me in control while the dragon slept on my back. I suspected the recent boldness of the beast must have been a result of it sensing the impending shift in power.

Aunt Marianna assured me that if the ritual was carried out at precisely the right moment, both my dragon and I would survive with little more than a sunburn, and I would permanently become a woman first and a dragon second. She'd been through the ritual herself as proof that it could be done. In fact, she'd assured me that there were many others who'd survived the ritual in order to take control of their destinies.

Will it hurt? I'd asked her nervously, assuming there was some dragon thing that would protect me from the agony of being burned alive.

Her answer was less than comforting. *There is a tonic that can be taken an hour before the ritual. It will dull the pain. Most say the pain is minimal, but mine was extreme.* Then she leaned in and told me that her freedom was worth every excruciating second of that pain. After that, she stood up to leave and said, *Katie or Katarina. The choice is yours.*

Katarina was the name given to me by my parents. I'd forgotten it, but the moment it came out of her mouth that day at Lou's Diner, the memories of my father came rushing back. That was the hook that kept me from climbing out of the booth and walking out the door.

We exchanged numbers that day, and she promised to help me through whichever decision I made. Then she was gone, and I wondered if she'd keep that promise or disappear from my life forever.

I snapped out of the thought and came back to the here and now. Jackson took the last bite of his burger and eased back into the worn vinyl booth, studying me intently as he chewed. Since walking back into the shop and retrieving him for our lunch date, he hadn't said a word about my impromptu meeting with Fin Cooper. That's one of the things I loved about him. He knew when to pry and when to back off.

"It's okay to ask," I said. "You have a right to know what your crazy girlfriend is getting herself into."

His brows arched. "Crazy?"

"You know what I mean." I couldn't help but relax a little from the way he was looking at me. Jackson had the gift of calm. It took a lot to ruffle his feathers. Maybe it was his considerable size, which was a natural deterrent to anyone looking for confrontation. But I suspected it was just his personality. He didn't give a shit what others thought about him, and I imagined that must have been liberating.

"You want to tell me what Cooper wanted? I promise not to tear his head off."

It was a joke, but he was capable of it. Among other things, the imposing male sitting across from me with the badass Harley parked outside my shop had the strength of Thor. So far I'd only gotten the condensed version of his history, but now that we were a bona fide couple, I had a feeling whatever secrets we still had between us were about to bloom like a mushroom cloud. He already knew about my dragon, and it was time to tell him about my twenty-fifth birthday and what his girlfriend was facing if she didn't play her cards right. After all, it would affect him too. I'd fallen for him about as hard as I'd ever fallen for any guy, and I suspected the feeling was mutual.

I pondered for a moment and decided Lou's Diner wasn't the right place to tell him about my birthday surprise. "Looks like the Crossroads Society has a war on their hands," I finally said, choosing to divulge the business with Fin but table the discussion about my fate for another time.

"A war?" He balked and straightened back up in his seat. "I'm not sure if I want to hear this."

"A witch war," I clarified. "There was a murder Saturday night. Some rich socialite offed her husband in the middle of a dinner party. Just stood up and shot him in front of everyone. She claims she doesn't remember doing it. The society suspects that black magic was involved, and guess which coven everyone's pointing a finger at? Apparently, the murderous wife was sleeping with a priestess from Blackthorn Grove. There's going to be some sort of tribunal, whatever the hell that means."

By the look on his face, he wasn't balking anymore. "What does this have to do with you?"

"Fin wouldn't give me the details. He just said they needed

my help and invited me to an emergency meeting at the society tonight." I bit into my sandwich and tried to enjoy it, but all I could do was move the food around my mouth and try to swallow. Eventually, I pushed my plate across the table. "You want the rest of mine?"

He ignored my offering and continued to stare at me. "Maybe I should move into your place for a while." He shrugged and attempted to play off the concern written all over his face. "Just for a while."

"Really, Jackson? You're not trying to play the alpha-male card with me, are you? Because you know how much that pisses me off."

He held up his hand to stop me. "I know you can handle your business, Katie, but it would ease my mind knowing you had a little backup. Just a precaution." He disarmed me with his intense green eyes, scattering my brain. "It took a little work to get you to appreciate my uncanny charm," he joked. "I think I'd like to keep you around a little longer."

I grinned from the memory of our rocky introduction. "I'm not going anywhere, Jackson. And you're not moving in."

He chose his battles well and decided not to push the subject as we stood up to leave. We exited Lou's and headed back across the street to MagicInk. Sugar was standing in front of the shop window when we arrived.

"Don't you think you might wanna put up one of them neon signs in the window or string up some of them flashing lights?" she said. "You need a big ol' glowing sign that says 'MagicInk' in big flashy letters. Pink would be nice." She waved her hand across the window and glanced at the other shops up and down the block. "You just disappearing over here. Ain't nobody going to notice this place without something to get their attention."

"Nice to see you too, Sugar." I walked past her into my "disappearing" shop.

"Well, excuse me," she said, bobbing her head across her shoulders. "I'm just trying to educate you on running a business that ain't going to be dead in six months."

Jackson nodded, I assumed in agreement with her.

"Stop it. You're just encouraging her."

"You better be nice to that boy, Katie."

I glanced at Jackson. "I don't see any boys around here, Sugar."

"You got that right," she muttered, following my eyes. He caught her looking at his backside and grinned. "I'll take you home with me, baby. Treat you right."

"Jeez!" I shook my head and headed for the front desk. "You two are incorrigible."

"Better watch out, Jackson. Katie be pulling out them *big* words today."

There wasn't a single customer in the shop. "See? What did I tell you?" Sugar dropped into a chair and straightened her short skirt that was beginning to inch its way up toward the danger zone. She caught a glimpse of Abel watching her and darted her eyes in his direction. "I got something you wanna see, baby?"

Embarrassed, he quickly looked away.

"On that note, I'm out of here," Jackson said, heading for the door. "What time are you getting home tonight?"

I glanced around the room and cleared my throat. "Uh . . . I've got that thing tonight," I reminded him, trying to be discreet about the business with the Crossroads Society. Sea Bass snorted and looked over at Mouse. "What?" I asked.

"Well, it's kinda obvious. Fin Cooper shows up here out of the blue after weeks, and you two go all 007 and head across the street for a little private conversation. You're heading over to Lillian Whitman's house tonight on a little society business, aren't you?" Lillian's palatial estate was home to the Crossroads Society.

"Yeah, you got me, Sea Bass." I was a little annoyed that my privacy came at a premium these days. "Congratulations, Sherlock."

He huffed and shook his head, going back to cleaning his station with a little more gusto than necessary.

"You got a problem with that, Sea Bass?"

The instruments in his right hand came back down on the table while his left hand straddled his hip. "You didn't just ask me that, did you?" Before I could reply, he continued. "We damn near all died about a month ago in this very room because of Crossroads Society business. I think we all deserve to know if we're about to experience a little déjà vu."

"Sea Bass, I was—"

"Not to mention the fact that I'm your best friend." He glanced at Sugar who was giving him a dirty look. "And you don't trust me enough to tell me what the hell is going on? Damn it, Katie! I got feelings, too."

I felt like I'd just been ambushed by an intervention team. "You're right. I should have said something. And I apologize if I hurt your feelings." By now, Sugar was standing and giving me the same look as the rest of them.

"Katie," Jackson said, still standing next to the door with his hand on it. He pointed toward his bike. "I'm just going to . . ."

"I'll call you when I get home," I said as he walked out the door. Then I turned my attention back to the inquisition behind me. "Just so everyone in the room knows, I'm going to Lillian's house tonight to find out for myself what the hell is going on." I looked at Sea Bass. "Maybe you should ask your grandmother." Davina McCabe was a card-carrying senior member of the Cross-roads Society. He backed off a little when I said it. "All I know is that there's been a murder, and Blackthorn Grove is somehow involved. Fin has asked for my help. I guess tonight I'll find out why."

Sugar looked like she was about to spontaneously combust

when I glanced over at her. Obviously she wasn't privy to the information either, and considering that her ancestral connection to the Crossroads Society made her an honorary—though silent —member, I imagined she was pretty pissed about being left off the need-to-know list. I think she was actually shaking with indignant anger.

"I—I'm gonna kill that man!" she managed to squeak out along with the invisible steam coming out of her ears. I assumed she meant Fin Cooper. Her mouth tightened as she shook her head. "Come on, Katie. We got us a meeting to get ready for."

I guessed that meant she was coming with me.

3

Sugar followed me to Lillian Whitman's house, just in case she decided to leave early after tearing Fin Cooper a new one for leaving her out of the loop. I wouldn't want to be Fin right about now.

"You better be careful with that car," she warned the young man who Lillian had hired to valet for the evening. "It's a classic."

He glanced at the Eldorado and then examined her daisy-yellow jumpsuit. "Yeah . . . uh . . . I'll take real good care of it."

"Mm-hmm. I find one scratch on that car and Lillian will be buying me a new paint job." She clamped down on my arm and steered me toward the steps.

"Jesus, Sugar! Lighten up!" I shrugged my arm out of her death grip and followed her up the steps.

Sugar riled pretty easily, but I hadn't seen her this irritated in a while. Things were going to get interesting fast if someone didn't have a good explanation for why she hadn't been informed about the latest society business. I suspected it was because unlike the business with the grimoire that nearly got us killed a month ago, Blackthorn Grove business didn't have any real connection to her or her family. Sugar and her mama were honorary members, without all the formality of attending meetings or making appearances at the society's social events. Up until now, Sugar seemed to be perfectly happy with that little arrangement.

Fin was standing in the doorway when we reached the top of the stairs. He looked right past Sugar. "Miss Bishop." When he finally acknowledged her, he immediately went into defensive mode. "Now Sugar, you need to settle down and check yourself before walking through that door."

"Oh, God," I muttered.

"*Check* myself?" Sugar repeated, nostrils flaring as her eyes demanded that he clarify what he'd just said. "I'll show you who's gonna be *checked* in a minute here."

Having no patience for their bickering, I stepped around them and headed through the door. My goal for the evening was to find out what was going on and decide whether I wanted to be a part of it. After that, I just wanted to get home to my cat and spend a quiet evening on the patio with a glass of wine in my hand.

"Katie," someone said.

I turned toward the soft voice calling my name and spotted Emmaline standing at the window in the living room. It was the same spot where I'd first laid eyes on the demure and ghostly girl who happened to be a powerful priestess with Blackthorn Grove. I imagined the scandal hanging over the coven was taking a toll on the sensitive witch. She'd sensed my dragon the first night we met by blindly touching my tattoo. I could only imagine how a witch war—as Fin put it—was tearing at her delicate psyche.

"Emmaline." I headed for the window. Her breath caught as I pulled her into a polite hug. Tensing a bit at first, she relaxed as she allowed the warm greeting to continue. I guessed she wasn't used to being touched by people she hardly knew, and I remembered the way Fin had very gently grasped her arm the night he introduced us at the society's annual ball. "I'd ask how you're doing, but that's probably a stupid question with all this stuff going on with the coven."

Fin interrupted us before Emmaline could respond. "If you ladies don't mind, we'd like to get started. It's a weeknight, and everyone has a mundane life to get back to in the morning."

We followed him into the library where we'd convened the last time the society needed my help. "Where's Sugar?" I asked, glancing around the room. The group was smaller this time. José was missing of course, seeing how he was now dead and decaying underground due to his failed deal with the devil. Several of the others I'd met the first night I was here were also absent from the room. I was surprised to see Davina McCabe sitting at the table.

"Don't you worry about Sugar," Fin said. "We've made our peace, and she decided that sitting around a table with these fine folks wasn't so appealing after all. She wanted me to let you know she'd see you later on this evening."

Good thing she had the foresight to follow me. I'm sure the valet was relieved to hand back her car keys.

A snide laugh came from the other end of the table. It was Agnes Freemont, the owner of Le Petit Gateau, a bakery a few blocks down from MagicInk. "Lucky you," she said. A cross between rust and pomegranate seeds, the color of her hair was clearly from a bottle, and her blunt fingernails showed traces of bread dough dried around her cuticles.

I glared at her, having at that very instant been shown exactly what kind of person she was. Agnes Freemont was a bigot.

We took our seats and waited for our hostess to arrive. A minute later, Lillian Whitman entered the room and headed for the bar against the wall. She was wearing a black sheath dress that matched the onyx stone pin securing her gray hair into a neat chignon. She poured two glasses of liquor and walked over to me. "If I remember correctly you prefer scotch, Miss Bishop?" I gladly took the glass. The other one was for her. "I only have two hands, so I hope no one minds fending for themselves."

There was a scurry of people getting up from the table to get their own drinks, while Lillian sat down and stared at me unabashedly from across the table. By the time everyone settled back into their seats, I was about to break out in a cold sweat from the way her eyes were burning a hole in me.

Fin poured himself some bourbon and downed it. He refilled the glass and headed over to the desk to retrieve a cigar, to the annoyance of Dr. Greene. Halfway back to the table, Lillian stopped him. "Hell Fin, bring one for me." Fin returned to the table and lit Lillian's smoke.

"I guess I'll be seeing you in my office for a stress test in the future, too," Dr. Greene said to Lillian. As a cardiologist, I imagined cigar smoking, fried chicken eating Southerners were the bread and butter of his practice.

She glanced down at the generous glass of Wild Turkey in his hand. "You don't hear me preaching about that little habit of yours, do you, Moses?" She took a puff of her cigar. "Besides, what good is living if you can't treat yourself to a little vice now and then."

Moses Greene shut his trap and set his drink down on the table.

"Now that everyone's comfortable, we'll get down to business," Fin announced, wrangling the meeting to order. "We have a dire situation on our hands, folks. As everyone is probably aware by now, there's been a murder."

I looked at the unimpressed faces listening to Fin describe what anyone in Savannah could have picked up by turning on their televisions. Sadly, we'd all become immune to the headlines of someone pulling out a gun and executing a philandering spouse or significant other, but it was the next thing he said that raised the eyebrows around the table.

"A priestess of Blackthorn Grove has been accused of practicing the dark arts in order to compel Rita Cavanagh to shoot her husband, in the middle of a room full of witnesses." Fin paused and looked around the table before revealing the name. "Esrial."

Agnes Freemont set her glass back down on the table with a heavy hand and appeared to be a little stunned. "Esrial?" Fin nodded once. "But why would—"

He held up his palms to rein in all the mumbling around the table. "Now before everyone starts throwing questions out," he continued, "let me put all the facts on the table first." He proceeded to educate the council on the case. "The only thing everyone knows for sure is that Harry Cavanagh is dead and Mrs. Cavanagh is the one who pulled the trigger. Now, she's sitting over there in the Chatham County jail charged with murder, but she's pleaded not guilty. Claims she doesn't remember anything that happened between handing someone a drink and seeing an army of police officers charging through her front door."

A collective murmur traveled around the table as suspicions grew. Fin relaxed deeper into his chair and listened, letting the news sink in.

"For the love of God, Fin," Davina groaned. "Get to the good part."

"The good part?" I repeated. "There's something good in all this?"

Moses spoke up next. "Esrial may be a lot of things, but I've never known her to practice the dark arts for anything more than a little incantation on someone who damn well deserved it. Even then she's usually ethical in her handling of that kind of power. As a matter of fact, I can only recall one time when she resorted to slightly unethical magic. It was when her asshole of a neighbor tried to poison her dog." He snickered at the memory. "I believe he moved shortly after a series of unfortunate events took place in his house. Can't blame the woman. I'd do the same thing if someone tried to harm my Gunter."

"That monstrosity can take care of itself," Davina said, referring to the doctor's mastiff-coonhound mix.

Lillian slapped her palms down on the table. "Settle down, everyone. We'd all like to get out of here at a decent hour."

"I'm lost," I said, feeling like I was the only one in the room who wasn't getting the connection. "What does Blackthorn Grove have to do with Harry Cavanagh anyway? Other than the fact that one of its priestesses is sleeping with his wife."

A gasp spread through the room.

"Now don't act so surprised," Davina piped in. "We all know who Esrial has been entertaining for the past few months."

"Why would Esrial frame Rita Cavanagh for her husband's murder?" I continued. "It can't be for money. Rita's never going to see a dime of any life insurance policy, and it's going to be hard to enjoy the rest of the estate from a jail cell."

"She didn't," Lillian said. "I've known Esrial since we were children, and I can assure you she did not do this."

Fin continued. "We believe a sorceress with questionable integrity has decided to invade our town and frame Esrial. However, we suspect the real target was the coven. Blackthorn Grove is the most powerful coven in Savannah, and we have no doubt that this witch has every intention of taking over that throne. Harry and Rita Cavanagh were just a couple of convenient props. In fact, we have a witness who can testify to the presence of this intruder."

I glanced at the faces around the table. "Who?"

Emmaline sank deeper into her chair as her shoulders inched up. Uncomfortable with the sudden attention she was drawing, she sheepishly raised her hand to acknowledge herself as the mystery witness. "I—I've seen the sorceress. Well, I haven't actually seen her, but I can feel her. Her energy is frightening."

"Emmaline is a sensitive," Lillian clarified.

I remembered how she knew I was a dragon the night we met at the Crossroads Society's annual ball. She'd picked up on it when she hugged me and her hand grazed the back of my dress. Lillian explained that Emmaline's uncanny ability to see the dragon was due to her being a witch, but I always suspected it was more than that.

"There's something monstrous about her," Emmaline continued. "She's as dark as a bottomless pit, and her fire is . . . terrifying. I can't see her face, but I can feel her like she's standing right next to me." Her face suddenly soured. "And she smells awful!"

And they needed my help with this? After listening to Emmaline describe the witch, a chill ran down my spine. "I'm afraid to ask, but what does the society need me for?"

Fin snuffed out his cigar. "As Emmaline just mentioned, we're dealing with a fire witch. We need your help, Miss Bishop, because it's going to take fire to fight fire. This intruder is a beast of fire, just like you."

Lillian got up from the table and went to the bureau to retrieve the bottle of scotch I was so fond of—the one equivalent to a month's rent. She slid it across the table toward me and continued. "The Council of Southern Witches is sending a group to Savannah as we speak. There will be a tribunal, and that dragon of yours is our only chance of ridding the city of this sorceress and clearing Esrial of conspiracy to commit murder." She leaned across the table and stared me down like a hungry hawk. "I will not let them destroy Esrial—or the coven."

I glared back at her, trying to hide the fact that every limb of my body was vibrating with adrenaline. Lillian Whitman's ferocity was pissing off my dragon, and I did not need it to make an appearance in a room full of people. The closer I got to my twenty-fifth birthday, the harder it was to control. A diversion was called for.

"So," I began, trying to get Lillian to back down and lower the heat she was generating. "What do I get in return?" For my role in capturing the last outlaw the Crossroads Society was charged with apprehending, Fin handed me the deed to my shop, although it was a surprise gift I never asked for.

"You mean payment?" Fin asked.

I didn't expect to be paid. I just wanted Lillian to back off before I sprouted wings. "No, Fin, I don't expect payment. But it would be nice if she-wolf over there"—I nodded to Lillian—"would back the fuck off."

Lillian grinned back at me. "My apologies, Miss Bishop. I get a little passionate when my family and friends are threatened. Right now, I'm downright dangerous."

"Good," Fin said to me. "I prefer it when people choose to volunteer their services for their community. You are a member of the society, after all."

Right. A membership I never asked for. It was more like an ultimatum if I wanted to stay alive. I could have refused, but our arrangement had proven to be convenient, and I was now a card-carrying member.

"Do you have any proof that this witch is responsible for framing Esrial?" I asked. "I'm all for getting rid of her if she's as bad as everyone seems to think she is, but I believe in the principle of innocent until proven guilty. No offense Emmaline, but I'm going to need something a little more concrete than a bad smell in your nose."

Davina stood up and pulled a small cloth pouch from her purse. I could hear chair legs drag across the Persian rug as everyone moved away from the table. With a flick of her wrist, she tossed the contents on the shiny mahogany surface, sending an ivory-colored object sailing toward me.

"Careful with that, woman!" Lillian warned.

"Why don't you go play some bridge, Lillian," Davina shot back.

The piece of bone stopped before flying over the edge into my lap. "Is that proof enough for you?" she asked. I leaned in to examine it. Written on the side of the bone in something that looked like dried blood was a series of symbols I didn't recognize. "Those marks are from the book. The grimoire," Davina clarified.

It hit me like a lead weight. The grimoire was where the rogue god, Legvu, was imprisoned. I'd helped recaptured him so he could be shoved back in the book and buried a hundred feet under the very house we were sitting in. The Crossroads Society's primary mission was to find a set of powerful bones Legvu had buried at a crossroads somewhere in Savannah. The bones of the god Adro. It was a place where the worlds met and the veil between them was paper thin. A doorway where all kinds of bad things could step over the line. We'd recaptured Legvu, but the bones were still at large.

"Is that—"

"You bet your sweet ass it is." Davina snatched up the bone and shoved it back in her bag. "We found it in Esrial's house, in the center of her altar. Poor Esrial didn't even know she was a conduit for the spell that put a gun in Rita Cavanagh's hand. In fact, she wasn't even in the country at the time."

I must have looked confused, because Davina offered answers for the unspoken question on my mind. "You're wondering how Esrial could have been an unwitting party to the murder from thousands of miles away," she said. "It doesn't matter if Esrial was in Savannah or on the moon at the time of that murder. It's the emotional connection between the two women that facilitated the spell. A lover is always an effective conduit for magic."

"You're not afraid to touch it?" I asked, wondering why Davina seemed to be the only person in the room who wasn't afraid of that bone in her purse. The way they all talked about those bones, I figured just looking at them could set your eyes on fire.

"Don't worry. It's all used up," Davina said. But everyone in the room seemed to have their doubts. "No doubt it was stolen from the crossroads, but that spell sucked the power right out of it." Davina had a way with bones. Coming from the Ozarks, bone magic was second nature for her. She was the one who'd procured the hyena bone that we used to trap Legvu. I wondered what she had to give as payment for it.

A thought suddenly occurred to me. "Where is Esrial right now? I'd like to meet the woman I'm trying to save."

Fin inhaled sharply. "That is a very good question, Miss Bishop. We'd all like to know where Esrial is hiding."

4

By the time I got home, all I wanted to do was hit the sack. It was barely past ten, but my head was spinning from all the information I'd been handed. But by the looks of my driveway, that wasn't going to happen.

"Great," I muttered. "I only pay the rent." I parked on the street and eyed Jackson's Harley parked in my spot. I could have easily parked next to his bike, but Sugar's tank was in the way.

"It's about time," Sugar said without looking up from the frying pan as I walked through the front door. Jackson was sitting at the kitchen island eating something. "We was beginning to wonder if Lillian was throwing a slumber party over there at the society." She turned to Jackson and lifted a curled brown piece of meat from the frying pan and dropped it on a slice of toast. Then she put another slice of toast on top of it and handed it to him just as he was polishing off his first sandwich.

"Is that bologna?" I asked.

"Yes, ma'am. Nothing like a fried bo-log-na sandwich," she declared, sounding out the word.

I glanced at Jackson who was eagerly chewing his mouthful. "You know that stuff's been in the fridge for a while. I'm pretty sure I should have thrown it out by now." I tried to eat sensibly, and that pack of processed meat product was a bad decision I'd made months ago. His mouth paused as he considered my words. Then he shrugged and swallowed, pushing the plate away as he decided to heed my warning. "Smart move," I muttered.

As I sat on the stool next to him, his palm rubbed against my back. His hand went still from the chaotic movement taking place under my shirt. My dragon was restless. "What's going on?" he asked, easily reading the changes in my body. He was one of the few people who knew my dragon personally. Knew its moods.

Instead of addressing his question, I looked at Sugar, who was doing her damnedest to avoid my eyes. "What the hell was that all about, Sugar?" I demanded. "Why did you leave?"

She turned back to the sink to wash the pan. "I told you I might leave early. Why'd you think I followed you? Me and this man of yours was having us a real nice chat while you was over there at the society playing Nancy Drew. Weren't we, Jackson?"

I gave her a pointed look, silently questioning what that chat might have been about. "Early? You barely made it through Lillian's front door. And what exactly have the two of you been chatting about while I was gone?"

She rinsed the clean pan and dried it with a paper towel before turning back around. "Baby you getting yourself mixed up in things you ought not mess with." Sugar was one of my closest friends, and I knew that look. Her cocky attitude was absent, which made me uncomfortable on so many levels. "Mama's been sending me some strange vibes, and I ain't never second guessed one of Mama's messages. And you *damn* sure better not either."

Unlike Sugar, I didn't have a direct line to Pearl May Mobley's mind. "Does that mean what I think it does?" I asked, wondering if we were going to be taking a drive out to her mama's house real soon.

Sugar nodded firmly. "I'd drive you out there right now, but

Mama would kill me for knocking on her door this late at night. She likes to get her beauty sleep. Now, if this was a full moon—"

"You two planning to let me in on the crisis?" Jackson interjected. Sugar opened her mouth, but I gave her a look that shut her up. "I thought we were past the point of keeping secrets. I guess I was wrong," he said with a look that made me feel like a deceitful piece of shit.

I shook my head, but he just kept staring at me like I'd committed a cardinal sin. He was there for me the last time the Crossroads Society needed my help, and I had no doubt he'd be able to handle anything I threw at him, seeing how he had a pretty strange and fantastic background himself that included a history of riding with a pack of shifters back in Atlanta. But I was afraid the latest round of crazy would be too much too soon, and he'd get sick of a woman who attracted catastrophe like flies. If it were any other guy, I'd say *don't let the door hit you in the ass on your way out*, but Jackson was a keeper.

His brow arched as he read my very poor attempt at a poker face. "How much have you been keeping from me?" Now he was getting off his stool. At six foot seven, he was a mountain of a man. It was only natural to give him a wide berth, and his deep baritone voice only enhanced the menacing illusion.

"I—" I stammered, suddenly wanting to come clean about not just today's revelations, but the sins of the past, too. But I just didn't have the guts to tell him everything. I figured certain secrets were appropriate discussion points after a month or two of dating, but the darkest secrets were better left for the one-year anniversary mark. For instance, I hadn't told him that he was sleeping with a murderer. Or that the body of my victim had never been found. He knew I was somehow connected to my ex-lover's disappearance, but to this day he'd let that ghost lie. I figured he was willing to wait until I was good and ready to talk about it. Well, I wasn't good and ready to tell him about Christopher Sullivan just yet.

Sugar was ready to burst when I glanced over at her. I could tell by the look of contempt in her eyes that if I didn't tell him, she would. And then it happened.

"You better tell that man," she warned. "Or I will." I begged her with my eyes to have mercy on me. "Tell the man, Katie," she demanded again through clenched teeth.

Jackson's expression turned grave. "Tell me what?"

"Fine," I said. "You want to know what I am? I'm a murderer!"

Sugar's eyes flew wide. "Well, hell, baby. I was just going to tell him about Rita Cavanagh and that nasty witch you plan to help the society get rid of. You'll need this man to help keep you alive."

My mouth must have been hanging open, because Sugar walked up to me and gently cupped my chin, raising it back up. "I guess I better be leaving now, on account of that discussion you two are about to have." She brushed the hair out of my eyes and whispered, "Just tell him. Jackson's a good man."

"Just . . . leave, Sugar," I said, closing my eyes in anticipation of what I was going to say to him. The cat was out of the bag. Either I'd be sleeping alone tonight, or I'd be relieved in the morning that there truly were no more big secrets between us. I prayed for the latter.

Sugar walked out the front door, and I turned to Jackson who was grabbing the bottle of wine off the counter and heading for the patio door. I stopped at the kitchen cabinet and grabbed the bottle of scotch before following him outside. I loved my red wine, but this discussion called for something a little stronger.

Jackson sat in one of the metal chairs and looked at the bottle in my hand. "You want some?" I asked. He shook his head, opting for the wine. "Suit yourself." I took a fortifying swig straight from the bottle and then sat in the other chair. How was I supposed to tell the man I was sleeping with that the last man in his position was now dead—at my hands. Christopher Sullivan —assistant DA for Chatham County and my former lover—had become possessed with the demon I was hunting. He tried to kill me, but my dragon killed him first. It was self-defense. His life or mine. Fin had cleaned up the murder, and to this day the body had never been found. Despite an anonymous call placing me with him the night he disappeared, the police had no case against me.

"Is this about your ex-boyfriend?" he asked. "The one who disappeared?"

Paralyzed with fear, my eyes managed to meet his. "You know what happened to Christopher?"

He finished off his glass of wine in a single chug and reached for the scotch. He was about to pour it into his wine glass when he got up and started to pace across the patio. "Fin told me the guy is missing." He took a deep breath and strode up to my chair, cupping my chin to bring my gaze up to his. "Jesus, Katie, what the hell are you hiding from me?"

"I killed him," I replied in a shaky voice, shrugging my shoulders and pulling away from his hand. "He was going to kill me, so my dragon—"

"Where I come from that's called self-defense." He grabbed my arm as I stood up to walk away and pulled me against him, burying my face in his chest. Then he lifted me off the ground and sat me on the table, guaranteeing I wouldn't take off before we had a chance to get all the secrets out in the open. "You think I haven't done things that make me a monster?" he said. "Don't forget who I used to run with. Whatever you'd imagine an outlaw biker club is like, it's worse."

I got a visual of the Hells Angels or the Mongols, only with the ability to shift into dangerous creatures. "I guess I never thought about it." I pushed him back and looked into his eyes. "Have you ever killed someone?"

Without hesitating, he answered. "Yes. But it was justified."

Who was I to judge? The crime I committed was justified, too. And although I'd barely been with Jackson for two months, I'd stake my life that he was a decent—if not formidable—man who just happened to have a past. We all did.

"Can we leave it alone for now?" I asked. "We can talk about our mutual crimes on a better day, because right now I have something else I need to tell you." It was time to tell him about my twenty-fifth birthday. The cruel gift that would be waiting for me on that day. Then we'd see if he wanted to stick around long enough to continue the conversation.

Twenty minutes later, Jet strolled out the door and hopped into Jackson's lap, right on cue as I finished giving him the details on the ritual that would either free me from a life of circling the sky in a foreign land or leave me one step closer to living pretty much as I did now. I'd always been more woman than dragon, but lately that was beginning to change. The beast was restless, and every day I worried that it could spring out of me from the slightest annoyance, or manifest from too much excitement.

He stroked Jet's back for a moment and then set him on the ground, pulling my chair closer to his. With those large hands that I loved so much, he pushed his long hair over his shoulder and leaned onto his knees, filling the space between us with the familiar scent of leather and the soap that lingered on his skin. Even his sweat was intoxicating.

"You have to stop doing that, Jackson."

"Doing what?"

What exactly was he doing? He was just looking at me. But that mundane act, performed by millions of people every day, was powerful. Complete strangers looked at each other all the

LUANNE BENNETT

time. Enemies looked at each other, too. So why did it disarm me so easily when Jackson looked at me?

I sat straight up and tried to muffle the small gasp that came out of my mouth. My limbs began to discreetly shake as a rush of warmth washed through me, right about the time I felt a little nauseous. I wasn't just infatuated with him. I was falling in love with him—hard.

I stumbled out of my chair, nearly knocking him over in the process of trying to put some distance between us. I didn't have time for this. There was a deviant witch to catch, and I had a business to run. Love would only complicate my life. I'd learned that lesson the hard way.

"Katie?" The puzzled look on his face turned to concern. "What's wrong?" He whirled around as if there might be an intruder standing on the patio behind him, but the only thing standing in the shadows was Jet.

"Nothing's wrong, Jackson!" I replied defensively. "I just got a little overwhelmed for a minute. Must be all this society stuff." Yeah, that was a good excuse. I'd been free from the craziness for weeks, and all of a sudden Fin walks back into my life and shoots it all to hell. "Jeez. Can't a girl have a little moment of anxiety without you guys assuming something's wrong?" I was starting to sound like a bag of hormones.

He looked completely bewildered, but when he ignored my standoffish body language and reached out to hug me, I felt his torso go stiff. He hesitated as our rigid bodies met. Then I felt his muscles relax and turn to soft clay as I melted into him. Something was different about him—his smell.

His smell?

That's when I knew that *he* knew. Don't ask me how I figured it out, but that smell was meant for me. Must have been my dragon sniffing it out.

After a few minutes of standing there in the glow of what we both knew was happening, he let go of me and took a step back to look at my face. "You okay?" he asked.

"I guess I should be asking you that question." I searched his eyes for a glimmer of regret but saw nothing but heat. "You're taking on a hell of a lot if you walk down that road with me, Jackson. There's your exit if you want to take it." I motioned toward the patio door. "No hard feelings." On the one hand, I was hoping he'd leave. On the other, I would die if he did.

"If it eases your mind," he said, cupping my face and giving me a look that made me weak, "your dragon gets me hot."

———————

I HANDED my clothes to Jackson and looked in his eyes as if it might be the last time I ever saw him. Flying always made me feel that way. There was always that unexplainable pull, that risk that I wouldn't come back down. Or I might crash into the sea and sink to the bottom like a stone.

With the approach of my twenty-fifth birthday, my dragon was taking more of my will every day, demanding to be set free at regular intervals. Midnight on the beach seemed to be a good time and place to let it loose.

Jackson took my clothes and nodded for me to get on with it. I headed toward the water, enjoying every second of the freedom to walk naked under the moonlight before the beast took control.

Impatient, the dragon came out faster than usual. I buried my feet in the sand and gripped it firmly between my emerging talons, unfolding my wings to catch the sea breeze. A second later, I lifted into the air and sailed over the water. The first few seconds were always the most jarring, when the scales protruded from the pores of my skin, and my body heated up to a hot one hundred and thirty degrees. Most reptiles are cold-blooded, but not creatures of fire. Not dragons.

I flew over the ocean through the dark blue sky, sailing toward the waxing moon as it peeked through the forming clouds, my reflection soaring over the surface of the water below. As late as it was, there were still people out on the beaches of Tybee Island, so I flew farther out to sea and became nothing more than a bird in the distance to anyone spotting me.

As good as it felt to be free in the sky, I turned back toward the beach. This was the part where I struggled with the temptation to keep flying until I reached my father on the other side of the world, to become the beast. But my instinct to be the woman was stronger, and Jackson was waiting patiently to take me home, to lie back on the bed while I devoured him and let the energy of the beast slowly extinguish until the next time it consumed me and demanded to fly.

5

The first thing I did when I walked into the shop the next morning was look for an available set of hands. Sea Bass wasn't in yet, and Mouse was already working on a client's neck tattoo. I looked at Abel who was coming back from the kitchen with a cup of coffee in his hand, and I motioned for him to follow me.

"What's this?" he asked, staring at the sketch of a scorpion I'd rendered while I ate my bagel with cream cheese after Jackson left that morning.

"What does it look like?"

He scratched his bald head as the unspoken request sank in. "You're not asking me to—"

"Oh, yes I am." I sat in the chair at my station and inched my tank top up to just below my breasts. "I want you to put it right there." I pointed to my bottom rib, the spot where the pain would be a solid ten. I'd had an epiphany, right about the time I realized I couldn't bear to see Jackson Hunter leave that morning. I would not turn into that stupid, irrational girl I'd become the last time a man made me feel like that. The only way I knew how to distract myself—at least for an hour or two—was to submit myself to something even more demanding of my attention.

"Boss, I've barely put on my training wheels. I ain't ready for this."

I glanced at the tattoos covering his arms, neck, and head. The ink he didn't personally apply to his own skin but drew with his own hands. Abel was a talented artist, and while he'd only been apprenticing for a few months, I knew he was capable of applying that tattoo. And right now, I was more than willing to be his first guinea pig.

"Come on, Abel. If you fuck it up, at least it'll be covered by my shirt." I grinned as his face sobered. "You know you can do this. Piece of cake."

He swallowed hard. "You're the boss." Then he went to gather supplies. "You sure you don't want to put it on an easier spot?" he asked from across the room. "Might look better on your arm." Not for the faint of heart, the ribcage was one of the most painful places to get a tattoo—which was the point. I imagined he was uncomfortable with the idea of his first victim squirming under his nervous hands.

"I'll be fine. It's not about the damn tattoo," I added under my breath.

A few stations away, Mouse was snickering as she concentrated on the intricate spider web she was wrapping around her client's neck. "You got balls, Katie."

"Ain't that illegal?" her client asked. Tim Monroe had been coming into the shop since it first opened, so he knew Abel was the shop's apprentice.

"Not if he's being supervised by a licensed tattoo artist," I replied. "That would be me."

Abel returned with a tray full of everything but the kitchen sink. I suspected he was preparing for the apocalypse of tattoo sessions. Remembering what it felt like the first time I put a needle to a client's skin, I kept my mouth shut. I would have been more concerned if he came back with a half empty bottle of ink and no gloves.

I climbed on the table and lifted my shirt over the cup of my bra, which only made it more uncomfortable for him. But like a true professional, he ignored my half-exposed chest and applied the stencil to the spot where I instructed him to put it. The tattoo machine hummed as he turned it on, but as he lowered it toward my skin, the front door opened.

A crashing sound got the attention of everyone in the shop. Sea Bass was standing near the back door with a large object lying on the floor near his feet. "What in the hell—" he began as he stared at Abel crouched over my torso, gloved and ready to puncture my skin with the needles. Suddenly realizing that the bulky object was no longer grasped between his hands, he glanced at the floor. "Shit! See what you made me do."

I jumped off the table and headed for the strange object. "What is that?" I asked as I bent down to help him stand it back up. It was some kind of large pot or jug. It had to weigh fifty or sixty pounds and stood a good two feet tall. Each side had a handle in the shape of a snake.

"It's a face jug," he replied. "Damn! Its nose broke." He looked around the floor for the missing pottery chip. "I can't believe the thing didn't shatter when I dropped it." He glanced at Abel who was still sitting at my station with his gloves on. "What the hell are you doing, Katie?"

"It looks fine. Gives it character," I said, ignoring his question and grabbing the chipped nose between my index and middle knuckles. "Why is it here?"

"I was on my way over and I got so distracted in my thoughts that I missed my turn. Ended up on the wrong street and spotted a yard sale." He hefted the heavy jug off the ground and carried it to the table in front of the window. "It was sitting under a table looking all sad and dusty, so I offered the lady twenty bucks for it."

After examining the giant jug a little closer, its age was obvious. The face was primitive and had two *X*s painted above it, probably indicating its twenty-gallon capacity. I considered myself fairly knowledgeable about antiques and collectibles, having amassed a substantial collection of eclectic odds and ends over the years, and I knew that jug was worth a lot more than twenty dollars.

"Good thing I didn't ride my bike today," he said, referring to his old Triumph Bonneville.

"Yeah, good thing," Mouse snorted.

Sea Bass glared at her. "Shut up, Mouse. You ain't got no taste in the finer things."

"You call that fine?" she retorted. "Bet that woman was laughing when she stuffed that twenty in her pocket."

"God, you're like an old married couple," I said, breezing past Abel's waiting hands to get a cup of coffee.

"We doing this, boss?" he asked.

I sighed. "Sorry, Abel. Changed my mind. Don't think I'll be needing that pain after all." The jug debacle had been enough to distract me. "But don't worry. I'll let you experiment on Sea Bass next time."

Sea Bass scoffed. "Like hell." He adjusted the position of the jug, turning it a few times to play with the orientation of the face. "Maybe I should face it out the window. Make folks stop to get a closer look at it." His face brightened up as an imaginary light bulb went off in his head. "We could put it on the sidewalk out in front of the shop. You know, like them wooden statues you used to see in front of stores. Bet that would get some people to come inside."

"You mean a cigar store Indian?" I said. "Sea Bass, this isn't a cigar store, and that jug isn't any kind of signage for a tattoo parlor. And I guarantee you, if you leave it outside it'll disappear before the day is up."

He adjusted the jug so its face was staring at the spot where people entered the shop. Then he walked over to the front desk to get a good look at it from a distance. "Okay," he said, looking at it thoughtfully. "I guess it'll just have to stay inside then. Over there on that table is perfect. Makes a good conversation piece."

"Fine with me." I looked at the strange ceramic face sitting on the table under the shop sign. With its big ears and chipped nose, it reminded me of a Mr. Potato Head toy. "I think it's kind of cool. Let's just hope Beth Hendricks doesn't walk in here with those hellion kids of hers. I can guarantee one of them will knock it over, and the last thing I need is a kid with a concussion—and a lawsuit." Kids weren't allowed in the shop, but Beth Hendricks had a bad habit of ignoring that clearly posted sign on the wall.

"Harold," Sea Bass declared. "That's his name."

The door opened and a man walked in. The first thing he did was head over to the jug and bent down to get a better look. "My granddaddy used to have one of these, but it was about half the size." He examined its features and ran his finger over the damaged nose. As if he'd suddenly realized where he was, he straightened back up and looked at the framed tattoo art hanging along the wall. "You guys take walk-ins?"

"Yes, sir," I said, happy to keep the distractions coming. I motioned him over to my station.

He looked back at the jug as he headed for my chair. "Is that thing for sale?"

"Nope," Sea Bass was quick to reply. "That's our newest employee."

Just before closing, Sugar walked past the shop window toward the entrance. But the door never opened. She did a double take and backtracked to the window to stare at the face sitting on the table. She cupped her eyes against the glass to get a better look at it before coming inside.

"Hey," I said as she blew through the door like a tornado and headed straight for the front desk where I was closing out the receipts for the day. "I'll be ready in a minute." We were heading out for a late evening visit with her mama. Pearl May Mobley was a fierce conjure woman who possibly had information on this intruder who was causing so much trouble for Blackthorn Grove. Sugar had said her mama was sending her messages, so we were heading out there to find out what she knew.

"What the hell is that?" She nodded toward the jug.

"That's Harold. Sea Bass decided we needed a mascot for the shop."

She strolled over to Sea Bass and gently moved a lock of his hair away from his forehead with her middle finger. "You know I love you, baby, but sometimes I wonder about that little head of yours."

He sighed and pulled away from her intrusive finger. "Sugar, you need to stop doing things like that every time you walk in here. People will start wondering about us." He glanced around the empty room. "Good thing we're closed."

She smirked but respected his boundaries and took a step back. "One of these days you'll admit that you love me." She took on a more serious note and glanced at the jug. "That thing ain't right. Where'd you get it?"

Abel muttered something about *ugly* under his breath and went back to the business of sweeping the floor.

"Yard sale." He shot Abel a dirty look and then directed that look back to Sugar. "Some people just don't see the unique character of things. It was calling to me, so I bought it."

"I don't know," I said. "It kind of grows on you. It already brought one new client into the shop today. Like you said, Sea Bass, it makes for a great conversation piece. See, we're already talking about it."

Sugar snorted. "Well, it gives me the creeps. I swear the damn thing's eyes are following me around the room." She headed toward the front door. "Come on now. Mama's waiting."

I handed Abel the bank deposit bag. We didn't handle large amounts of cash, but anyone out there looking to rob someone with a bank deposit bag in their hands didn't know that. I preferred to drop it in the night deposit box myself or hand it off to our resident ex-cop.

We climbed into the Eldorado and headed out. Pearl May Mobley lived on a little patch of property on the outskirts of town. Her house was small and looked more like a shack, but inside it seemed twice as big as you'd expect.

We pulled up to the front and climbed the few steps to the porch. I noticed the darker plank in the center, remembering Sugar's demonstration of how the trick board bowed and nearly split when stepped on. That was the one meant to keep the solicitors from crossing what appeared to be a dangerously unstable porch to knock on May's door.

Satisfied that I wasn't about to put my foot through the trick plank, Sugar reached for the door and opened it without knocking. "Mama," she called into the living room. There was no sign of her. "She must be out back."

I followed her to a doorway that led into the kitchen. The room was tiny and cramped, and every inch of wall space was taken up by shelves containing jars and baskets. There was a large cast iron skillet on the stove and a massive stock pot sitting on the opposite burner. It was simmering with its lid vented.

Sugar headed for the screen door on the other side of the room. As I followed her through the kitchen, something grazed the top of my head. It was a clump of dried sage. Suspended above us were bundles of herbs hanging upside down by strings laced around a sprawling tree branch bolted against the ceiling. The thin limbs stretched a good six feet in all directions. It was like walking through an indoor forest.

"That's Mama's hazel tree," Sugar said, following my eyes up to the ceiling. "Helps her concentrate and keeps out the riffraff."

"Riffraff?" I repeated.

She nodded. "When you do the kind of work Mama does, a lot of undesirables try to get in to siphon a little power. Can't be too careful in these parts."

"Guess not," I agreed as we dodged the drying gauntlet of herbs.

Mama was on her hands and knees with her back to us when we walked outside. I glanced at the garden on the side of the house and then back at the bare patch of dirt she was digging through.

"Come over here, boy," she ordered before we announced ourselves. "I need me some leverage."

May never could accept who Sugar was. She gave birth to who she thought was a son, and despite a lifetime of Sugar living her truth, she would always be Raymond to her mama.

Sugar let out an exaggerated sigh. "Mama, you need to get up off them knees." She shook her head before complying with May's request. "One of these days I'll come out here and find her face down in the damn dirt," she muttered out of her mama's earshot.

May braced herself against Sugar's arm and rose to her feet, brushing the dirt away from the apron of her skirt.

"It's nice to see you again, Mrs. Mobley," I said, forgetting about her aversion to being called that. She preferred to be called May over Mrs. Mobley, or even Pearl.

I took an involuntary step back when she turned around. Her

eyes were slightly squinted against the waxing moonlight, but the cloudy white orbs looking back at me were jolting. Absent were the sparking hazel irises I remembered vividly from the first time we met, and her pupils were gone, too. Her eyes appeared to be rolled back in their sockets.

Sugar saw the startled look on my face and furrowed her brow in question, as if May's strange eyes didn't need an explanation. Then it must have kicked in, because she quickly recovered from her state of ignorance and clarified what was happening. "Oh that," she said, flipping her wrist to dismiss my surprise. "Mama does that sometimes. Usually when she's got the sight." She looked at the ground where May had been digging. Then she bent down and plunged her hand into the disturbed dirt and felt for whatever May was looking for. When she straightened back up, she was holding a brown chicken egg in her hand.

I glanced at May whose void eyes were still fixed on me. She didn't make a sound or move an inch through it all. "I wasn't expecting that," I muttered as I examined the egg nestled in Sugar's palm.

Suddenly May came back to life, blinking several times as her bright hazel irises returned. She grabbed the egg from Sugar's extended hand. Then I heard a sound come out of her mouth that made my blood run cold. She screeched like an owl and threw the egg on the ground, crushing the shell and releasing the black yolk inside. The oozing contents spread over the dirt at our feet and began to grow bigger and move in a funnel shape. A minute later, a tornadic cloud of black rose up from the mess, and a buzzing sound filled the air as thousands of flies circled us.

I tried to step back from the commotion of the whirling insects, but May grabbed my arm. "Stay put, girl!" I couldn't have moved if I wanted to because my arm was being gripped by a tiger. The lines on my back stirred, and I knew I had to get out of there before my dragon came out. "Get a hold of that beast!" she said, still holding me in place.

My eyes darted to Sugar's, but all she could do was shake her head frantically as a warning not to move.

The black cloud of insects rose above our heads and into the dark sky. It hovered above us for a minute and then scattered in a thousand directions as the flies disappeared into the night. May dropped my arm and bent down to pick up the broken pieces of shell. Sugar leaned over to help her, but based on the venom in May's tone, I thought she was going to strike her child. "Leave it! Ain't I taught you better?"

Sugar looked startled standing in May's shadow, stung by the words. I could sense the wound her mama so easily inflicted. I glanced away when she noticed me looking at her.

May stood back up and smiled, her intermittent remaining teeth gleaming against the light reflected from the sky. As she read the pieces of eggshell like tea leaves, she mumbled quietly under her breath. "Buried is buried," she kept repeating.

"Mama? What are you saying?"

"You see that?" May said, holding her deeply-grooved and calloused palm out to me. I looked closer, but all I saw was a bunch of broken eggshells. She pointed to one in particular and flipped it over. Stuck to the membrane on the inside of the shell was a tiny cluster of dirt shaped like something that reminded me of a rune. Next to it was a fly. Its wings buzzed, futilely trying to escape the sticky substance, and then it just stopped dead. "That's the devil," she warned with an odd grin. "It's comin'."

6

We spent another half hour with May as she told us about her vision. She'd been having it for weeks, this itch at the back of her mind warning of a sorceress who was neither here nor there. What she meant by that wasn't clear. All I knew was that something terrible was heading straight for Savannah, and that something had played a major role in Harry Cavanagh's death.

Sugar implored her mama to look deeper and find out who this devil was. But all May could give us was a name—Ijibah. She just kept staring at me with a glazed look in her eyes, like she was seeing right past me to the dragon inside. But May knew more than she was telling. Why she felt the need to hide crucial information was a mystery, but I had a feeling we'd be back here sooner rather than later when the shit hit the fan.

On the drive back, Sugar was unusually quiet. "What's on your mind?" I asked.

She accelerated the engine, and we took off down the empty road with a jerk. "I was just thinking about how it might not be such a bad idea for that big ol' man of yours to move into your place for a while."

"Don't even go there—" I began, but she cut me off.

"But I figure it don't matter, since you could probably kick that boy's ass across the state line with that dragon of yours."

I snorted a laugh. Jackson was a real force of nature, but I doubted his superhuman strength could match mine when the beast came out. The only time we ever went to battle was in the bedroom, to see who got to be on top.

We were getting closer to the city limits when something stepped out from the trees into the road. About thirty feet in front of us, a figure stood in the headlights. "Watch out, Sugar!" I braced my hands on the dashboard in anticipation of a collision.

Sugar slammed on the brakes, sending the Eldorado sideways as we careened right through the man and then spun around to face him. My lungs felt like collapsing from the force of the air rushing out of them, and I'd never heard Sugar scream as loud as she did the moment she thought she'd just committed vehicular homicide.

"We missed him," I said, looking at the man standing in the road about twenty feet in front of us. "Wait a minute." I blinked my eyes a few times to make sure I wasn't seeing things. "We plowed right through him."

Sugar looked a little irritated. "Damn right we did." She reached for the door handle and stepped outside. "What the hell you want?" she demanded to the man who was looking a little pale. I got out and stared at him as he began to fade in and out of the beams coming from the headlights, like an apparition. "Damn spook!" she spat. "Go on now. Get your sorry ass outta here." She shooed him like you would a dog.

"Spook?" I did a double take when I got a good look at his face. His eyes were round, with thick brows that arched up toward two little flaps on the side of his head, and his nose looked oddly thin and tapered to a point just above where you'd expect to see his mouth. But he didn't have a mouth, and I could see the silhouette of the trees through his transparent form. "Is that what I think it is?"

"Damn right it is," she said. "I don't mind me a spook every now and then, but that one crossed the line when it just about wrecked my baby." Sugar loved that car. Had it for God knows how long and babied it like it was brand spanking new off the dealership floor instead of a thirty-year-old relic. She preferred *vintage* over *old* when describing it.

She took a few steps toward the apparition when it refused to leave. But as she got closer, she looked nervous and stopped within a few yards of it. Its eyes shifted over her shoulder and looked directly at me with a cold stare, sending a shiver through me.

Sugar turned around abruptly and ordered me back in the car. "What's going on, Sugar? Did it say something?" Without a mouth, that would be a feat.

"Just get your ass back in the car." She was usually fearless, but at that moment she looked downright alarmed. I froze from the thought of what had the power to intimidate her like that. "Now, Katie!"

Sugar was a little overbearing at times—well, usually—but she'd never spoken to me like that before. It made the hair on the back of my neck stand up as I got back into the car. She wasted no time jumping back into the driver's seat and turning the car around, flooring the gas pedal a second later. By the time she eased off, we must have been doing ninety down that deserted road.

"Talk to me, Sugar."

Her mouth tightened into a grimace. "That ain't no ordinary ghost."

I looked back through the rear window and saw it floating behind the car, like it was catching a ride on our airstream. "Shit!

It's right behind us!" Then I saw the two wings stretched out at its sides. It wasn't floating—it was flying.

"Buckle up, baby!" she said. "We gonna lose that damn thing." She hit the gas again, and I prayed the ancient engine could handle the torque.

"Damn it, Sugar! What is that thing?"

"That's an owlman," she declared. "Coming to escort us straight to hell if we don't lose it real fast."

We were right on the edge of town. I could see lights in the distance as we got closer to the city where at least there'd be safety in numbers. Maybe it was selfish to lead it right into the epicenter of Savannah, but that thing tailing us was frightening, and I'm nothing if not practical.

The adrenaline rushing through my veins was making me queasy. My hands were trembling and starting to scale over, and I could feel my needle-sharp talons pushing through the tips of my fingers. "I think I'm going to have to let the beast out, Sugar," I warned in a shaky voice. "And I might throw up. Unless you want your car destroyed, you need to pull over."

"The hell you will!" She glanced over and noticed my claws braced against the vinyl dashboard. "Don't you tear my dash, girl!"

Good thing it was late, because we kept running red lights and ignoring the yield signs around the square we'd entered. The next thing I knew, Sugar hit the brakes as we dead-ended into Abercorn Street, nearly sending us both through the windshield. Thank God for seatbelts. The owlman flew straight over the car and kept going, not looking back as it sailed over the iron gates of Colonial Park Cemetery and disappeared into the trees and tombs.

"Yeah, you better keep going!" Sugar yelled out the window. "Damn death marcher."

My shift had stopped, but I was still shaking from the excess energy and adrenaline that always took hold of me when I became the dragon. Sugar must have been yelling at me, because I could see her mouth moving and her face bobbing back and forth, but all I could hear was the deafening sound of a high-pitched ringing in my ears.

"Ow! Jesus, Sugar!" That took care of the ringing. I rubbed the spot where she'd slapped the shit out of me. "What the hell was that for?"

"Baby you needed a little help coming back from that dark place you was at." She shifted the car into park in the middle of the street and reached over me for the glove compartment to get a cigarette. She lit it and held her hand out the window as she shifted the car back into drive and headed toward the shop.

"You need to explain what just happened, Sugar. An owlman?"

She took a drag of her cigarette, replying through the exhaled smoke. "Don't you know nothing, girl? Hell, I figured you'd be educated on things like that, having that witch friend of yours back in New York City." She dropped the lit cigarette into the opening of the can of Coke in the cup holder. "Remind me not to drink that."

"You need to quit," I said for the hundredth time.

Ignoring my nagging, she continued. "Sometimes an owl is just a cute little bird with fluffy wings and big eyes. But sometimes them cute little birds is waiting to escort you right to your grave. Messengers for the dead. That's what they is." She pulled into the back lot behind MagicInk and shifted the car into park. "You ever see an owl during the day?" she asked.

Come to think of it, I'd never seen an owl with my own two eyes at any time of the day. I'd only heard them at night making those hooting sounds. "Your point?"

"Creatures of the night. You ever see one during the day, get ready to die."

I scoffed. "I doubt that's true."

"You calling me a liar?"

"Gullible, maybe," I said with a nervous grin.

Her sober expression put an end to any ease I'd managed to garner. "I ain't never seen one of them things up close and personal before. Mama used to tell me stories about the owlman lurking in the trees when someone was fixin' to die. Said the whole community would take turns watching over sick folks to make sure that thing didn't fly in and try to carry them off before their time."

We sat in the car in silence, neither one of us willing to admit that we were still spooked. A few minutes later, Sugar surveyed the dark lot and nodded toward my car. "Go on. I got you covered." I climbed out and headed for my Honda. "And don't stop nowhere on your way home," she yelled out the window. "Text me when you get there."

Sugar had successfully given me the creeps. I knew better than to dismiss what she'd told me about that thing, because I'd seen it with my own two eyes. In fact, I'd probably have nightmares about it for weeks, and I'd never look at an owl the same way again.

Safely locked in my car, I headed home. Sugar tailed me most of the way but eventually took a right turn and disappeared when I was a few blocks from the house. I'd left some pretty fierce friends back in Manhattan, shoes that weren't easy to fill. But Sugar had stepped right into those deep shoes and had proven her loyalty time and time again. We watched each other's back. Even with the gifts of my dragon, she was fiercely protective. Friends like that were hard to come by, and I'd struck the mother lode since moving to Savannah.

When I pulled up to my house, I was disappointed to see an empty driveway. That morning, I'd told Jackson to go home and promised to meet him for lunch the next day, but a part of me was hoping he'd ignored my request and was waiting inside. After my little meltdown that morning over the epiphany of how easily he made my heart flutter, all I wanted to do was curl up next to him and block everything else out. For a single night, I wanted to lose myself in Jackson Hunter. And then there was the fact that I was still a little spooked about the owlman encounter.

"Suck it up, chicken shit," I muttered, scurrying toward the front door with my eyes darting around the sky.

Jet greeted me enthusiastically when I walked inside. I scooped him up and carried him to the kitchen. When I put him back down, he stared at me with his tail twitching, making that odd little gurgling sound he always made in lieu of a typical purr. "Don't look at me like that," I said, glancing at his full bowl of kibble. "You're not starving."

I gave him a generous plate of his favorite canned food, then texted Sugar to let her know I was home safe and sound. Then I dropped down on the sofa and turned on the TV. I usually avoided the local news like the plague, but something got my attention before I could change the channel.

"Witnesses say they hear ghostly moans and screams coming from the tree, along with apparitions of men hanging from this particular limb." A female reporter was standing under a large tree, pointing to a thick branch several feet above her head. "Over the past forty-eight hours, police have received a staggering eighty-six calls from people reporting possible suicides." Savannah was an infamous ghost town, so stories of sightings were rarely covered on the news. But eighty-six calls in the span of two days was definitely unusual. "Dozens of people have captured apparitions or strange orbs on camera, begging the question—Do ghosts really exist?" The reporter gave her best camera-ready smile. "Reporting live from Wright Square, I'm Amanda Stokes."

I raised the volume and flipped to the next channel. The story being covered by that news station was just as bizarre. A woman had killed her own sister, claiming to have no memory of stabbing her sibling over thirty times. Either the Rita Cavanagh case had spurred a copycat killing, or the havoc created by this intruder witch was beginning to spill over to the general public.

It was the third channel that got my undivided attention. The iron cemetery fence was visible in the background near the building the reporter was standing next to, as where the gabled domes of tombs. "The building has been steadily sinking since last week when a construction crew unearthed a section of old graves around the perimeter of the site. It's too soon to speculate on the potential number of graves that extend beneath the foundation of the building, or to identify any of the remains, but authorities are estimating that the number could be in the hundreds."

I'd heard the rumors about bodies buried under the city streets, especially the area around the cemetery. But Savannah is filled with master storytellers, so everything I heard was taken with a grain of salt.

"The property is owned by a company called Cavanagh Holdings," the reporter continued.

The anchorman cut in. "Is that the same company owned by Harry Cavanagh who was allegedly shot to death by his wife?"

"That's correct, Phil. A source downtown has also confirmed that the primary investor on this development project is Finley Cooper, a prominent Savannah businessman." The reporter was obviously trying to hide his enthusiasm over divulging the next little bit of information. "Coincidently, Mr. Cooper is also the ex-husband of the woman who was allegedly involved sexually with Rita Cavanagh at the time of her Husband's death."

I nearly dropped my glass of water on the floor. The reporter didn't mention Esrial by name, but I was an insider and knew exactly who Rita Cavanagh was sleeping with. What the society had failed to mention to me was the part about Fin being her ex-husband.

"Trying to protect Blackthorn Grove, my ass!" I hissed at the TV. I'd been played. Fin wasn't trying to protect the coven. He was trying to protect his ex-wife.

I reached for my phone to dial his number while I was good and hot under the collar. It rang half a dozen times before going to voicemail. I dialed it again but got the same annoying message. "Pick up your *fucking* phone, Fin!" I spat out after the beep. The last time he didn't answer one of my calls, he was entertaining someone in bed. Lillian wasn't answering her phone either. I glanced at the time—11:43 p.m. "Where the hell is everyone?"

Jet ran out of the room when I stood up and growled. Shaking off the adrenaline, I grabbed my keys and headed for the door. I had no idea where Fin lived, but I knew where to find Lillian, and she was on my shit list too.

7

L illian's house was dark when I drove up, except for the lamps lining the circular driveway and a couple of dimly lit rooms on the first floor. It was just past midnight, and I did debate the appropriateness of knocking on her door so late. But I knew Lillian was the nocturnal type, and I had a strong feeling Fin was somewhere in that house. And based on the number of cars parked outside, either Lillian was having a slumber party, or there was a meeting going on inside.

I climbed the steps and stood in front of the large double door, steeling myself before knocking. I considered ringing the doorbell, but a knock at midnight was intrusive enough. As angry as I was, I still had some manners, and that bell would sound like Big Ben ringing through that cavernous house. Firmly, I rapped my knuckles against the wood and listened for footsteps. When no one answered, I knocked louder.

A woman peered through the side window of the door before deciding I was innocuous enough to open it. She was wearing the same gray dress I'd seen on one of Lillian's other house staff. For a rich woman with a heavy imprint on Savannah's society crowd, she had surprisingly few servants. These days "servant" was a word frowned upon. Domestic employee was probably more appropriate.

"May I help you?" the woman asked, clearly annoyed at my audacity to knock on the door at such a late hour.

"I'm here to see Mrs. Whitman," I replied. "I know it's late, but it's important. Tell her Katie Bishop is here, and she wants answers. I'm sure she'll be willing to see me."

"Mrs. Whitman is asleep. You'll have to come back tomorrow."

"I doubt that," I said, glancing at the cars parked in the circle. "What? No valet tonight?" I breezed past her and headed straight for the library where Lillian's meetings usually took place, but when I pushed the door open the room was empty.

"You can't just barge in here," she said with a huff.

"I think I just did. Where's Lillian?"

She came toward me but decided to back off when I turned around and gave her a psychotic glare. While I waited for her to answer my question, I got a whiff of something in the air. It was musky and sweet. I sniffed again and followed the smell coming from the hallway.

"Don't go down there," she warned as I turned around and followed the scent. "Miss Bishop!"

My heart fluttered wildly as the smell grew stronger, and the woman's voice muted in the background. I focused on the door at the end of the hall, pulled toward it by that scent. A low murmuring sound came from the room it marked. Each step toward it made my blood pump a little faster. It was a double door, the kind that marked elaborate halls and grand rooms.

When I reached it, I extended my trembling hand toward the handle. I had no idea why that room was giving off such an ominous vibe, but my gut instinct told me to prepare myself for whatever I found beyond that door. But this was Lillian's house. What could be so bad?

Somewhere in the background, the woman continued to protest as I turned the handle and pushed the double doors open. The room was dark except for the glow of candles, and the smell that had drawn me to it hit me like a wave. In the center of the cavernous space stood a group of figures wearing black robes. They turned in unison to see who had interrupted them, and then they stepped aside and allowed me a clear view inside the circle they'd formed.

"Miss Bishop," Fin said, standing at the edge of the altar. Lillian was standing next to him with a large dagger in her right hand and a velvet bag in her left.

I must have looked stunned or unsteady, because Emmaline suddenly stepped from the circle and took my hand. "Are you all right, Katie?" she asked. "I know this must all seem very strange, but I'm glad you're here." A modest smile graced her demure and ghostly pale face. She was lovely in a gothic way, and her voice always seemed barely above a whisper. But tonight it held a little more volume than usual.

"What is this?" I asked. But I knew what it was. I glanced back at the altar, with its candles and tools of worship. I'd just barged my way into some kind of ritual, and Lillian and Fin were the ones conducting it.

"I think you know what this is, Miss Bishop," Lillian replied. She placed the bag and dagger on the altar and pinched out the candles with the tips of her thumb and middle finger. "Madge, would you get the lights, please. We'll have to start over tomorrow night, seeing how the rite has been disrupted."

Suddenly feeling embarrassed at barging in on such a private moment, I started to apologize. But then I remembered why I was here and realized they'd been hiding a hell of a lot more than just Fin's connection to the latest local scandal. I looked at Fin and then back at Lillian. "You two are—"

"Members of Blackthorn Grove," she interjected. "Well, of course we are. We're in charge."

Emmaline spoke up. "Lillian is our high priestess."

"And you are?" I asked Fin before Emmaline could state the obvious.

He gave me a forced smile that reeked of contempt for my intrusion. "High priest," he said. "You just interrupted an important working intended to help us find our missing priestess, Esrial."

"You mean your ex-wife. You failed to mention that to me, among other things."

If he was surprised by my statement, he did a damn good job of hiding it. "My intention was not to deceive you," he said. "My fear was that you'd be thinking exactly what you're thinking right now." He glanced at the circle of people standing around us. "Let's take it down, ladies and gentlemen. I need a damn drink."

I followed Fin as he disappeared through a door on the other side of the room. "Don't walk away from me, Fin." I regretted it the second I stepped inside the small room and got a look at his naked body. "Shit!" I spun around and squeezed my eyes shut, as if it could undo what I'd just seen.

"It's all right, Miss Bishop. I'm not shy." I could feel his eyes looking at me while he slipped his clothes on. He walked up behind me and spoke, his breath rushing over the skin of my neck. "Let's go have that talk now."

I left the changing room without saying another word and headed back toward the hallway. Agnes Freemont crossed my path and slipped the hood of her robe off her head. The sight of her face was startling as she glared back at me with a sneer, clearly resenting my presence. I never liked the bigot anyway.

The woman who'd tried in vain to keep me from barging into the house gave me a chastising look. I ignored her and headed for the living room where Lillian was waiting for me with a glass of that fancy scotch. I took it and quickly polished it off.

"Would you like another?" she asked.

"I'd like several, but I'd prefer to keep my edge for this conversation." I put the glass down on the table. Fin came in behind me and headed straight for the bourbon. On the way, he grabbed my glass. He handed me a refill and then took a seat in the overstuffed chair next to the sofa.

I barely noticed Emmaline standing by the window. She had a way of doing that, disappearing into the drapes of the room like a chameleon. But as soon as she turned her gaze on me, I felt the unmistakable draw of her haunting eyes.

"What I can't figure out is why everyone in this room felt the need to lie to me," I said. "I thought I was a member of the society, but I guess I'm just a handy tool when something needs fixing."

My favorite bartender from MacPherson's pub came into the room with Dr. Greene. "I figured you were under one of those hoods, Fiona." I'd recently found out that Fiona was Lillian's granddaughter, and it didn't surprise me one bit that she was a member of the grove. She looked like a witch, with the horned god tattooed on the top of her shaved head. And her evasive demeanor the first time I mentioned Blackthorn Grove made me wonder. I would have been surprised if she *wasn't* a member.

"Nice to see you again," Moses Greene said to me.

"Didn't expect to see you under one of those hoods," I replied.

Not one for small talk, Lillian hijacked the conversation and got straight to the point. "What do you want, Miss Bishop?"

"What do I want?" I repeated, incredulous to her blunt question.

"Well, I'm sure you didn't drive over here after midnight just to disrupt our little ritual. That was rather inconsiderate, by the way."

"How about the truth," I said.

Fiona nearly choked trying to stifle a snicker. Lillian glared at her. Out of her Grandmother's line of sight, she grinned at me in solidarity. That friendship of ours was getting stronger by the minute. We needed a girls' night out real soon.

"The truth," Fin said, "is that Esrial is indeed my ex-wife. Now I know what you must be thinking, and that's exactly why I left that little detail out of our conversation when we discussed the society's interest in the Cavanagh murder case. I suspected you'd think this was nothing more than a personal matter." He leaned forward and set his empty glass on the table. "I can assure you this is not about my affection for my ex-wife, but it is personal."

Fin always seemed a little cocky, even when his anger came out. But the look on his face at that moment was anything but arrogant. It was solemn and resolute, like a man taking an oath.

"This is my church," he continued. "I will not have it destroyed by some intruder who thinks she can walk into my city and start a war."

I was still a little bit taken aback by the thought of Fin Cooper in a black robe. Who would have thought that the shrewd businessman sitting a few feet away from me was also the king of Savannah's most prominent coven? And speaking of that, my next question came out.

"And your business relationship with Cavanagh Holdings?" My mention of Harry Cavanagh's company seemed to surprise him. "I watch the news, Fin."

His solemn look turned back to the arrogant one I knew so well. "Miss Bishop, are you suggesting that I might be involved in a conspiracy to murder my business partner over a little piece of land? Surely you realize that I'm way downstream on the list of his beneficiaries."

"How convenient that his beneficiary is sitting in jail and will probably die there," I replied. Actually, that wasn't what I meant at all. I just wanted him to cut the crap and be straight with me about everything, including the Crossroads Society's real interest in Cavanagh's death. Of course, now I understood his fierce instinct to protect the coven, having outed himself and Lillian as the head honchos.

"My only interest in that land," he continued, "is the building going up on top of it. And since you watch the news, you know that building is sinking like a ship into a pile of old graves." He got up to refill his drink. "Now, let's just lay it all on the line. Get the facts straight so there's no more innuendo dividing our efforts to defeat whoever has been wreaking havoc on our town. Yes, Esrial is my ex-wife. Yes, I do business with Cavanagh Holdings." He looked at me with a resolute stare. "But neither of us had anything to do with Mrs. Cavanagh putting a bullet in Mr. Cavanagh's head."

"This witch heading for our city must be pretty powerful," Lillian said. "To be capable of compelling such diabolical acts from beyond the gates of the crossroads is damn impressive, if not troubling. All kinds of strange acts have been taking place around this town lately. If she can do that before she even gets here, imagine what she'll do when she steps over the line between the worlds." A wary sigh shuddered out of her as she lifted her glass to her lips. "It's like the dead are waking up."

Buried is buried. Pearl May Mobley's words resonated in my mind. "What are you not telling us, May?" I muttered to myself.

"What's that, Miss Bishop?" Fin asked.

I shook my head. "Just thinking out loud."

Dr. Greene cleared his throat to get everyone's attention.

"Maybe we should discuss the impending arrival of the council." He noted the question on my face. "For the tribunal."

"They'll send at least three," Lillian said. "Three inquisitors who will decide the fate of our Esrial. By my estimation, they should be here within a few days."

"You mean you don't even know when they'll arrive? Aren't there rules about disclosure to allow the accused to prepare a proper defense?" In the mundane world people had set trial dates.

Lillian let out a short laugh. "They like to sneak up on you. Gives them the upper hand. If I didn't know better, I'd swear they enjoyed finding scandal and delivering punishment." She took a deep swallow of her drink. "Hell, I need to shut up. They could fry me for just making a disparaging remark like that."

The doctor continued. "They'll be expecting accommodations, and I just don't have the space in my house for three guests."

"Well, don't be ridiculous, Moses," Lillian said. "Vivian!" The woman who answered the front door when I arrived appeared around the corner. "Make up three guest rooms when you get here in the morning. First thing."

"In the east wing?" Vivian asked.

"North. Let's roll out the red carpet." Vivian nodded her head and turned to leave the room. "Why don't you go on home, Vivian. It's late and everyone will be leaving shortly. Let's just hope they don't show up before morning."

Regardless of when these "inquisitors" showed up, it would be hard to interrogate a missing suspect. "Has Esrial resurfaced?" I asked.

"Not yet," Fin replied. "But she will. She always comes home when she needs fixing, and with her current muse locked up in the Chatham County Jail, home means me."

Lillian stood up and sighed heavily. "Miss Bishop, have we

answered all of your questions? I'm tired and I'd like to go to bed."

"Just one more. Are there any other secrets the society is keeping from me?"

"I think you've passed your vetting period, Katie," someone said from behind me. Davina McCabe was standing in the doorway when I turned around, still donning her black robe.

"Jesus," I said. "Is everyone at the society a member of Blackthorn Grove?"

Davina smirked. "Honey, Blackthorn Grove *is* the Crossroads Society. Although we do have members who are not initiated into the grove, such as yourself."

Ignoring my shocked reaction to what Davina had just revealed, Fin smoothed right over it with an invitation. "We're having a little get together at MacPherson's on Saturday. A cookout in the back lot sponsored by the grove. You should stop by. Jackson too, of course."

I needed to find out more about the people I was working with, especially the ones I'd never met. "What time?"

8

I tried to call Sea Bass to let him know I'd be a little late getting to the shop that morning, but he didn't answer. Lack of sleep was finally catching up with me, and getting home at three a.m. had turned me into a zombie. I probably would have slept even later, but I smelled bacon coming from the kitchen. Either Jackson was making me breakfast, or some intruder was in my house.

"Morning, sunshine. Sit down and have you a real breakfast."

"How'd you get in here, Sugar?" I asked, taking a seat at the kitchen island.

She dumped the bacon on a plate next to a pile of her signature scrambled eggs. "Same way I always do."

"I need to get that door fixed." My sliding patio door was a burglar's dream, and for the life of me I couldn't remember to put that metal rod in the track at night. One of these days I'd come home to a ransacked house if I wasn't careful.

She fixed us both a plate and joined me on the other stool. "I'm going to get my cousin out here to give you an estimate on a new door."

"You never mentioned a cousin before," I said around a mouthful of food.

"Baby I got cousins all over the state. Mobleys is what you call prolific."

I bobbed my head and chewed. "Must be nice to have a lot of family."

"Oh, it's nice all right. Till they need money."

I glanced at the offending door. "I'm a renter, Sugar. The only person who's going to replace that door is my landlord."

"Well, you give me his number, and I'll have me a little talk with him."

I noticed we were missing something. "No coffee?" I was truly grateful when I looked over at the counter and spotted a full pot. I got up and poured us both a cup. Handing one to Sugar, I confronted her. "Were you planning to tell me that the Crossroads Society and Blackthorn Grove are practically one and the same?"

It wasn't easy to surprise Sugar, but based on the way she momentarily froze mid-chew, it appeared I'd managed to catch her off guard. "I guess the cats out of the bag. How'd you find out about that?"

"Because I walked in on them last night. I was watching something interesting on the news and decided to pay Lillian a personal visit when I couldn't get a hold of Fin. They were in a back room, wearing black robes and performing some kind of ritual."

She looked confused and reached for her phone on the counter. "What the hell day is this?" she muttered. "Ain't no damn full moon."

"Fin called it a 'working' and said it was to help them find Esrial. She's still AWOL."

It occurred to me that she had no intention of telling me. "You weren't even going to tell me, were you?"

She took a sip of her black coffee and winced. "Have some mercy on me, baby, and get me some of that half and half from the fridge."

I grabbed the carton and held it at arm's length from her. "And I also suppose you weren't planning to mention the pertinent fact that Esrial is Fin's ex-wife?" That caught her off guard for a second time.

"You know about that?" she asked in a nervous voice as I handed her the carton. She lightened her coffee by about twenty shades and darted her eyes around the counter. "Got any sugar in this kitchen?"

"Answer me, Sugar." The revelations kept coming. "I bet you even knew about Fin's business relationship with Harry Cavanagh, didn't you?"

She looked genuinely surprised. "Now I didn't know about all that, but it don't surprise me."

"But you did know about Fin and Lillian being head of Blackthorn Grove, and Esrial being Fin's ex-wife?" I shook my head and gave her my best shame-on-you glare. "Really, Sugar. I thought you were my friend."

The deer-in-the-headlights look disappeared from her face. "You know why I'm your best friend?" she said. "Because I keep your secrets. Ain't nothing you tell me going to end up in anyone else's ears."

"Make your point, Sugar."

"My point is that Fin and Lillian's secrets ain't your business till they make it your business. And vice versa," she added as she put me in my place. Then she calmly reclaimed her coffee cup and took another sip.

Then another thought entered my mind. "Damn it, Sugar. Are you one of them, too?" I didn't care if she was a Blackthorn Grove witch, but it did bother me if she hadn't trusted me enough to tell me.

She set her cup down roughly. "Now what the hell do you think? Do I look like one of them white-folk society witches? I got me enough juju with Mama and them." She shook her head and muttered under her breath, "A hell of a lot more powerful than them incense burning . . ."

I sat back down next to her and took a few more bites, but my appetite had vanished. "I know you didn't come over here just to cook me breakfast," I eventually said to break the uncomfortable silence we'd suddenly fallen into. "Which is fabulous by the way. You might as well get to it."

She took a bite of her eggs and tapped her fingernails against the counter in an annoying machine gun rhythm. Never one to give a rat's ass about what anyone thought, Sugar usually just came out with whatever was on her mind. But this morning she seemed a little hesitant. "You got any plans after work?" she asked.

I shrugged. "Just planning to sit around with Jackson. Maybe cook him dinner." We hadn't had an uneventful night since Rita Cavanagh killed her husband and Fin Cooper walked back into my life. "Why? Are you making plans for us?"

"I'm working at the club tonight and thought you might want to stop by." Sugar performed at the Blue Light Club over by the river. In the time I'd known her, she'd never invited me to see her perform, and for some reason I was anxious about it. It was kind of like thinking about your parents having sex—you knew they did it, but you didn't need to see it. Sugar wore her truth inside and out every day, but the thought of seeing her up on a stage dressed in an elaborate costume made me oddly uncomfortable. Like a voyeur.

"I don't know, Sugar. If I could, I'd stay in bed and sleep for the next twenty-four hours. Maybe some other night."

She glanced at me from the corner of her eye. "I got someone you need to meet. Someone who knows all about the crazy-ass shit been going on around here lately. Knows about them owlmen, too."

I swallowed and put my fork down, sagging against my elbows on the counter. "Fine, but it'll be after ten before I can get there."

"Shit, the clubs just warming up by ten," she replied. "Don't worry. I'll get you home before you turn into a pumpkin."

A CROWD WAS GATHERED in front of MagicInk when I finally got there. As I turned my car to go around to the rear lot, I saw the back of Abel's head. He was waving his hands in the air and yelling over the group of people trying to get a look inside the shop through the front window.

"We need to clear the sidewalk," I heard him say as I came around the corner of the building to see what was going on. "Everyone just move on now."

"What the hell is going on?" I asked.

He whipped around and sighed. "That goddamn nutcase in there is what's happening." He nodded toward the shop, but I heard it before seeing it through the window. "It's been going on for half an hour."

"And you didn't pick up the phone and call me?" I said, irritated and ready to go inside and physically harm Beth Hendricks. She was screaming so loud it carried out to the street. Her voice was muffled but I could hear something about devils. A second later, I heard something crash.

I swung the front door open, ready to walk inside and end a client relationship that had become more liability than benefit. And if those bratty kids of hers were inside wreaking havoc like their psychotic mother, I was calling the police.

"What the fuck, Beth!" I said when I spotted her to my left.

She was standing on the table next to the window, with Sea Bass's prized yard sale find lying on the floor below her feet. The jug was still rolling back and forth before coming to a stop with its face staring at the ceiling. The three-foot drop from the tabletop should have shattered the heavy ceramic vessel, but it appeared to be intact without a single crack.

Sea Bass looked stunned. "I ain't never laid a hand on a woman," he said, glancing at the jug on the floor and then back at Beth, "but I'm about to——" He shut his eyes and tightened his lips, letting the anger seep out before continuing. He'd known Beth Hendricks since high school, and he wasn't above putting her in her place. But the look on his face was downright homicidal.

I stood between them and gave her a warning look. "You want to get off that table, Beth?" That's when I caught the destruction out of the corner of my eye. I turned to look at the shattered mirror in the middle of the room, next to the over-turned tray of ink and equipment. "What in God's name happen——"

Before I could complete my sentence, she grabbed me by my hair and yanked me backward. "You *fucking devil!*" she spat, digging her fingernails into the sides of my scalp and nearly puncturing my skin. She yanked harder, and my head hit the edge of the jug as I fell to the floor. My eyes squeezed shut from the pain radiating up the back of my neck, toward the top of my skull. When they popped back open, the pain was gone and the room was a sea of brilliant color. I was looking at it through the eyes of the dragon.

"Jesus, Mary and Joseph!" Abel said as he rushed inside and got a look at my eyes. The other client in the shop ran straight past him and out the front door.

My back arched as my skin tightened. It began to harden, and a layer of shiny emerald shields covered me.

Beth was suddenly on top of me as if oblivious to my trans-formation. Her eyes bore down on mine, and for a second they looked like two black holes devoid of any white. "I knew there was something wrong with you!" she sneered. Her left hand found my throat. It barely reached around my growing armored neck, and all I could think about was how that scrawny little woman suddenly had the strength of a tiger. Beth Hendricks probably weighed a hundred and ten pounds soaking wet, but today she was a beast. Then she pulled the game changer from her pocket—a folded knife that she flicked open with her free hand. She stuck her fingers in my mouth and tried to pry it open. "Let's see how dangerous you are without that tongue, you fucking torch mouth!"

As my shifting continued, my hearing started to fade due to the freight train running through my head. The room was getting smaller, and Beth began to seem more like a pesky gnat than a threat. Even that knife in her hand felt like a toothpick as she jabbed it against my armor.

From the corner of my eye, I saw Abel flattened against the left wall, frozen with fear. Mouse was at the back of the room, transfixed with her jaw gaping. Sea Bass was the only one who seemed calm. Well, calm was probably the wrong word to describe his demeanor. Controlled was more like it. Of course, he knew what I was. But he'd never seen me in full dragon glory, so I imagined it was difficult to maintain his composure.

I felt the ceiling against my back, and Beth Hendricks went flying across the room, slamming face first into the wall. She slid to the floor like a limp rag doll, out like a light.

"Now, Katie," Sea Bass said, holding up his hands, signaling for me to back off. "Let's just all calm down."

The room rumbled. It was me growling in the back of my throat. My wings stretched across the room as my instinct to fly kicked in. I needed to get out of there, but the only way out was to take half the building with me. My wings began to beat against the walls, shaking the room and sending picture frames crashing to the floor.

Mouse's eyes flashed wide as I took a step forward and nearly demolished one of the chairs in the middle of the room. A strangled gasp left her mouth as she stumbled and fell trying to reach the back door.

"Damn it, Mouse! Stay put!" Sea Bass growled. "It's Katie."

At the mention of my name, Mouse glanced at him with an incredulous look on her face. "K—Katie?"

"That's right. I'll explain everything later. Just stay put." He glanced at Abel's frozen form. "You too."

My wings crashed against the walls of the shrinking room. I was about to outgrow it, which sent me into a panic. Trapped like a caged animal, I continued to thrash, sending all three of them toward the back wall. A shriek built in my throat. It was ready to come roaring out and announce my presence to the entire neighborhood. But as I opened my jaws, I heard a familiar voice.

"Katie!" Jackson said from the doorway. He took a few steps closer and caught the edge of my right wing before it could smash against the wall again. His strength was impressive, rivaling mine due to his own unusual gifts. He'd become my guardian when I needed to shift, to release the beast that seemed to be growing more powerful and unpredictable by the day. But this was not the appropriate time or place for that. This wasn't the seclusion of the beach where I could spread my wings over the ocean. I was about to do some serious damage to the shop that would cripple my business and out me to the entire city.

A deep growl resonated off the walls as I swung my head around and lowered it to meet Jackson's eyes. His voice become a trigger that could ease the beast and send it retreating to its place on my back. Staring into my eyes with an unspoken command, his palm smoothed over the thick armor of my jaw. My lids grew heavy and eventually closed as the fire in the core of my stomach grew weaker, dimming with each stroke until it extinguished. I felt like a feather swaying back and forth toward the ground. And then the feather became a brick, falling a hundred stories a second until I hit the floor.

I lay there for a few minutes with my eyes closed until I felt Jackson's arms reach under my legs to scoop me up. He sat me in a chair and got down on his haunches, lifting my chin to examine my eyes. "What do you see?" he asked.

"Superman," I said in a shaky voice. "What just happened?"

He glanced at Beth's inanimate form sprawled on the floor. "Good question." Then he kissed my forehead and stood up, throwing a questioning look at Sea Bass who was the only other person in the room who knew my secret—until now.

I cocked my head and looked at the still body lying on the floor at the other end of the room. "Sea Bass, did Beth Hendricks just try to cut me?"

He shook his head. "I've seen Beth do some crazy shit, but this was epic." Furrowing his brow, he scratched the stubble on his cheek. "She seemed normal when she walked in here. Said she wanted a tattoo, but then her face kinda changed and her nostrils started flaring like she was smelling something nasty."

"Smelling something?"

"Yeah, it was weird. She looked around the room and asked for you. I told her you weren't in yet and she went all apeshit. Started screaming and busting up the shop." He nodded toward the area by the window. "Broke the mirror and jumped on that table over there. She had a piece of that broken mirror in her hand when I tried to talk her down." He turned his wrist over to show us the cut Beth had inflicted on his arm. "She started screaming that you were the devil, and she was going to cut your tongue out. To stop the fire."

I glanced nervously at Jackson and then back at Sea Bass. They were both thinking the same thing I was—How the hell did Beth Hendricks know about the dragon?

Suddenly realizing Abel and Mouse were standing comatose near the back door, I took a deep breath and contemplated what to say to them. How do you explain to your employees that their boss is a beast? "I guess I have some explaining to do." Abel just nodded his head while Mouse had that same transfixed look on her face. She looked more curious than scared. "But right now I think we've got more important things to deal with." I glanced at Beth's crumpled form and then back at my two dumbstruck employees. "You guys know I would never hurt you, right?"

"Of course you wouldn't," Sea Bass said.

"I guess we better check Beth's pulse," I suggested. Last thing I needed was a dead client in my shop. I already had one dead body on my conscience. Even if Christopher Sullivan's murder was an act of self-defense, another death attributed to me was more than I could live with and would probably land me in prison this time.

Jackson bent down and confirmed that Beth was very much alive. He picked her up and carried her to the table at the back of the room while I flipped the sign on the door to CLOSED. Then we all just stood around her watching for signs of life. Eventually she stirred.

"Well, look who just woke from the dead," Sea Bass said when she opened her eyes.

She gasped when she saw us hovering over her. "What the hell happened to me?" she felt her face where she impacted with the wall. "Jesus! Did one of you assholes punch me?" Then she looked at Jackson and jerked backward. "What the hell are you? A damn vampire?" Jackson had that effect on people, with his intense eyes and long black hair, not to mention his pale skin that resembled porcelain. As long as you didn't mess with him, you were safe. But Beth Hendricks had just tried to excise the tongue from his girlfriend's mouth, so all bets were off.

"Whatever you do, Jackson," I said while I glared at her, "try to keep it neat. I'm not in the mood to clean up a bloody mess today."

She looked at Abel. "You're a cop. You can't just stand there and do nothing."

"Ex-cop," Abel corrected. "I don't have to do jack shit."

Jackson allowed her to sit up but stopped her from climbing off the table. "Look," he said with a disarming tone. "I just want to know why you walked in here and tried to cut Katie's tongue out of her mouth." The deceptively warm smile he gave her was almost frightening.

Her mouth began to tremble. At first it was just a twitch at the left crease, but it spread across her lips until I thought she'd burst into tears. "I don't know!" her head shook frantically. "I came in for a tattoo, and before I knew what the hell was happening, I was smashing things. Last thing I remember was yanking you by your hair!" She looked at me with a remorse I'd never seen in her eyes before, and I believed her.

Nervously, her eyes panned around the room. She did a double take as they passed over the jug on the floor. "That thing is creepy." Then she startled a little as if her memory had been jogged. "Where'd you get that damn thing?"

"Harold!" Sea Bass exclaimed, suddenly realizing the jug was still lying sideways on the floor. He went to hoist it back onto the table, inspecting it for damage. "That ain't none of your business, Beth. You're lucky you didn't break it. It's an antique, and you'd be getting the bill for it if you did. And here I thought it would be one of them wild kids of yours who would knock it over."

"Don't you talk about my kids, McCabe!" she spat back.

"Beth," I said, reclaiming the conversation, grateful that she didn't remember the dragon. Abel and Mouse could be trusted, but Beth Hendricks would spread my secret across town like wildfire. "I believe you had a momentary bout of insanity this morning, but now I'm telling you to get the hell out of my shop."

Her jaw dropped. "You mean I can't get my tattoo?" She glanced at the No Small Children In The Shop sign I'd prominently displayed and warned her about the last time she showed up with one of her hellions. "I paid a sitter to watch my kids so I could get over here."

I thought Jackson was going to pick her up and carry her out the front door, but he knew better than to deprive me of the pleasure of kicking her out myself. "No Beth. No tattoo today—or any other day," I added for clarity. "You see, I have a strict rule. When people try to mutilate me, we're done. Now get out and don't come back."

"Yeah," Sea Bass said, pointing toward the door. "And don't even think about walking past that window in the future."

After escorting her out, I watched her stomp down the sidewalk and out of view, hopefully for the last time. Jackson came up behind me and put his hands on my waist. "You okay?"

I sighed deeply and thought about what was really bothering me. "No, I'm not okay." He turned me around and gave me a questioning look. "I couldn't control it at all. It didn't even warn me this time. It just came out like it was controlling me." My twenty-fifth birthday was right around the corner. I hadn't really taken my aunt's warning too seriously because until now nothing had happened to make me believe that the beast was taking control. Maybe I was just in denial.

Abel walked up and eyed me from my shoulders down to the edge of my short skirt. His eyes continued down to my strappy sandals with the spiky heels. "How do you do that?" he asked.

"Do what?" I asked back, following his eyes.

"Keep your clothes on after all that? Shouldn't they be

shredded or something? I'd expect you to be naked after turning into something ten times your actual size."

Mouse snorted. "You wish."

Abel shot her a perturbed look. "Quiet, you little pervert."

"The clothes kind of shift with me," I said, keeping it simple. Going into detail would only complicate a delicate situation that still needed to be explained to them.

Aunt Marianna had explained it to me the night she introduced herself at Lou's Diner. Apparently, the art of dragon shifting included the ability to absorb our clothing as part of our human skin, and then expel it back out once we shifted back into our human form. She said it was some kind of evolutionary thing. It got pretty frigid in the Slovenian Alps where we were from, especially during winter. Dragons spent centuries dying from exposure after shifting back into human form, with nothing but their birthday suits to protect them from the elements. Our ability to retain our clothing just sort of evolved as part of our metamorphosis, out of sheer necessity.

Thank God for small favors, because I'd never be able to look my employees in the eye again if they saw me sprawled on the floor buck naked. Not to mention the time I shifted in the middle of hundreds of people in Washington Square Park back in New York City.

"I guess it's time to make that call to your aunt," Jackson said. "You know I'm not going anywhere."

He was right. My time was almost up. I had to choose my destiny.

9

When I turned around, Mouse was still standing near the back door with that same curious look in her eyes. Her family had been Savannahians for generations, so I suspected she'd seen some pretty strange and unexplainable things over the years. You couldn't walk a block without being reminded of the rich history and the notorious reputation of the paranormal in this town.

"I think we need to have a staff meeting," Sea Bass said, glancing at his two stunned co-workers.

Abel nodded his head in agreement but was having difficulty finding words.

Jackson squeezed my hand in solidarity and then took a seat in one of the chairs in our makeshift waiting area, which was really just a couple of chairs and a table covered with old magazines. It was a good thing he showed up when he did, because I don't think anyone else could have talked me down before my wings broke out the front window and drew another crowd even bigger than the one Beth Hendricks amassed earlier.

"Well, what do you think?" I replied, irritated that he even had to ask.

His head bobbed as he contemplated what to say next, but since it really wasn't his show to run, I took the reins and spoke up. "I guess you two are wondering what the hell just happened." I laughed weakly since I really didn't know how to explain it other than to just rip the Band-Aid off and show them. "The tattoo on my back isn't just ink." I turned around and lifted my shirt high enough to give them a good look at what they already knew was inked on my back. Until now though, they'd only seen glimpses of it peeking out from under the edges of the fabric.

"That's a real live dragon," Sea Bass said in an authoritative tone, nodding toward my skin. "Welcome to the club, folks. Ain't too many people that know about that. Of course, I did," he said, snorting. Mouse and Abel both shot him a look, and I'm sure there'd be some heated conversation after I left the room about why he'd been keeping that information from them. "Well, I am her best friend."

Sugar and Sea Bass vied for that designation on a regular basis. The truth was, they were both worthy, and each had my undivided trust and loyalty.

"I was born with it," I said, drawing their eyes back to me. "It's a birthmark. Sea Bass is right. I have a dragon inside of me. You just saw it up close and personal." I took a moment to look into both of their faces for signs that I might have judged them wrong. Signs that my trusted employees, who were also my friends, were about to turn on me. "The question is, can the two of you keep my secret?"

Abel was the first to respond, scratching his bald head and snorting an ironic laugh. "When I was a cop, I got a call on a guy running through the cemetery with nothing but a cape covering his naked ass. When I got there, he was running around, all right. Had a sword in his hand, too. Fucker disappeared when I got within ten feet of him. Just vanished like mist." He shook his head at the memory. "But I've never seen anything like what you just did. I know you're a decent person, Katie. I don't understand it, and I don't plan on telling anyone what I just saw. Hell, no one would believe me anyway."

"Why?" Mouse asked.

"Why what?" I asked back.

"Why do you do that? Turn into a dragon?" She approached me and touched my arm as if feeling for the roughness of scales. Then she stepped back quickly. "Sorry."

I held my arm out. "It's okay. You guys can touch my skin, but it's no different than yours right now."

"I'll take your word for it," Abel said, declining my offer. He glanced at Jackson who was sitting quietly in the chair, taking in the conversation like it was the weather forecast we were discussing. "What are you?" he asked Jackson. "Some kind of dragon whisperer? Is that why you showed up in town? Are you the dragon's handler?"

Jackson laughed. Then he stood up and displayed his impressive height. He walked over to where we were standing and draped his arm over my shoulders. "Nobody handles Katie."

Someone knocked on the front door, and we all turned to see who was outside.

"Shit," Mouse said. "It's my eleven o'clock." The door was locked, and the sign was still flipped to CLOSED. We all glanced at the mess around the room—the glass from the mirror that Beth had shattered during her psychotic episode, overturned trays, ink everywhere. "I guess I need to reschedule her appointment."

"That would be wise," I said.

Mouse slipped out the front door to make up an excuse for rescheduling her client, while the rest of us got busy cleaning up the mess left by two women who had both shown their true colors that morning. If I ever saw Beth Hendricks again, she'd be lucky to survive it.

I bent down to pick up a few pieces of large broken glass. As I grabbed the last piece, something had the hair on my arm's standing on end. I glanced up and found those eyes staring back at mine. For an inanimate object, that jug sure could talk, with its beady eyes and that chipped nose. I decided right then and there that it had to go. Now I just needed to figure out a way to convince Sea Bass that it would look better in his apartment.

THE BLUE LIGHT had a nondescript entrance that shouted anything but drag club. The door looked more like the entrance to an old warehouse. In fact, we walked right past it on our first attempt to find it. Had it not been for the faint beat of music snaking through the thick walls of the building, we might have ended up all the way down on River Street.

We were met at the door by a tall woman with a mountain of curly hair. Her eyes appeared twice as big as they actually were on account of all her makeup. "That'll be twenty dollars, honey," she said to Jackson with a smile.

"They're with me," I heard a familiar voice say. "No charge." Sugar threw her arm over my shoulders and hooked the other one around Jackson's elbow. "Welcome to my world, babies. Let's get us a drink." She ushered us through the crowd toward the right side of the room and nodded to the young man behind the bar. "Scotch," she said, holding up two fingers. "And not that cheap shit. These are my friends."

"You don't drink before you perform?" I asked.

She took a step back and looked at me, surprised. "Baby, I ain't getting up on that stage tonight. Ain't got no time for it. I got other business to attend to."

I was relieved. There'd be plenty of other times to see Sugar perform, but tonight I was too preoccupied to enjoy it.

She handed us our glasses and leaned back against the bar. Jackson downed his drink and surveyed the room. It was filled with an equal mix of men and women. There was a group of people dancing to the music between acts, wearing colorful plastic leis around their necks and looking sufficiently drunk. Tourists, I figured.

One of the performers, who looked just like Britney Spears, walked past us and ran her eyes over Jackson. "Hey, baby," she said, sipping the drink in her hand. "You a big boy." He grinned as she passed, her eyes glued to him.

"Good thing you got Katie B with you, Jackson. You about to get eaten alive up in here," Sugar said, giving Miss Spears a warning look. "Yeah, you *better* keep moving," she muttered under her breath as the woman walked away.

She pushed off the bar and motioned for us to follow her. Through a cloth veil covering a doorway, we walked down a long hall. We climbed the stairs to the next floor and stopped at the second door on the right. Sugar knocked once. Without waiting for an invitation, she opened it and motioned us into the room.

On a tall chair with the name QUEEN MOLASSES written on a canvas panel draped across the back, was a dark-skinned woman with her hair slicked back tightly against her head. It was secured with a flesh colored headband and a sheer cap.

"This is my friend, Katie," Sugar said. "The one I've been telling you about." Queen Molasses smiled at me and then glanced over my shoulder at Jackson, a grin reaching up the right side of her face. "That's her man, Jackson."

"Well, of course he is," she said, grinning wider. "Fine man like this always got a woman."

Jackson reached his hand out. She took it and gripped it firmly. "Nice to meet you," he said. "Do you prefer Queen or Molasses?"

"Baby, you can call me whatever you like."

"All right, now," Sugar said, breaking up the innuendos that didn't bother me one bit. "Queen's got some information about all this crazy shit been going on around here lately."

Queen turned back to the mirror and continued applying her makeup. "Don't mind me. I go on in a few minutes. Sugar tells me you work with the Crossroads Society. True?" She looked at my reflection in the mirror and waited for me to answer.

"That's right. Card-carrying member."

"Then I guess you know all about Sugar's connection to the society." Sugar was an honorary member, a descendant of some of the earliest slaves brought into the Port of Savannah in the mid-eighteenth century. My first "assignment" with the society was to hunt down a rogue god who'd hitched a ride in the body of an unborn slave child. That unfortunate child's mother also happened to be one of Sugar's ancestors. The ghosts of those ancestors saved both of our asses when the god we were hunting nearly killed us earlier that summer.

"Intimately," I replied.

Sugar got up and handed her a pink lipstick. "That red makes you look trashy. And it don't go with that dress either." She appraised the flamingo-pink sequined gown before continuing. "You know why I brought Katie here, so get to the point so I can take the girl home. She got her a business to run in the morning."

Queen glared at her through the mirror. "Easy for you to throw your uppity-ass weight around here, Sugar. Like it ain't nothing to let them skeletons out of your closet." She tightened her lips and went back to the business of painting them with the red color she preferred. Between strokes, she spoke. "Some people got good ancestors, and some people got bad." She snapped the cover on the lipstick and tossed it on the table. Then she grabbed a powder puff. As she moved it down the length of her nose, she continued. "And then there's those who got the evil ones." She swiveled around and smiled. "How do I look?"

Sugar seemed impatient with Queen's beating around the bush. "You look like Diana Ross without her wig! Now get to it before we get up and walk out of this damn club!"

I glanced at Jackson. He seemed perfectly content to watch the two go at it, but the buildup to whatever she'd brought us here for made me nervous. Sugar didn't suffer fools, so I knew that behind all the stalling there was something important about to come out of Queen's mouth.

Queen went back to primping and finally got on with it. "My family goes way back, just like Sugar's. Only mine was the kind you stayed clear of unless you needed something special. Us Bassets were the ones you came to for a little juju when things needed fixin'. Basset men are about as useful as any other, but Basset women are resourceful. Ain't no stopping one of us when we want something." She glanced at Jackson and then back at me, losing her cocky grin. "She's coming. And she ain't gonna stop until she gets what she came for."

"Who?" I asked.

"Ijibah. Now there's a real queen."

She suddenly stopped powdering her face and looked at my reflection again. Then she put the puff down and swiveled back around in her chair, looking genuinely amused. "Sugar tells me you're a dragon."

Jackson stifled a laugh, but I was more shocked than amused by the sudden revelation that I'd been outed for the second time in one day. I gave Sugar a dirty look and then eyed Jackson, who for some unknown reason found it all very entertaining. He sobered up and smiled sympathetically.

"Jesus, Queen! Ain't you ever heard of discretion?" Sugar looked at me and tried to explain. "I had to tell her, Katie. Wasn't no other way to convince her to talk to you."

Queen pressed her hand to her chest. "Did I say something wrong? Honey, your secret is safe with me."

Sugar leaned in and whispered. "Baby, that old queen got more secrets than you. You can trust her." She straightened back up and raised her voice. "All right now. Tell her the rest."

Queen continued with her story. "All this crazy shit going on around this town is the work of Ijibah, including that murder over there at the Cavanagh place. The question is why? That old witch is coming home, and whatever it is she wants, she'll get."

"We know what she wants," I said. "She's trying to frame one of the witches of Blackthorn Grove so the Southern Council of Witches will sanction the coven. It's her way of getting rid of them so she can step in and take over. She wants power."

"Oh, she got that." Queen huffed. "But honey, you got to understand. A witch like Ijibah doesn't waste her time on a middleman. If she wants to take over, she'll take over. A witch like Ijibah takes what she wants. No match for a bunch of mortals." She shook her head in thought before continuing. "Harry Cavanagh was a revenge killing. I'd stake my kitty on it."

"Revenge?" I said. "For what?"

"Don't ask me. I'm just the messenger."

"How do you know all this?"

"Queen's got the sight," Sugar said. "Like me and Mama."

"Ijibah is my people," Queen continued. "I've been getting orders. Ijibah's been telling me to do things." Her head shook as she tightened her lips and took a deep breath through her nose. "Uh-uh. I won't."

"Like what?" Jackson asked before I could open my mouth.

She smirked but quickly lost her cocky smile. "Like get me a gun and get ready to use it. Ijibah's been flooding my mind with instructions, giving me dreams and bad thoughts. I was shopping at the Kroger the other day, and I saw this woman with a little baby in her arms. I heard this loud voice in my head telling me to snatch that baby from its mama's arms and take a bite out of its fat little leg. Can you imagine? Biting a little baby? But I'm strong. Got me a good life, and I won't mess it up for some old witch who can't stay dead. And I don't give a shit whose side of the family she comes from. That's when I decided to have a little talk with Sugar, to let the society know what was going on."

I could tell Jackson was still skeptical about all the sharing going on in the room. "Why you?" he asked.

"Because I'm the last one. Alive, that is. I'm the last of my line. The rest are all dead and buried. Ijibah's dead, too. But something woke her up." She took her time looking at me, like she was debating whether I was up to the task or if her ancestors would eat me alive. "Ijibah's got the fire just like you, but something tells me she's got a better hold on it than you got on yours. No offense, honey, but you look a little artsy-fartsy for this kind of dirty business."

Sugar spoke up in my defense. "Don't let them tattoos and pretty blue eyes fool you. Katie B ain't no bored suburban chick trying to piss off her daddy. Got her a beast inside that'll scare the Jesus outta your ass."

Queen gave me a second look. "You want to stop a witch like Ijibah, you got to take her power. My bet is she's back because she's got her sights on more." She continued to get ready for her performance. She swept some blush over her high cheekbones and then reached for the waterfall of curly black hair sitting on a wig form on the table. "You need to find out where she's planning to get it, and then get to it before she does. If I was you, I'd start by looking at that building that's been sinking. The one that's been all over the news."

"Why's that?" I asked.

She finished running a second layer of red over her top lip and studied the final product in the mirror. "Because that's where they buried her, so they say."

Based on the look on Sugar's face, she was thinking the same thing I was. *Buried is buried* her mama kept repeating when she read the eggshells. I knew May was holding back, but why she felt the need to was a mystery.

"Damn it, Mama," Sugar muttered. She grabbed my arm and steered me toward the door. "We're going for a ride."

"Hold it, Sugar. What about the owlman?" The mention of it caught Queen's attention. "Sugar said you could enlighten us on that thing that nearly chased us straight through the cemetery fence last night."

Queen wouldn't look at me. She adjusted her wig and only gave me a fleeting glance through the mirror. Then she arched her brow at Sugar. "You seen it, too?"

"I seen it, all right. Like Katie said, damn thing chased us and flew right over the car into the cemetery. Chased us halfway from Mama's place."

I could see the silent conversation taking place between the two of them. Something had hit a nerve, and they weren't interested in telling me what it was.

"Come on," Sugar said. "We got to go. Mama's going to kill me for showing up this late as it is. The later it gets, the more I'll regret it."

I was tired but decided not to argue with her. The three of us left the club and climbed into Sugar's Eldorado. Then we headed out of town to pay another visit to Pearl May Mobley.

10

May's house was dark when we pulled into her driveway around midnight.

"Where the hell are we?" Jackson asked as he climbed out of the Eldorado with minimal difficulty, which was unusual since most cars had his long legs smashed against the dashboard or the back seat. But Sugar's ride seemed to accommodate him nicely.

"Mama's house," Sugar replied evasively.

"Yeah, no shit." He opened his mouth to say something else, but I shook my head at him to quell the confrontation. Something had his hair standing on end, and the dark aura coming off of May's house jacked his guard up even higher.

Sugar pointed out the trick board when we reached the top step. "Don't step on that one, Jackson."

"I'll explain later," I said as I stepped around it to follow Sugar to the door. I stopped a few steps behind her and cocked my head. "You hear that?" It was faint, but I could have sworn I heard voices coming from the side of the house.

Sugar and Jackson both stopped to listen. "All I hear is the wind rustling them privet bushes over there," Sugar said, nodding to the stand of gangly shrubs growing next to the house. Jackson shook his head in agreement with her.

Satisfied that there was nothing out there, Sugar reached for the door handle and tried to turn the knob. It was locked. Her brow furrowed. "Mama don't ever lock her door."

"Not even at night?" Jackson asked.

"Uh-uh. Don't need to. Ain't no fool stepping over that threshold without an invitation."

I gave her a questioning look because that's exactly what we did the night before, and we were about to do it again. "So you're leading us into some juju booby trap?"

She shook her head. "Don't apply to blood. Now if you or Jackson was to open that door, you'd be in for a surprise."

"Booby trap?" Jackson muttered to himself.

"I bet Mama's out back again." She led the way down the steps and around to the back of the house. When we passed the side garden and turned the corner, May was on her shins in that mountain of dirt, just like she was the night before. The waxing moon was even brighter, shedding a glow over her dark skin that made it look like polished ebony. She was leaning her body into a smaller mound of dirt, pushing it back into a hole where she must have dug it up for some reason.

May usually felt our presence before she could see us, but tonight she seemed too engrossed in what she was doing to sense our arrival, a dangerous chink in the armor of the elderly woman living out in the boondocks on her own.

"Mama, what are you doing?"

Before we could get within breathing distance of May, that dirt tucked under her bosom went flying into the air, spinning like a funnel cloud. It burst into a million tiny particles of earth that swarmed in our direction. All three of us flew backward a good five feet and landed on our backs, with that cloud of dust altering our vision as we tried to open our eyes.

"Goddamn it, Mama!" Sugar rolled over and grabbed me by my shoulders. "Baby, you okay? Talk to me, Katie!"

Jackson stood up and towered over us, blocking out the moonlight and making it even more difficult to see. He brushed the dirt from his face and clothes and then reached down to pull me up, offering his other hand to Sugar.

"Don't you curse me, boy!" May said. "Come sneakin' up like that."

"Mama, you could have killed us!"

May grinned at me. "You okay? Got a little dirt between them teeth." Then she turned her eyes on Jackson. They flashed as wide as her smile. "Who are you?"

"This is Jackson Hunter," Sugar said.

May walked up to Jackson and reached up to run her dirt-crusted hand along a strand of his black hair, slowly working her fingers through it down to the ends. "Well, look here," she said, seeming fascinated by him, gazing at his pale skin and green eyes. The top of her head barely reached his chest, so she had to crane it up to look at his face. Then her palm rested flat against the spot over his heart. "You a big boy, ain't you? Strong, too."

I glanced at Sugar and smiled. May was reading him like a book.

Jackson looked down at her and cupped her hand with his. "It's a pleasure to meet you, Mrs. Mobley." He squeezed her hand gently but allowed it to remain on his chest.

A few seconds later, she lowered her hand but kept her eyes on his. "I bet folks scare easy around you. All that dark and light fightin' each other under your skin." Jackson gazed down at May, fixed in some silent conversation with her that Sugar and I could only speculate about. A reading of his soul it seemed.

"You layin' with my boy?" she eventually asked with a look of genuine curiosity.

Sugar's chin quivered, and a barely audible gasp came from

her mouth. Although May was still having an issue with the *girl* word, I got the feeling this was one of those rare instances when she not only acknowledged Sugar's truth but seemed to approve of it too.

Jackson glanced at me and laughed. "No," he said to May. "But I am laying with Katie." I arched my brow, daring him to continue discussing our sex life with Sugar's mama.

May had already moved on before he had a chance to dig his hole deeper. "Got you a good one, Katie," she said as she turned back around to continue with what she was doing in the garden before we interrupted her.

"Mama, what the hell you doing out here in the dark again?"

She turned to look at Sugar, the light from the sky exaggerating her hazel irises, giving them an almost ghostly pale shimmer. "Cookin' me up some ju."

Before Sugar could respond, something crashed inside the house. Some kind of explosion. Jackson took off toward the back door and pulled it open. A cloud of white smoke came pouring out of the kitchen, rolling over him like a dense fog until we could hardly see him anymore. By the time it passed, he was inside. Sugar and I were right behind him, while May stood back and looked on like it was nothing.

"Stay put, Mama," Sugar ordered.

We walked inside and stopped cold when we spotted what Jackson was staring at. It was a giant hole that took up most of the kitchen floor, leaving only a foot or two around the perimeter. The tree branch suspended across the ceiling, the one that May used for drying herbs, was heavily singed, filling the room with an odd smell of smoldering rosemary twigs and something else. It almost smelled like burnt hair.

Sugar shook her head, incredulous as May appeared in the doorway. "Mama, what are you up to?"

May smiled a wide toothy grin, but it was more sly than

93

joyful. She stared at the hole in the middle of her kitchen floor. "That's just the juice workin'," she said, glancing at the oversized stockpot laying sideways on the stove, emptied of its contents.

I stepped closer to the hole and looked down. Jackson and Sugar did the same but quickly stepped back. Jackson wrapped his arm around my waist to pull me back from the edge because I was leaning precariously over it to get a better look at what was at the bottom. But there was nothing to see. The hole seemed to go on forever, to stretch to the center of the earth.

May pushed past us and walked to the edge, bracing her hands on her hips as she leaned over and spit into the dark hole. After a minute of examination, she nodded her head. "That devil 'bout to bust through the crossroads," she proclaimed. "We in for trouble now."

Sugar's eyes flew wide. "Who you talking about?"

"Who do you think?" I said before May could say the name.

Sugar suddenly remembered why we were here, in her mama's kitchen at midnight. "Why the hell didn't you tell us everything you knew about Ijibah?" she asked May.

May's face hardened. "You better watch your mouth."

"I'm sorry, Mama, but this ain't no game. You should have told us everything last night. Saved us a whole bunch of grief." She stood a little taller and shook her head slowly, clearly irritated by May's lack of disclosure. I was a little annoyed myself, but I had my manners and thought it best to be respectful and keep my mouth shut. Disrespecting a conjure woman, who'd just managed to cast a spell that blew a hole through her kitchen floor the size of a Jacuzzi, was just plain stupid.

"I'da told you if I knew," May said. "I didn't know who she was till just now. These things take time." She pointed toward the center of the hole. "See that?"

All three of us followed her extended finger, but all I could see was a void of bottomless black. I fixed my eyes on the spot and tried to see what May was seeing. That's when I realized that the dark circle of what initially looked like nothing but an empty space was actually turning. My eyes were drawn to the edges of the hole where I could see the black void slowly circling, spinning in a counterclockwise motion, creating a small funnel in the center like an emulsion of liquid in a blender. "Why is it doing that?" I asked. "Pulling inward."

May shook her head and reached inside the pocket of her apron. "It ain't." She revealed a penny in her hand and held if out toward the hole. "Stand back," she warned, tossing it in the center. The penny hit the vortex, but instead of being swallowed up by the black whirlpool, it flew into the air, ricocheting off the ceiling and shooting toward Jackson at a dangerous speed.

We all gasped in that split second it took to realize what was about to happen. Like it was second nature to catch a bullet, Jackson snatched it out of the air with his bare hand and turned to May, tossing the penny back to her. "You want to tell us what we're dealing with?" He nodded to the whirling black hole and waited for an explanation.

"Damn, that boy's got skills," Sugar muttered.

"Ain't pulling nothing in," May said. "'Bout to spit something out." Her nose crinkled as she took a whiff. "Something rotten. That witch been dead too long to be coming back now, but she done found a way to cut herself a door. By the amount of stink coming out of that hole, she'll be here real soon. Powerful juju drawing her out. Bone magic."

"Bones from the crossroads?" I asked.

"Mm-hmm. Them's the only bones strong enough to get you over. Regular old bones won't even get you to the gate. Something's calling her back. Got to pay for them bones with something precious. Something personal."

I thought about what Queen had said about Ijibah being buried on the land where Harry Cavanagh's construction project was sinking. "You said something last night about *buried* being *buried*," I said. "Were you talking about Ijibah?"

May opened her left hand, which had been clamped shut since she walked into the kitchen. In the center of her palm were the eggshells she'd read the night before, that dead fly still stuck to the dried membrane. "Shells don't lie," she said. "Ijibah be dead and buried, but them eggshells say different. I can see it."

"Is her grave just outside the cemetery in town?" If that construction project had disturbed her burial spot, it could be what woke her up from the dead in the first place, followed by her need to seized control of Savannah. Murdering Harry Cavanagh and implicating Blackthorn Grove through Esrial was probably just killing two birds with one stone—revenge for desecrating her grave, and a means for eliminating the competition.

"Mama," Sugar said, "Fin Cooper's got him a building project over there by the cemetery. It's sinking into the ground. Found them some graves underneath it. You telling us one of them graves is Ijibah's?"

May grinned with a devilish look in her eyes and chuckled in a gravelly voice that gave me the chills. In that moment, standing over the giant black hole in the middle of her kitchen floor, that small woman who gave birth to Sugar looked about as formidable as a rattlesnake. Even Sugar took a step back.

"What the hell's wrong with you two. I ain't gonna bite." She smiled at me again, but this time her expression seemed more excited than dangerous. "You done good, Katie. You is quicker than May." She must have been referring to her own lag in detective work. "You saving us a lot of time trying to find the source."

"The source?" Jackson said. "Source of what?"

She looked at him thoughtfully for a moment. "You a big, strong man, but you ain't got the sense us women folk got." Her smile widened as she continued. "But you're still useful."

Jackson nodded, accepting the less than flattering comment graciously.

She turned back to me. "You know what I mean, don't you?" I did. The dead were usually tied to their final resting place—their source. "When you're dead and you decide to come back, you come back to where you left from. Ijibah will bust through the crossroads and head straight for the land that building is sitting on. To her grave. That's where we'll find her."

"Maybe she just wants some peace," I said. "If they get the construction of that building done quickly and her grave is left alone again, maybe she'll go back to being dead." Seemed reasonable. Now all they had to do was hurry up and complete construction before she killed someone else—like Fin Cooper—because I doubted Cavanagh Holdings or Fin would be willing to take a loss of millions and scrub the construction project altogether. "Maybe she's not as evil as we're making her out to be."

"Oh, she evil all right," May quickly countered. "Witch like Ijibah got bad blood. She ain't stopping till she gets her a pound of flesh, and that power she wants so bad. Too bad them folks didn't put that building up on a good witch's grave." She shook her head slowly. "Best can be done now is to keep her out. Keep her from getting through. But she gettin' a lot of juju from somewhere. Got to find the cone."

"Cone?" I asked.

"Cone of power. If Ijibah gets enough juice from the cone, she be flying through that crossroads faster than a hawk eyeing a fat squirrel," she said, nodding toward the black hole at the edge of our feet.

That hole in the floor was making me nervous. I expected Ijibah to come catapulting out of the center at any moment. "Shouldn't we try to close that thing? Maybe start dumping some wheelbarrows of dirt into it?" It was a ridiculous suggestion, seeing how it appeared to have no bottom, but stupid things tended to come out of my mouth when I was nervous.

May followed my eyes to the hole and then looked at me like I had two heads. "That ain't the damn crossroads, girl!" She continued to eye me in a puzzled way, like I was thick in the brain or something. "That there is just a thought."

"A thought?" I repeated. "What are you talking about, May?"

"That's what I said. That hole is just a manifestation, but the real one be opening up soon."

Before any of us could process what May was saying, she took a step over the edge of the hole.

"Mama!" Sugar yelled, frantically reaching for May before she could plunge into the vortex that would either swallow her up or send her crashing against the ceiling like that penny.

Out of Sugar's reach, May continued across the room toward the stove, each step seeming to banish the wide hole back into her mind, like it was nothing but a shadow fading away as she crossed it. By the time she reached the stove and righted the heavy stockpot back onto the burner, the hole was completely gone. Vanished.

"Got to find me a new tree," she said, looking up at the singed limb bolted to the ceiling. "That one's spent. Been a good tree, but it's done now. Got no more magic." She glanced at Sugar who was still standing on the other side of where the hole had been, looking relieved that her mama was still intact. "Will you help me find a new one?"

Sugar just nodded her head, unable to speak for the first time since I'd known her.

We spent a few more minutes helping May clean up the mess in the kitchen. With his impressive height, Jackson took down the damaged limb from the ceiling and headed out back.

"Toss it on the dirt pile," May instructed. "Got to dispose of it in the proper way."

As we climbed into the car, Sugar promised to come back in a few days to help May scout for a new limb. "Moon's got to be just right," May said. "I'll tell you when to come."

We said goodbye to May and headed back to town. On the way, I mentioned the cookout at MacPherson's the following afternoon, knowing that as an honorary member of the society Sugar would be on the guest list. I also figured she'd rather have her teeth drilled than go to one of their events.

"I'll drop by and pick you up at the shop," she said. "What time?"

I was shocked but glad she'd be joining us. Jackson was coming with me, but you could never have too many reinforcements at one of these things. The more the merrier as far as I was concerned.

11

S ea Bass was having a conversation with that jug when I walked into the shop the next morning.

"Morning, Katie," he said.

I dropped my purse on the counter and looked at his friend sitting on the table next to the window. "Sea Bass, tell me you are *not* having a conversation with that thing."

He adjusted its face a little toward the window and then stood back and folded his arms, eyeing the position of the jug with his head cocked. "Harold and I have a little talk now and then. But as long as I know he ain't actually listening, I'm just as sane as you. Ain't no different than when you talk to yourself driving down the road. As long as you don't think someone's listening, you're all right."

"I see," I replied. "You just let me know if he starts talking back to you. Okay?"

"If you need confirmation that he's crazy, I can vouch for that," Mouse said as she prepped a tray for her nine o'clock client. "Been crazy since high school."

He pointed his finger at her. "You ain't got no room to talk, you little rat." His head bobbed up and down as he smirked, feeling full of himself for having such a witty comeback. "I got plenty on you." He redirected his pointed finger to his head and continued. "It's all up here. Blackmail."

Mouse threw a plastic bottle of ink across the room and hit him square in the chest. "You ever call me that again, I'll cut your balls off!"

The front door opened as she said it. "Not if I cut them off first." Maggie walked over to him and gave him a kiss on the cheek. "Baby, you been giving Mouse grief again?" She smiled and winked at Mouse.

"Nothing she didn't ask for." He headed for the front desk to check his schedule while Maggie took a seat and grabbed a magazine. "I got a client coming in at noon, but it shouldn't take more than a couple of hours to finish him up. Let's plan on heading over to MacPherson's around two thirty."

Sea Bass and Maggie had been invited to the cookout, seeing how his grandmother, Davina McCabe, was a senior member of the society. I normally wouldn't allow two of us to be out of the shop at the same time, but apparently the event was an annual tradition, and Sea Bass had practically begged me to give him the time off. Besides, we'd cleared our schedules for the afternoon. Mouse knew where to find us if the shop was suddenly inundated with walk-ins demanding tattoos. I was looking forward to the day when Abel was ready to graduate from his apprenticeship and take on his own clients, which would allow more flexibility for everyone at the shop.

Maggie stood back up and joined us at the front counter. "Okay. I'll stop by the bakery and pick up a cookie platter on my way back over this afternoon."

"We don't have to bring anything," Sea Bass said. "They'll have enough food to feed half the state of Georgia. Fiona will be sending us home with a load of leftovers."

"I know that, but it's the polite thing to do. I don't ever show up at a party empty-handed."

"Shit," I muttered. She was right. Maybe I could call Jackson and have him pick up a cheese platter on the way over.

Hearing my reaction, Maggie glanced over at me. "If you haven't already picked something up, Katie, I can just say the cookies are from the shop. I'll get an extra fancy tray."

A little embarrassed by my lack of etiquette, I shook my head and tried to politely decline. "That's nice of you to offer, but you don't have to compensate for my bad manners."

"I insist. I have to get the cookies anyway. It's no trouble at all."

I pulled a couple of bills from the money drawer and handed them to her. "You're the best, Maggie, but I'm buying."

She took one of them from my hand but refused the other. "We'll split it."

Sea Bass walked her to the door and gave her a peck on the lips. On the way back, he couldn't help but stop by the table to adjust that damn jug one more time. He was obsessed with that thing, and it was starting to get a little bit weird.

"Morning, sunshines." Abel came strolling through the back door, wearing a wide grin and a pair of shades.

"Morning, yourself," I said back. "You're awfully cheerful today." Abel was not a morning person, so seeing him bounce through the door looking all chipper either meant he'd won the lottery or gotten himself laid. My money was on the latter.

"What's her name?" Sea Bass asked.

Abel stopped in his tracks and pulled the sunglasses from his face. "What? Can't I walk in here in a good mood without you thinking something salacious?" He glanced at me next, noting my expression of curiosity. "You too, boss?"

I leaned my elbows on the counter and noted the glow coming off his face. "Hey, I'm happy for you, Abel. In fact, that smile on your face is downright infectious. See?" I shot him an exaggerated Cheshire cat grin.

"Darla," he said, heading for the coffee. "I met her at a martini bar."

"Martinis?" Sea Bass said, his face twisting like a pretzel. "Since when do you drink martinis?"

"Since I followed her inside that bar the other night." He tossed his glasses next to the coffeepot and poured himself a cup. "She's the real deal, man."

Abel had been divorced for nearly a year. I'd never met his ex, but from what I'd been told, it was a rough split. Of course, I'd never heard of a smooth one, no matter how amicable a couple tried to part ways. His kids were grown, and he'd taken full advantage of his newfound freedom by shelving his old life as a cop for the pursuit of happiness, and the impoverished life of a tattoo apprentice. But I had a feeling he had money stuffed away that helped bridge that transition. It was one of the benefits of getting a second chance later in life, after you'd had years to pad the retirement and bank accounts with a little extra every payday.

"Well, I'm happy for you," I said with a wary glance, remembering the last time he fell for a woman on the second date. "But take it slow, Abel. Slow and easy."

"Yes, ma'am," he replied.

Mouse's nine o'clock client arrived, followed by a walk-in wanting a pretty elaborate tattoo applied to the side of his leg. I gave it to Sea Bass, because at that moment, I was too distracted to create a permanent mark on someone's skin. I also had my own client coming in at eleven, so I needed to clear my head before she walked through the door. I was hoping that a couple of hours of tidying up and paperwork would do the trick. All I could think about was Ijibah and the conversation with May the night before. We needed to find the cone of power she'd mentioned, and I intended to make good use of the party that afternoon to find out exactly what that was. What better place to do that than a party full of witches.

———————

JACKSON WALKED into the shop fifteen minutes early and took a seat while I finished ringing up my client. He grabbed one of the crumpled magazines from the table and began flipping through it.

"You need a receipt, Jen?" I asked as she handed me her credit card.

"What for? It's not like I can return it."

I took that as a no. "You want to make an appointment for the next section?" I asked, referring to the final part of the tattoo that would wrap around her left arm. She'd been coming in for the past four months to get a boa constrictor wrapped around her body. It started on her right arm and continued around her waist. The final section ended on her left arm with the snake's head reaching up to the cap of her shoulder. It was an interesting piece that made her look like she was either getting the life squeezed out of her, or she had an unusual pet that she carried around under her shirt.

"Let me see how I feel in a week or two," she said, shuddering at the thought of the pain. Today was ribcage day, and any tattoo that came that close to the bone was unpleasant, to say the least.

Jackson watched her walk out the front door. "I knew a guy who had one of those things as a pet. Used to carry it around just like that tattoo. He even rode his Harley with it wrapped around his waist under his shirt. It got out of its tank and disappeared for months. You know where they finally found it?"

"In the toilet bowl?" I joked. I'd heard urban legends about snakes swimming through sewer lines.

"Curled up inside the empty gas tank of his bike. Brought it in the garage for maintenance over the winter and had the cap off the tank."

"Poor thing." Unlike some people, I didn't have an issue with snakes.

He shrugged at the memory and dropped the magazine back on the table. "Snake was fine. Hungry as hell though."

Sugar came through the front door, wearing a pair of calf-length white jeans and a striped shirt with its unbuttoned ends tied into a little knot just below her navel. Her blond wig was tied back with a leopard print scarf, and she had on a pair of white sunglasses that completed her ensemble.

"Don't you look picnicky," I said.

She pulled the large frames from her face and smoothed her hand over her hair. "Well, I wasn't sure if these stripes would clash with my scarf. But then I said, who the hell cares." She gave Jackson a wink and leaned over the desk. "You ready to head over to MacPherson's?"

"By the way," I said to Jackson. "Sugar's riding with us."

She shook her head. "You riding with me. Better park that fancy bike behind the shop, Jackson, just in case you partake a little too much and have to leave it overnight. Them crackheads coming around after dark won't waste no time helping themselves to a nice Harley-Davidson parked on the street."

He seemed annoyed at the mere suggestion. I recalled the first night he invited himself over to my place. Without my permission, he parked his Harley on the grass on the side of the house for fear of just what Sugar was talking about. "Tell you what," he said. "You drive, and I'll follow."

"Done! Problem solved." I glanced at Sea Bass across the room. "I guess we'll see you and Maggie a little later."

He nodded without taking his eyes off his client's skin.

"Thanks for holding down the fort," I said to Mouse and Abel. "I own you both an extra afternoon off."

"Don't worry about me," Mouse muttered, engrossed in the drawing she was preparing for her next client that was due any minute. "I need the money. With the two of you gone, it means more of it for me."

Mouse wasn't much for socializing, but when she did let her hair down, I'd been told she let it *all* the way down. One of these days I'd have a party at my house to witness it firsthand. The holidays were right around the corner, so that opportunity wasn't far off.

The three of us left the shop, and I headed for the Eldorado. "I'll ride with Sugar." Jackson took no offense and climbed on his bike and cranked the loud engine.

"Jesus, Lord!" Sugar said, covering her left ear with one hand while she reached for the door handle with her right. "Got to be some kind of ordinance against that."

Jackson grinned at me as he backed out of the parking spot. He lifted his feet off the pavement and sped away. Seemed like an eternity before the growl of his engine faded, and I had to admit I disliked the deafening sound as much as Sugar did. But I sure loved the way it felt to be on the back of that bike on a sweltering night, when nothing else could cool you down but the rush of that machine cutting through the humidity. I was sure I'd feel different when winter arrived.

Sugar turned the key, and the engine coughed for a few seconds before dying. She did it again, but the result was the same. "Now come on, Hazel." I raised my brow at the name. "Don't make me scrap your ass at the junk yard."

Third time was a charm. The car rumbled to life and sputtered, threatening to conk out again. It finally managed to maintain a steady purr as she put it in reverse and backed out into the street. She shifted the transmission into drive and hit the gas before it could stall again, sending us both back against the seat in a violent jerk.

"Jesus, Sugar! Don't you think it's time to start thinking about parting ways with this old thing?"

Looking at her profile, her lips tightened ever so slightly. "This here is a classic," she said, firmly patting the faded vinyl dashboard. "And we all getting a day closer to the grave every time we wake up. This car ain't no different."

"It's just a car, Sugar."

Her mouth tightened even more. "I'm going to just let that comment roll right off my back, because you one of them millennials who ain't got no appreciation for the classics."

Not wanting to fuel the fire, I changed the subject. "Who am I going to meet today? Tell me about these mysterious witches of Blackthorn Grove." Of course I already knew a lot of them, but I had a feeling I had yet to meet the majority.

"Most of them are regular folks," she said. "You wouldn't know they slipped on them black robes and danced under the moon once a month."

"I doubt they do that, Sugar."

"I don't know what the hell they do in that room over at Lillian's house. They go out in the woods sometimes, too."

"Have you ever been invited?" She took her eyes off the road to give me a look. "I guess that was a stupid question," I muttered. Sugar had made it clear on more than one occasion that society business was less fun than a case of poison ivy. Suffering through a full moon ritual with Fin, Lillian, and the rest of them would probably make her head explode.

"Emmaline's a little strange," she said, loosening her tight lips. "But I'd be a little strange too if my mama and daddy tried to kill me." She nodded toward the glove compartment. "Hand me that pack of gum in there. You want a piece?"

I handed her a stick of gum and waited for the details, but she just drove in silence. "Are you kidding me? You can't say something like that and then just brush over it. Emmaline's parents tried to kill her?"

She stuffed the gum in her mouth and rolled the window all the way down to stick her elbow out. "Hot as hell today. Should have worn a skimpy little sundress instead of these tight jeans."

"Come on, Sugar."

She finally relented and gave me the details of Emmaline's unfortunate past. "Marlene and Jimmy Gilbert. A couple of nature's unfortunate accidents. Them two was crazy motherfuckers." She shook her head. "Emmaline is special. Got her some crazy-ass skills with that third eye of hers. She ain't like you, Katie. Can't sprout no wings or fry someone's ass with fire, but I swear that girl could conjure up an earthquake if she wanted to."

"So . . . Emmaline is psychic?"

"Telekinetic, baby. Among other things. That girl could wipe out half this city if she put her mind to it. Her mama and daddy knew it too and tried to end that poor little girl's life. Told her Jesus would fix her on the other side, right before they tried to stick a knife in her belly to speed things up."

I was confused. "Weren't her parents members of the Crossroads Society?" I couldn't imagine people like that as members, but Fin had told me her family had strong roots in the society.

"That was before some backwoods preacher got a hold of them and messed with their heads. They just went crazy and tried to kill her."

The image made me shudder. My own family was pretty messed up, but the thought of a mother and father trying to kill their own child was beyond comprehension. "Well they obviously failed. How did she survive?"

"Some kind of funnel cloud came tearing through the house before they could do it. That's what the police said. Found them bodies all ripped to shreds half a mile down the road." Sugar laughed briefly. "That little nine-year-old girl was standing in the same room when it happened. Didn't have a scratch on her. Lillian raised her up after that."

"Shit," I whispered.

"Something like that would make anyone a little odd, but that girl's got her a heart of gold."

"And then she killed *them*," I added absently.

Sugar quickly changed the subject. "And then there's Carmen," she said, smacking her gum. "Mm-hmm."

"Something I should know about this Carmen?"

"She's a man-eater. A *witch* man-eater, and you know what they say about them."

Actually, I didn't.

"Better keep Jackson on a short leash this afternoon."

"I don't own Jackson." I snorted and looked out the window as we rounded the corner near MacPherson's. My motto was, if a man cheated on me, good riddance. I had no desire to try to keep someone who didn't want to be kept, and that wasn't about to change because of some witch who liked to make sport of poaching other women's boyfriends.

Sugar stretched her arm over the seat, brushing her hand over my shoulder as it came to rest behind me. "You ain't got nothing to worry about, girl. Ain't no man gonna throw away filet mignon for a piece of chuck steak."

I glanced at her and laughed. "Thanks, Sugar—I think."

We passed the front of the pub and turned down the side street toward the back lot. Between the cars parked along the street, I spotted Jackson's bike. Then I saw him deep in conversation with a woman I'd never seen before.

"That right there," Sugar said, climbing out of the car and nodding toward Jackson's companion, "is Carmen."

12

Jackson was laughing at something Carmen had said when we came up from behind. Her hand was on his forearm, and they both seemed to be enjoying each other's company. Had I been the jealous type, there might have been a problem. But I didn't waste my time on useless emotions, even if it did kind of irritate me.

"Hey, baby," Jackson said, kissing me briefly on the lips before making an introduction. "Katie, this is—"

"Carmen," Sugar said. "Yeah, we know." She gave the witch a warning look and took Jackson by the arm, steering him toward the drinks. "Come on, Katie. Let's get us some juice. And I don't mean no apple juice."

Jackson complied with her manhandling and headed for the generous bar at the other end of the lot. It was covered with bottles of wine and every kind of liquor you could imagine. Next to it was a tub of ice and beer. This was Savannah after all. A party was nothing but a crowd until you had a drink in your hand.

"Miss Bishop."

I turned around. "Fin, are you ever going to drop the formality? I think we're way past it. Don't you?"

"I suppose you're right, Miss Bishop," he said, nodding to Sugar and Jackson. Then he grabbed a bottle of scotch from the bar. It wasn't anywhere near the quality of the stuff Lillian spoiled me with at her house, but we were at a cookout, and I couldn't blame the Crossroads Society for not wanting to fund ridiculously priced drinks for every lush on the lot. "Scotch?"

"Probably wise to stick with wine today," I replied. "Red, please."

He handed me a glass and then looked at Jackson. "What's your poison?" While waiting for Jackson's reply, he poured a glass of vodka and handed it to Sugar.

"Why thank you, Fin," she said, taking the drink with a cocky grin. "You always know what this girl needs, don't you?" Fin held her gaze for a second and then turned it back to Jackson, making me wonder about the innuendo. Sugar had mentioned Fin's presence at the club before, but a club like the Blue Light was a magnet for all kinds of folks: tourists, college kids, your average native Savannahian looking for something a little different. That place probably attracted quite a mix of characters. "Now we got us a part*ee*," she declared. A second later, she waved at someone and disappeared across the lot.

After handing Jackson a cold bottle of beer, Fin motioned to the colossal smoker that was sending out the aroma of good old Southern barbecue. "You won't get ribs like this in any restaurant," he said. "Hope you're hungry."

"I think I'll wait a little while," I said, glancing around for Emmaline. I really did want to get to know her better, outside of the society's walls that seemed to keep her so reserved. Maybe that was just the way she was under any circumstances. "But you go ahead and eat, Jackson. I'm going to mingle a little bit."

Jackson headed for the food while I turned to make my way

through the crowd, but someone rested their hand on my shoulder before I could leave. I turned around and came face-to-face with a tall woman sporting a black fedora, covering a cropped blond bob that came to a stop just below her chin. Her face was covered with a thick layer of makeup that showed no hint of melting away in the sweltering heat.

"You must be our little dragonfly," she said, gazing at me like I was some kind of rare specimen trapped in a glass jar.

Fin introduced us. "Temperance LeBlanc, this is Katie Bishop." She kept staring at me, making me feel uneasy after the customary amount of time for an introduction had passed. "You can quit your gawking now," he said, noticing my discomfort. "Miss Bishop isn't a sideshow attraction."

"Oh, I'm sorry, Katie—I can call you Katie, can't I? Unless I'm addressing the mayor, I despise formality."

"I'd prefer it," I said. "I despise formality, too." I glanced at Fin, hoping he'd take note. "Temperance," I said, turning back to her and noting the tattoo on her neck. "That's an interesting name."

Lillian Whitman approached us and joined in on the conversation. "I see you've met one of our priestesses." She smiled at me in her usual genteel way, with her chin slightly lifted and her cheekbones never moving a millimeter. "Let's not overwhelm our guest, Temperance."

The woman ignored Lillian's suggestion, examining me from head to toe with little to no discretion. After she'd had a good look, she gave me a sly one-sided grin. "You are a *stunning* woman, Katie. Were you born with all this, or have you had a little help?" she asked, waving her hand over me.

Lillian gave her a subtle glare, compelling her to take a step back. "Well, it was a pleasure to meet you, Katie. I hope we have a chance to chat later." The philodendron pattern of her long skirt swayed to life as she walked away, conjuring images of a tropical rainforest. I caught her glancing back at me before disappearing into a group of people at the far end of the parking lot.

"She was interesting," I mumbled over the rim of my glass.

"Yes, that is one way to describe Temperance," Fin said, raising his own drink to his lips.

There was a collective murmuring of oohs and aahs behind us. When I turned around, a couple of men were carefully carrying a board across the lot, topped with a huge cake in the shape of something I couldn't make out. I walked up to the table where they'd placed the cake, getting a good look at the confectionary tombstone complete with an inscription. The fondant covering was colored in shades of gray and white, mottled and pitted artistically into an impressive illusion. If I didn't know better, I'd swear it was a weathered stone.

"Shit," Jackson said, coming up behind me with a plate of food. "Is that a cake?"

"It is indeed," Fin said.

I read the name inscribed on the sugar tombstone— ALTHEA NOBLE BOULEAU. "What's this all about?" I asked Fin.

"This is the reason we're here," Davina McCabe said before Fin had a chance to respond. "Nice to see you, Katie." She glanced at the cake, and then surveyed the crowd. "Where's that grandson of mine?"

"Maggie should have picked him up by now, so they should be here soon." As if on cue, they walked around the corner with that oversized platter of cookies. "Speak of the devil."

Davina waved to them, and then gave Fin an admonishing look. "I guess it didn't occur to you to tell Katie what this little gathering is all about."

Fin polished off his sizable glass of bourbon and winced from the burn. "Today is the anniversary of Althea's passing."

"Who's Althea?" I asked.

Lillian overheard the conversation and joined us at the table.

"Althea Noble Bouleau was our founding priestess. She ran the coven for nearly fifty years before her passing a couple of decades ago."

I looked at the cake and noted Althea's birthdate, but there was no date of death after the dash. "I think the cake decorator forgot something. The date of death is missing."

"That's because she ain't dead," Sugar said, sliding between Fin and Davina to reach for one of the edible stones scattered around the cake. "This shit is tasty."

"Have a little respect," Davina said, glaring at Sugar like she was some uninvited party crasher.

Sugar threw the look right back at her. "I'm just carrying out Althea's wishes."

My head shook in confusion. "Lillian just said she was dead."

"I said she passed," Lillian corrected. "We're not exactly sure where she passed to, but it's not here. A witch like Althea doesn't just die."

"Well, you have to admit, Sugar is right." Fin continued with the history of the annual event we were enjoying. "Althea always said she didn't want some fancy headstone marking her passing, unless it was made of cake and being served at a party. So you see, Miss Bishop, we come together every year to have a piece of that cake."

Sugar rocked her head back and forth in Davina's face. "Well, I guess we might as well dig in then." She grabbed a knife and cut a piece off the corner, plopping it on a paper plate and holding it in the air. "Who wants a piece of cake?" she yelled over the crowd.

"Man, that looks good," Sea Bass said, stuffing a cookie in his mouth as he held out his other hand. Sugar handed him the plate and cut another piece for Jackson. After serving me and cutting a piece for herself, she grabbed my arm and steered me away from the crowd lining up in front of the cake.

We pulled up a couple of chairs and watched everyone scramble to get a piece of the annual tradition. The way they were grabbing for the plates Davina was filling as fast as she could, you'd think she was handing out winning lottery tickets.

"Bunch of damn animals," Sugar grumbled, inhaling her cake like a ravenous dog. "It is good though."

"Sure is," I said, laughing at the frenzy that really wasn't that funny at all.

My eyes wandered, stopping on Emmaline who was standing by herself in the shade near the back of the building. Even with the oppressive heat, she wore long sleeves and a skirt that reached all the way down to her feet. At least she was wearing sandals so her toes could breathe.

"I'll be right back." I tossed my empty plate in the trash and headed across the lot. "I guess this is the only spot where the pavement doesn't fry your feet," I said to Emmaline.

She smiled meekly and grabbed the ends of her sleeves with her fingertips, tugging them down to conceal the backs of her hands. A nervous habit, I assumed. "It's good to see you, Katie. Did you get a piece of Althea's tombstone cake?"

"I did. It was delicious." She seemed to be the only one not fighting for a piece of it. "Not into cake?"

"Oh, I love sweets, but I'm not getting in the middle of that." Her eyes flashed wide as she nodded to the mob lined up in front of the table. "I'll get it when the line calms down."

"Want me to get you a piece?" I offered. "It might be gone if you wait too long."

She let out a rare laugh. "Did you see the size of that cake? Half of it is left over every year."

I looked up as several people approached. Emmaline spotted them a second later and tensed up. Either she was uncomfortable with the prospect of socializing with a large group, or she didn't care for these particular folks.

"You want to introduce us to your friend, Emmaline?" one of the men said. I recognized him from Lillian's house the night I barged in on their ritual. The other three looked vaguely familiar. "Well, we know who you are, but you don't know us." Not given a chance to open her mouth, the man proceeded to introduce himself. "Nicholas Hunt," he said, extending his hand.

"You're a member of the grove," I said, shaking it. "I recognize you from the other night when I walked in on the ritual at Lillian's house." There was no apology in my voice.

"That's right." He held my gaze—and my hand—for a moment, and then turned to introduce the others. "Cat, Mary, and Eric." He nodded to each of them as he said their names. "We're all members of the grove—and the society."

He was attractive more for his demeanor than looks. Although he did have stunning green eyes similar to Jackson's and a head of wavy beach hair that stirred thoughts of Tybee Island.

Emmaline looked a little panicked, which seemed odd considering these were her covenmates. "It's nice to meet all of you, but you'll have to excuse us. Emmaline and I were just about to go over—" I was halfway through my excuse to get her out of there, when my eyes caught Sea Bass standing by the bar. Temperance LeBlanc was hanging all over him, pressing her crotch area against his knee. I did a double take as he threw his head back and laughed, bringing his face back up to hers and running his hand down the length of her bare arm. She leaned in and brought her mouth dangerously close to his, the rim of her black fedora brushing against his forehead.

Emmaline and the others looked in the same direction when they heard the commotion that ensued, the scorn of a woman tearing through the air like thunder. You did not want to piss off a woman like Maggie Donovan. Even so, I'd never known her to make her temper public.

"Why don't you shove these up your ass!" Maggie threw the

platter of cookies at Sea Bass, sending the expensive array of butter, flour, and sugar confections flying through the air in a spray of color. "Here's a better idea." She bent down and picked up a handful of broken cookies from the ground. "You can shove them up your new girlfriend's ass, you sorry son of a *bitch!*"

"Time to go, Emmaline." I grabbed her wrist and headed for Sugar, who was laughing and watching the fireworks with a plate of barbecue in her hand.

"Ain't nothing good going to come out of that," Sugar said when we reached her. "Maybe now that boy will come home to Sugar." She rolled her hips in her chair like she was giving a lap dance and took a bite of pork. A few seconds later, her mouth went still.

I followed her eyes as they settled on the crowd. "What the hell is going on?"

There must have been something in the air, because I counted at least four other couples grinding against each other in the middle of the crowd. Lillian was standing over by the table, dancing in place as she conversed with a man I didn't recognize. A moment later, she was doubled over in laughter, nearly falling over the table.

"Katie," Emmaline said, drawing my attention away from the spectacle.

I turned back around and saw Sugar standing next to her chair, kicking off her shoes and untying the knot above her navel. Then she started to unbutton the front of her shirt. "Damn, it's hot! I got to get this shit off," she said.

"Uh… no, you don't." I grabbed her hands and yanked them away from the buttons before she could strip her shirt off. "You see Jackson anywhere?" I asked Emmaline.

She shrank back a little and raised her hand to point toward the street. Jackson was leaning against Sugar's car. Carmen was pressed against his chest with her tongue halfway down his throat. "Something isn't right, Katie."

"No shit!" I growled, glaring at my philandering *ex-*boyfriend.

"No, Katie," she said, shaking her head. "I think you better go talk to Davina."

I looked over at Davina, who was standing in front of the cake table with Fiona. They appeared to be saner than the rest and as shocked as I was.

"Come on, Sugar." I dragged her over to the table. "Is there something I should know about?" I asked the two of them.

"That's a good question," Davina said. She looked around the lot for some common denominator to explain why perfectly respectable folks were suddenly acting like sex-starved fools. The one thing we saw plenty of were empty cake plates littered all over the ground.

Davina closed her eyes and slowly shook her head. Then she turned to Fiona. "Where'd you get that damn cake from?"

It was a simple question, but Fiona seemed a little caught off guard, as if a revelation was occurring to her as she replied. "I got it from Le Petit Gateau. Agnes made it herself."

"Goddamn fool!" Davina spat out. Fiona looked startled. "Not you, honey. That… *idiot*, Agnes!"

Fiona shook her head frantically. "I don't understand. She called me a few weeks ago and offered to donate it. Saved the society a boatload of money. Jesus, Davina! She's a member!"

"One of you want to let me in on what's going on, and why Jackson is about to get laid on top of Sugar's car?" When they cocked their heads at me, I motioned toward Jackson and Carmen across the street.

"This is my fault," Fiona said. "If it helps, Jackson won't even remember Carmen in the morning."

"Agnes Freemont is famous for getting funny with her baked

goods," Davina explained. "Ever wonder why everyone raves about that bakery of hers? Hell, I can make a better cupcake than that overpriced crap she sells." Another round of food went flying through the air, Sea Bass being the target again. "Lucky for my grandson, Maggie won't remember a thing either."

"Wait a minute," I said. "I ate a piece, and I'm not climbing all over the first guy I see."

Davina smirked. "You're a dragon, girl. That spell is wasted on you. I'm surprised Jackson isn't immune on account of what he is." She glanced around the lot at all the exhibition taking place. "That spell must have been a whopper. Witches usually can't enchant their own coven members, and I don't think I've ever seen Lillian this happy."

We all looked over at the giddy socialite, with her hair freed from its conservative chignon and sprawled around her shoulders. Lillian would probably die from humiliation if she was unfortunate enough to retain any memory beyond consuming that piece of cake.

Fiona headed for her grandmother. "I guess we better get her home before she snaps out of it and looks in the mirror."

I noticed that Agnes Freemont was absent from the crime scene, which seemed kind of strange. "I would have thought Agnes would want to see her handiwork," I said. "But I don't see her anywhere."

"She wouldn't have the balls," Davina said. "But I'll hunt her down tomorrow and make her regret this little stunt."

I walked Sugar back to her chair and sat her down as she started to get sleepy. "You better not go to sleep on me, Sugar. I am not driving that tank home." The Eldorado was bigger than anything I'd ever driven, and I wasn't interested in learning how to navigate it.

Fin walked up to us with a grin edging up one side of his face. "You look beautiful today, Miss Bishop." His lips were parted slightly, and the warm look in his eyes made me uncomfortable on a number of levels. Agnes Freemont's spell had claimed another victim.

"Jesus, Fin," I muttered. "Don't even think about it."

Fiona mercifully came over and steered him toward her car where her grandmother was already secured in the front seat. "Let's get you home, big boy."

I looked around for Emmaline. I spotted her over by the table of food, discreetly wrapping a piece of that wicked cake in a napkin. Then she went over to the barbecue and filled a large plastic cup with smoked pork, securing a napkin over the top with a rubber band before stuffing it in a paper bag. I found that a little odd, considering the fact that Emmaline was a vegetarian.

She was feeding someone and doing her best to hide it.

13

J ackson sat up in bed. He squinted his eyes at me as I stared at him from the chair in the corner of the room.

"Morning," I said, taking a little too much pleasure in his discomfort.

He shook off the wooziness and swung his long legs over the edge of the bed. "What the fuck happened last night?"

"Actually, it was yesterday afternoon. You've been sleeping for about fifteen hours." It was around five o'clock by the time I got him home and dumped him in bed. "Your bike is parked over at MacPherson's. I can drop you off on the way to the shop." He looked panicked. His precious bike was sitting on a strange street just waiting for vandals to strip it down to the bone. Or worse, steal it. "Calm down, Jackson. Fiona had Johnnie pull it up to the back of the pub so no one could see it from the street."

Like a dog who'd just chewed up a pair of expensive shoes, he looked at me regretfully, expecting me to come down on him hard for something he couldn't even remember. "Are you going to tell me what I did yesterday, or should I just call a cab and wait outside?"

I got up from the chair and showed a little mercy. "Come on. I made breakfast."

He grabbed his clothes off the floor and got dressed, then he joined me in the kitchen. He went for the coffee first, and then hesitated at the sight of the eggs and sausage on his plate. "I don't know if I can eat that right now."

The poor guy was hungover. Not from the single beer he'd had the day before, but from that nasty spell Agnes had infused into that cake. The woman had an odd sense of humor. After the failed cookout, Fiona had told me it wasn't an isolated incident. Apparently Agnes Freemont had a reputation with the underground communities—the witch circles in town—of tampering with her product to make it sell better. She'd earned notoriety as one of the best bakers in town via those dirty little spells, and few outside of the mundane world would dare set foot inside that shop of hers.

A muted laugh slipped from my mouth.

"What's so funny?" he asked, looking a little irritated by the whole debacle.

"Baby, you've been screwed with. Remember that cake everyone couldn't wait to taste yesterday? It was poisoned."

"*Poisoned?*"

"Sort of. One of Blackthorn Grove's witches thought it might be funny to put some kind of food spell in the batter. Agnes Freemont. She owns that fancy bakery a few blocks down. Made everyone horny as hell. I thought you and that Carmen chick were about to have sex in the middle of the damn road." I gave him a sympathetic look and tried not to laugh. I'd never seen Jackson Hunter so vulnerable. In fact, I'd never seen him vulnerable at all. But yesterday afternoon proved that even Superman was not immune to a savvy little witch with one hell of a spell. "It didn't have any effect on me, thank God."

He closed his eyes as if painfully aware of what he'd done. "Katie—"

"Don't apologize, Jackson. You had no idea what you were doing—to that woman," I added for a little satisfaction. I'd already forgiven him, just like I was sure Maggie had forgiven Sea Bass. At least I hoped she had. He would throw himself into a hurricane of depression without his redheaded warrior queen, and neither of us could afford that.

"I really don't remember anything I did past Fin handing me a beer."

I smiled at him. "I know. Now if you're not planning to eat that food, I need to get to the shop."

———

JACKSON'S HARLEY was safely tucked out of view behind MacPherson's Pub, without a scratch on it. On the way over, I reassured him about ten times that I was already over the incident with Carmen, but if he didn't shut up about it, I'd be happy to reconsider hating him if it would make him feel better.

After Jackson drove off, I headed for the shop for what I knew would be an eventful day. Sea Bass's drama excluded, there was the business of Emmaline sneaking barbecue and a piece of that tainted cake into a bag, and I had a hunch about it.

"Morning, Harold," I hollered across the room. It was meant to be a humorous icebreaker since Sea Bass refused to look at me when I walked through the door.

When it didn't work, I decided on a different approach. "Sea Bass!" I yelled as he swept the floor.

"What?" he yelled back, startled.

"What's wrong with you? I've seen you do stupider things than what you did yesterday, so why won't you look at me?"

He leaned the broom handle against a chair and spoke

without turning around. "Damn it, Katie, because I don't remember what I did at that cookout. Maggie won't answer her phone, and I don't even know how I got home yesterday." His head cocked in thought. "I remember a woman—who was not Maggie—touching me… down there." When he eventually glanced over his shoulder at me, he whispered through tight lips. "She had black hair, Katie. And a *tattoo*."

It took me a moment to realize what he was inferring. It would have been laughable if the thought didn't make me so uncomfortable. "Sea Bass, you don't think we—"

"Does Jackson know?" he asked. I'd be worried too if I thought I'd just helped myself to the girlfriend of someone as imposing as Jackson Hunter.

"Her hair was blond," I replied bluntly. "You're remembering her black fedora hat. Honestly, Sea Bass!"

The look of relief on his face was priceless. He turned around and let the pent-up air in his lungs come rushing out. "Thank God! Maggie would kill us both."

"Maggie wouldn't be stupid enough to think you and I would be messing around," I replied to his ridiculous suggestion. Then I put him out of his misery and explained about the cake. "It was Agnes Freemont. She put a spell on that tombstone cake that made everyone lose their mind with lust. Don't worry. Maggie probably doesn't remember a thing either. If she does, I'll explain."

Mouse snorted. "Good luck trying to kill Katie."

Sugar came barreling into the shop a moment later. She headed straight for me with an irritated look on her face. "Where the hell is my car?" she demanded.

"Well, good morning to you too, Sugar. You want to try that again with some manners?"

She settled down and patted the sides of her head, as if she'd just realized she'd forgotten her wig. Her natural hair was plastered against her head by a nylon headband. "I'm sorry, Katie, but no one messes with my car. I got up this morning and nearly had a heart attack when I looked out the window."

"It's parked in my driveway." I pulled her keys from my purse and watched the relief roll over her face. "I had to get home after dropping you off. And let me tell you something, Sugar. I don't ever want to drive that thing again. Nearly took out my mailbox trying to park that tank."

"You ever get into an accident with that tiny little tin can of yours," she said, referring to my old Honda Accord, "you gonna wish you was driving that tank."

I gave her a wide grin to end the battle. "How's that head of your feeling this morning?"

She made a beeline for the coffeepot and poured herself a cup. "Had me a conversation with Fin when I woke up feeling like a freight train ran over my head. I know all about what that witch put in that cake. I'll be getting her back." She nodded firmly, lifting her brows. "You just wait and see. Agnes ain't going to see me coming."

"And here I was offended about not getting an invitation," Mouse said, snickering as she listened to the recap of the debacle from the day before.

"Remind me to never eat anything from Le Petit Gateau ever again," Abel said.

Sea Bass chimed in next. "Me neither. Might have to give her a one-star rating on Yelp."

"Yeah, that'll get her," I said.

Sugar was staring at me when I turned around, dangling her keys from her index finger. "What? You need a ride to my place?"

"Well, what the hell do you think?" she said. "I had to beg my neighbor to drive me over here. You expect me to pay for one of them Ubers?"

"I'll be back in half an hour," I said to Sea Bass, rolling my eyes as I followed Sugar out the back door.

As soon as we left the parking lot, I told her about my theory. "I saw Emmaline sneaking food into a bag at the picnic yesterday."

"Well, she is a scrawny little thing. Maybe she don't like to eat in front of people and was taking her some leftovers."

"Pork?" I said. "She was packing pork barbecue into a cup and stuffing it into a paper bag." Sugar still didn't seem to get it. "She's a vegetarian, Sugar!"

"Well, maybe she got her a dog."

I shook my head, letting that nagging hunch drive me. "I don't know. I've got a funny feeling about this, and I know better than to ignore that voice in my head. I think she's hiding Esrial."

She let out an exaggerated sigh. "Now look here, little Miss Nancy Drew. Just because she's sneaking a little meat don't means she's harboring a fugitive. That little girl ain't got a conniving bone in her body."

"There's nothing conniving about it. The way I see it, she's helping family. Hell, Sugar, I'd do it for you."

"You got a point, baby. And just so you know, I'd do it for you, too."

"I need to find out from Fin where she lives without making him suspicious. No sense putting ideas in anyone's head without any proof."

"Well, why didn't you just ask me? Emmaline lives over at Lillian's place. In the little cottage just down the road from the big house."

WE CLOSED at six o'clock on Sundays, which gave me plenty of time to pay an unannounced visit to Emmaline before dark. The cottage was about a quarter mile down the side road that led straight to Lillian's front door, concealed by the woods as you passed it. I'd caught a glimpse of it through the trees a few times, but having never seen a light coming from any of the rooms, it never occurred to me that someone actually lived in it.

I turned onto the dirt driveway and pulled up to the front of the house. Emmaline opened the front door before I even had a chance to climb out of the car.

"Hello, Katie," she said, stepping aside to welcome me into the house. She was wearing a knee-length green dress that allowed me a glimpse of her legs for the first time. Long and pale like the rest of her, they reminded me of the legs of a ghost. "I'm surprised to see you here. I thought it would be Fin knocking on my door."

I followed her through the living room and out the French doors to a surprisingly large garden for such a small house. The space was filled with every shade of green you could think of, and I imagined the colors of the flowers were magnificent in the springtime, before the oppressive heat of the Savannah summers knocked them back.

"Wow," I said. "This is really beautiful. I had no idea all this was hidden behind the road." I ran my hand through a tall bush of rosemary as I followed her down a path, leaving the scent from its oil on my fingers.

As we rounded a tiny shed, I saw a woman kneeling at the edge of a pond. Her hair was a bright shade of copper that shined in the fading sun, like a waterfall of newly minted pennies cascading down her back.

"We have a visitor, Esrial," Emmaline said in that quiet voice that always conjured up an image of a bird. "This is the woman I was telling you about. Katie Bishop."

Esrial didn't turn to greet me immediately. Instead, she reached into the pond and swished the surface with her flattened palm, sending the still water into a ripple of waves. Then she stood up and turned around, catching me off guard with the brilliance of her blue eyes. I'd never seen a shade so light. Like ice with a faint tint of sky.

"The dragon," she said, gazing at my face. Then she followed my eyes as I glanced down at the water, watching it shimmer and ripple in a wide circle that seemed to take on a momentum of its own. "Do you practice scrying, Miss Bishop?" she asked as the water continued to hold my attention, a faint image of something fading from its surface.

I pulled my eyes away from the pond and looked at her. "Call me Katie, please. I get enough of the 'Miss' thing from Fin."

She gave me a knowing smile. "That's Fin."

Beautiful and mesmerizing, I was surprised to see that she looked to be around the same age as Fin, possibly older, which in our culture was refreshing. Middle-aged men with money and stature like Fin Cooper usually opted for younger things in their beds. As a society, we'd grown to accept that as the norm. "Good for you, Fin," I muttered quietly.

Her head tilted to the side, and a faint smile acknowledged her reading of my thoughts.

"Why don't we go inside," Emmaline suggested.

We went back into the house and sat in the living room. Emmaline went to fetch tea while Esrial continued to study me. "I hear you've been a great help to the society," she began. "I've been in and out of the country for the past couple of months on family business, so I missed the whole grimoire incident." Her chest visibly inflated as she drew a deep breath. "I came back from my most recent trip to find this ugly business with Harry Cavanagh."

"I have to ask," I said.

She beat me to the question. "No. I had nothing to do with the murder. Does that answer your question, Katie?"

Focusing on my lips, she cocked her head curiously. "Is it true that you can breathe fire?"

"Well, my dragon can." I nodded to the coffee table between us. "But if you asked me to char that table right now, you'd be disappointed."

"I hope you like mint," Emmaline said, returning with a tray of steaming cups. "It's from the garden."

I got straight to the point. "I know about your relationship with Rita Cavanagh. I also know the council is on its way here to investigate your involvement in her husband's death."

As if the mention of the name was difficult to hear, Esrial set her cup on the coffee table and tried to steady her trembling hand. "What Rita did that night was not her fault. It was mine."

I broached the rest of the conversation carefully, because the woman sitting across from me suddenly looked a little fragile. "From what I've been told, it was a spell. Ijibah used you as the conduit."

She shot me a wild look. "Where did you hear that name?"

Without going into the details about Pearl May Mobley and Queen giving me that information, I continued. "I know it's likely that she's framing you to bring down Blackthorn Grove. I also know we need to prove that before the council gets here. You need to go to Lillian and Fin. Hiding only makes you look guilty."

She scoffed quietly. "Do you know what the council is really coming here for?" I just stared at her because it wasn't really a question. "A witch hunt—no pun intended. They're not coming here for the truth or justice. They need to make an example out of someone, to keep us all in line. They don't like messy problems that open us up to scrutiny by the mundane world."

"All the more reason you need the society to help argue your innocence. Once they know the truth, the council can go after the right witch. They can make an example out of Ijibah."

The condescending smirk on her face was a little offensive. "A sorceress like Ijibah doesn't play by any rules, Katie. She's dead. They can't control her, but they can sure as hell try to control me. Hold me up as a living effigy for all the witches who have gone bad."

"Well, running makes you look bad to everyone. If I could find you so easily, the council will smell you out the minute they arrive." I shook my head at the absurdity of it all. "Jesus, Esrial! You're on Lillian's property. Don't you think that's a little bit of a slap in her face. Coming forward will at least smooth the waters with your high priestess." I glanced at Emmaline. "And it'll keep Emmaline from being tried for conspiracy to hide a fugitive."

That got her attention. She thought about what I'd said for a minute and then stood up. "You're right. I've put Emmaline in danger. I'll pack my things, and then we'll go."

Emmaline's cup hit the floor. "Esrial, no!"

"This was a bad idea from the start," Esrial said. "I'll never forgive myself if something happens to you." She glanced at me nervously and hesitated before continuing. "There's more. Rita told me something right before I left for my last trip abroad. A few weeks before—" Her eyes closed as the words stuck in her throat. Then she turned toward the hallway. "I'll get my bags. I'll tell you everything when we get up to Lillian's house."

While Esrial was in the back room, I questioned Emmaline. "You shouldn't have done this. Why would you put yourself at risk?"

She reached for her spilled cup and set it on the table, dabbing the wet rug with a pile of napkins. "My parents did something to me when I was very young."

"I know about that," I said. "Sugar told me."

Placing the damp napkins on the tray, she sank into the sofa. "After they were gone, Esrial took care of me."

Sugar told me that Lillian had raised Emmaline after her parents were killed. "I thought Lillian raised you?"

She looked up with those haunting hazel eyes that seemed to implore me to try to understand. "Lillian put a roof over my head and food in my stomach. She made sure I had an education and lots of fancy clothes—which I never wore." She laughed half-heartedly. "But Esrial raised me. Esrial showed me who I was. What I was."

I gazed at the delicate bird of a girl sitting across from me and realized that what I knew about her was just the tip of the iceberg. I doubted I knew her at all. "Well, Emmaline. What are you?"

14

We drove the quarter mile up the road to Lillian's house. Before leaving the cottage, I'd called Fin to let him know I was bringing Esrial home. Lillian was standing at the top of the steps when we pulled up.

"Fin will be here shortly," Lillian said without taking her eyes off of Esrial.

"Don't look at me like that," Esrial said. "What is it they say about throwing stones?"

Clearly there was a history between the two women, and it was more than their common affiliation with the coven.

Lillian trained her eyes on Emmaline next, and the poor girl withered.

"Why don't we go inside," Lillian finally said. "I need a stiff drink."

I needed one myself. Thank God the shop was closed on Mondays, because I needed a day off so I could sleep in and get ready for the battle I could feel coming.

We followed her into the living room where she went directly to the bureau containing the booze. She poured a glass of scotch and two more of bourbon. After handing me the scotch and one of the bourbons to Esrial, she glanced at Emmaline. "Would you like one?"

Emmaline shook her head.

A moment later, Fin came rushing into the house. He stopped in his tracks when his eyes landed on Esrial, and I could tell he was holding himself back with great difficulty. I'd never seen him look so anxious and subsequently relieved. He loved her. That was obvious.

"Where the hell have you been?" he asked. His eyes wandered over to Emmaline. "Was she with you?"

"Of course she was," Lillian said. "We were just too caught up in this mess to see the obvious." She gave Emmaline that same look that made her shrink earlier, and I wondered why Lillian had so much power over her. I suspected it was the domineering parent and timid child dynamic doing a number on Emmaline. But then again, Emmaline was about as aggressive and confident as a scared rabbit. That made me want to protect her.

"She was just trying to help," I said.

Lillian looked at me like I'd just walked in on a private conversation. "Emmaline can be impulsive. Defending that type of irresponsible behavior is just reckless."

"I would appreciate it if everyone would stop talking about me like I'm not even in the room." We all looked at Emmaline, who rarely spoke above a loud whisper. "I'm not stupid. I know it was foolish to hide Esrial, but she's family."

Sensing her agitation, Fin walked over and took her hand in his, careful not to overwhelm her with something as bold as a hug. "You're loyal. It's what makes you special."

"Now that we've all had the opportunity to make Emmaline feel like shit," Esrial said, glaring at Lillian in particular, "we can discuss the reason I'm standing here."

Fin took the lead. "We know it was an intruder who got to Rita Cavanagh through you. She left the bone on your altar. Probably figured you wouldn't be returning from your little trip anytime soon, which was correct. The question is, will the council believe it?"

"By the way," I said. "When is the council supposed to arrive? Inquisitors you called them?"

Fin inhaled sharply. He let the air dramatically release from his lungs as he calculated the council's ETA. "My guess is they'll be here by tomorrow. They could have been here days ago, but the anticipation of their arrival is an effective intimidation tactic that puts folks at a disadvantage. A surprise attack, if you will."

"Her name is Ijibah," Esrial announced. "She's coming home to collect what was stolen from her and her people, and she's using a power source somewhere in the city to manifest herself right back into this world."

She gazed at Fin for an extended moment as if contemplating his complicity in something.

"Why are you looking at me like that?" he asked, seeming genuinely perplexed by whatever it was that had her visually questioning him.

"That project of yours near the cemetery," she began. "The one with the building that's sinking." She stopped to gauge his reaction. When he scrunched his brow in ignorance, she continued. "Where did Cavanagh Holdings acquire that land, Fin?"

An uneasy feeling filled my gut as my instincts told me we were about to find out the real reason for Ijibah wanting revenge.

"If you're suggesting what I think you are, that's a mighty bold accusation you're making." He held her stare for a moment before continuing. "Tread very lightly before pointing fingers at some pretty powerful folks in this town?"

"Harry Cavanagh is dead," I said.

"That is true, Miss Bishop." He stopped glaring at Esrial and

134

looked at me. "However, the other half of Cavanagh Holdings is still very much alive, and he doesn't like to be cornered."

―――――

FIN and I took a ride to meet Chase Stone at his house near Lafayette Square. He'd called Stone to arrange a late evening meeting to discuss the project. Had Mr. Stone known the true nature of the discussion we were about to have, I'm sure he wouldn't have been so accommodating at nine o'clock on a Sunday night.

"I guess Cavanagh Holdings isn't doing so bad," I said as I looked at the grand homes along the street.

We parked in front of the house and climbed the stairs to the front door. "If you don't mind, Miss Bishop, I'd like to do some talking before we go all Perry Mason on the man," he said before ringing the bell.

"What's that supposed to mean?"

Before he could reply, the door opened. A beautiful woman with light brown skin and eyes somewhere between blue and green greeted us with a polite smile. The curls of her sable hair were corralled by a headband that kept them off her face, and I detected mixed parentage of African American and Caucasian. Due to her youth, I assumed her to be one of Mr. Stones staff, because a man with money like Chase Stone had to be at least twice her age.

"Good evening, Marla," Fin said. "I hope we're not inter-rupting anything this evening." He placed his hand at the center of my back and moved me forward into the foyer. "Marla Stone, this is Katie Bishop."

Chase Stone's wife trained her lovely eyes on mine in a bold way. "Not at all, Fin. We were just finishing up dinner when you called. Chase is in the study. You know the way, right?"

We proceeded down the hallway toward a room at the other end. Although a fraction of the size, the rooms were just as spectacular as the ones in Lillian's palatial estate. Made me wonder how much money Cavanagh Holdings was raking in annually. More than I'd ever see in a lifetime, I figured.

As we approached the study door, I could hear Chase Stone talking on the phone. He glanced at us as we entered the room, his eyes doing a barely detectable double take when they skimmed past me.

Could you be any more obvious? With your teenage wife in the next room?

He was about Fin's age. Maybe a few years younger. Not bad looking. The first thing I noticed right off the bat was how blond his hair was—surfer blond—and the crispness of his shirt.

Motioning for us to shut the door, he finished his call and placed his phone on the oversized desk in front of a wall of bookcases.

"I hope you don't mind me bringing a colleague along," Fin said. "Chase Stone, this is Katie Bishop."

Chase moved backward, leaning against the edge of the desk. "Not at all." He finally managed to pull his eyes away from mine to look at Fin. "What is it you'd like to discuss, Fin?"

"How about the deed to that land we're building on. You know, the building that's sinking like the Titanic," he added with an undertone of accusation.

Talk about cutting through the bullshit. Way to go, Fin.

Chase's relaxed eyes narrowed as he straightened back up and pushed away from the desk. "I'm being rude. Would either of you like a drink?" He headed for a cabinet on the other side of the room.

"Nothing for me," Fin said. It was the first time I'd ever seen him pass up a drink.

Chase glanced at me.

"No, thank you."

"No sense beating around the bush," Fin began. "Is the title on that land clean, or did you steal it?" I could hear the anger in Fin's voice. This wasn't a social call, and I supposed Fin thought it wise to hit hard the moment we walked inside that house, before Chase had the opportunity to get his bearings and come up with an appropriate lie.

Chase Stone went still for a second as the whiskey hit the glass. Fin had struck a nerve. He popped the cork back into the bottle and turned around, taking a deep swig of his drink before answering. "The deed is clean." He glanced at me and hesitated.

"You can be candid in front of Miss Bishop," Fin said. "She's a partner of mine."

Well, I guessed you could say we were partners. Chase Stone seemed to question the unusual alliance though. Eyeing the tattoos peeking out from under the edges of my tank top, he probably wondered how much a younger woman like me could contribute to Fin's business. Maybe he just assumed I was sleeping with Fin. Either way, he seemed satisfied that it was safe to continue.

"You could say we ran into some complications during our negotiations to purchase the property," he said with a shrug.

"What kind of complications?" I asked.

Fin shot me a look that suggested I should leave the talking to him. After all, I was a stranger to this man, and it was likely he was about to confess things that might not exactly be legal.

"Go on," Fin prompted.

Chase turned up his glass and finished his drink. "The old woman died on us, and that land was just sitting there like a ripe peach waiting to be picked. No surviving family. No heirs."

Fin's face began to change as the magnitude of what Chase was implying set in. He liked his money, but he like his reputation and freedom just as much. "Are you telling me that you acquired that deed under less than scrupulous means? That you've put us all at risk of litigation—or worse?"

Chase glared at Fin for a few seconds, seeming to think about how to broach the less than ethical subject. When he finally spoke, his voice dropped an octave. "Do you have any idea how much work went into getting a building permit in the historic district of this town? You think Cavanagh Holdings was just going to walk away from the project because the old woman died on us?" He laughed and glanced back and forth between us for signs that we were sympathetic to his business predicament. "We were a couple of signatures away from making the deal."

"So you just forged her signature on the contracts." Fin shook his head. "Then you paid off her lawyers to keep their mouths shut."

Chase let out a short laugh. "Well, we didn't just take it. We paid for that land. The money was deposited into her bank account. What happened to it without any heirs, I don't know. And I don't care. There are no victims here, Fin."

The library door opened, and Marla Chase entered carrying a tray. "I hope I'm not interrupting anything important, but I thought you might like something to munch on while you talk." She glanced at the bar. "It's Sunday night, Chase. Why don't you take a break from the booze and have some sweet tea instead?"

"Thank you," I said, eyeing the cheese and crackers on the tray. Having nothing in my stomach but the mint tea from Emmaline's garden, I was starving. Insidious plot to steal a witch's land or not, a girl had to eat.

Chase gave her a peck on the cheek as she set the tray on the desk. "Marla and I are newlyweds. What's it been? A couple of months?"

She swatted him playfully. "You better remember our anniversary."

Then he looked her in the eyes, his smile remaining but no

longer reaching his cheeks. I noticed his grip on her forearm was getting tighter. "My lovely wife is new to all this business stuff. She likes to entertain. Don't you darlin'? But right now is not a good time. You can go now."

You can go now?

I smiled to let her know that someone in the room appreciated her hospitality.

She gazed at my skin, examining my shoulders where the ink peeked out on both sides. "Does that tattoo wrap all the way around your back?"

"It does," I replied. "I'd show you, but we're in mixed company."

Her head cocked, and for a second I thought she was going to reach out and touch it. "I always wanted one of those."

I thought Chase Stone was going to explode. His jaw tightened as he gave his wife a subtle look that shut her down quickly.

The lines on my back began to stir, like the dragon wanted to come out and give the bastard someone bigger to pick on. No joke. I genuinely feared I was about to be outed to the Stone family if that asshole didn't take his wife-beater tendencies down a notch.

"I own a tattoo shop," I said, trying to mollify the beast by lowering the tension in the room. "MagicInk. You should come in and get one."

Chase shifted his eyes to mine and smiled. But what he was really saying with that look was that I should shut my mouth like a good girl and stick to doing what women did best. He had the wrong girl.

A low growl slipped from the back of my throat.

"What the hell was that?" Chase said, glancing around the room for the source of the sound.

I looked to my right and met Marla's eyes, which were

watching me curiously, a slight grin edging up the side of her face. That's when I shot Fin a look that screamed *help*.

He must have gotten the message loud and clear, because he walked over to the tray and helped himself to a slice of cheese before taking a seat in one of the leather wing chairs. "I think I'll take that drink now. If you don't mind," he added with mock courtesy.

I followed Fin's lead and sat in the chair next to his. We weren't leaving anytime soon, and I felt a storm brewing between the two men, as Chase complied and went to the bar to pour Fin a glass of whiskey.

"Wild Turkey, if you have it," Fin said.

"Of course," Chase replied, successfully distracted. "How about you, Miss Bishop? Have you changed your mind too?" I shook my head. I wanted that drink, but something made me want to refuse anything that man had to offer me. Must have been his blatant disregard of women in general.

"Well, it was nice to meet you, Miss Bishop," Marla said, holding my gaze a little longer than necessary. "Good to see you too, Fin."

She headed for the door, and I couldn't help but wonder what would happen the moment we left. Based on the look her husband was giving her, I had a feeling her simple crime of inter-rupting a meeting and expressing an interest in something as uncivilized as a tattoo would land her in the path of his fist.

I despised men like Chase Stone—pretty on the outside, but ugly as sin underneath that facade.

After Marla had shut the door on her way out, Fin glared at Chase and continued with the business of the land. "You have no idea what you and Harry Cavanagh have done," he said. "That land has heirs all right. Dead ones. And they're back for what's rightfully theirs."

Chase scoffed, but when he saw the look on Fin's face, he

decided to listen with a more open mind. He handed Fin his drink and walked over to the window. "What the hell are you talking about, Fin?"

"I'm talking about those graves under that land. The ones we keep digging up. The ones that shut down the project."

Chase seemed unfazed. "There isn't a new construction project in this city that hasn't tapped a pocket of graves while digging." He was referring to Savannah's notorious reputation for being one big graveyard, with dead bodies rumored to be buried under just about every street from the river down to the Victorian district. "What's another body?" He shrugged.

"You know what we do at the society," Fin said. "The kind of things we deal with. Those graves we disturbed aren't ordinary graves. They're the ancestors of the woman you swindled, and one of them is back for blood."

That arrogance that Chase Stone had sported since the second we walked into his house, suddenly vanished. It was replaced by a subtle fear that I'd gotten good at spotting. Or maybe it was the dragon smelling it.

"We'll stop digging for a while," Chase said. "The city has temporarily shut us down anyway. This will all blow over eventually."

"It's not that simple," Fin said. "Her name is Ijibah, and now that we've woken her up, she has no intention of going back to her grave. She wants it all. In fact, she's already started her war by compelling Rita Cavanagh to kill her husband." Fin snickered and glanced at the door. "You might want to be a little nicer to your wife."

Chase said nothing as he stared out the window, like he was waiting for ghosts to come walking down the street.

Fin stood up and joined him at the window. "You're going to give me that deed. Then the Crossroads Society is going to try to fix this clusterfuck you and Harry Cavanagh have created." He finished his drink. "One other thing. I'm pulling my funding from the project."

"We have a contract. You can't just walk away."

Fin smirked and handed him his empty glass. "I believe I just did."

15

Jackson was waiting for me at the house when I got home. On the patio, with Jet sitting next to him, he was buried deep in a book.

"What are you reading?" I asked, peeking through the door.

He nodded toward the living room. "Dug it out of that box." A packrat with books, I couldn't bring myself to get rid of the ones I'd read. Instead, I tossed them in a cardboard box in the living room. "I didn't know you liked urban fantasy so much."

With a snort, I stepped outside. "Jackson, I *am* urban fantasy."

"I see your point." He stood up and tossed the book on the table before greeting me with a kiss.

I sat down and relaxed into the cool metal chair. "Well, this has been an interesting day," I began as I dropped my head back and gazed at the stars. "I found out where Emmaline lives, and that our missing witch, Esrial, has been holed up in one of her bedrooms. I also found out that Ijibah is here to reclaim some land Harry Cavanagh's company apparently swindled from her last living descendant." I straightened back up in my seat and reached down to stroke Jet's back as he brushed against my leg. "Oh, I almost forgot. I nearly shifted in the middle of a complete stranger's house."

He got up and pulled his chair around to face mine, leaning his elbows on his knees the way he always did when we were about to have a serious discussion. I averted my eyes from his and focused on his chest, but he lifted my chin to bring them back up. "Don't disappear on me, Katie. We're having this conversation."

"You mean the one about me becoming a full-time, card-carrying member of the beast club any day now?"

I could tell by the way he ignored my flippant remark that we were about to have a come-to-Jesus moment about the decision I had to make. According to the calendar, I had about a week to decide whether to pick up the phone and call my aunt or roll the dice to see if this whole twenty-fifth birthday thing was an elaborate hoax made up by a deluded relative I barely knew.

"You know she's telling you the truth, Katie. You're already showing signs that the dragon is getting more determined, and we're going to have to deal with it before it's too late."

"We?" I pulled away from him. "There is no *we* in this equation." I put on my best mask of indifference to give him those options he deserved. I'd made it clear before that I'd understand if he didn't want any part of this, and he'd made it clear that he wasn't going anywhere. But I couldn't help but keep drilling it into his head that it was okay to walk away. Who were we kidding? We'd only known each other for a couple of months. He didn't owe me a damn thing, and I refused to drag him down into the abyss of my dark future because he was too decent to get on his bike and head back to Atlanta.

He reached for my hand and squeezed it gently, spreading a warmth into my palm that traveled up my arm and down my torso, nailing me in the gut. Such a simple gesture from any other guy would have been mildly titillating at best. But Jackson was a force of nature, and the slightest touch reduced me to a bag of butterflies.

"How many times do I need to tell you that I'm not going anywhere? We can fight this and win." He laughed softly and shrugged. "I'm Superman, remember?"

God help me I wanted to believe that, but the truth was I was scared shitless about the alternative to that happy ending. I just wasn't used to relying on anyone but myself to survive life's little catastrophes, and I think the possibility of turning into a dragon permanently qualified as a catastrophe.

"I think you should go." I pulled my hand away from his. "I'll call you when it's over—if I'm not on my way to the Slovenian Alps," I added with a nervous laugh.

He stood up and glared down at me. "You've gotta be fucking kidding me." There was enough aggression in his tone to stir the dragon on my back. "Aren't you tired of this shit, Katie? It must be exhausting pushing people away." Lost for words, I said nothing. In the time we'd been together, he'd never spoken to me like that, and I had no idea how to respond to his anger.

We'd reached an impasse, with him waiting for a response, and me going quiet while I stared into the night sky. When I wouldn't look at him, he reached into his pocket and pulled out his keys. He removed my house key from the ring and tossed it on the table. "If you decide to fight for your life, call me." A few seconds later, he headed back into the house and out the front door.

A minute passed, and I heard the sound of his bike starting up. A sharp pain hit me in the center of my chest. I'd gotten exactly what I'd asked for. I'd pushed Jackson away and guaranteed myself a lonely battle, if and when I faced the dragon on my birthday. At that moment, I wanted to lose.

Sugar took one look at my puffy eyes when I opened my front door the next morning and barged her way past me toward the kitchen.

"You know what time it is, Sugar?" Judging by the dim light coming through the window, it was too early for a social visit.

She ignored my question and started the coffee. Then she grabbed a carton of eggs from the fridge and proceeded to make me a breakfast I couldn't possibly eat.

"You want toast?" she asked.

I shook my head, trying to hold back the tears that were threatening to well up in my eyes. What the hell was wrong with me?

"Jackson's gone," I said. "I was a world-class asshole last night and finally got what I deserved. I told him to leave." I shrugged. "So he left." Instead of food, what I really needed was a tall glass of water to help me swallow that thick lump obstructing my throat.

With her back to me, I detected her shoulders stiffen as she mumbled something under her breath. For the next few minutes, she cracked eggs into a bowl and whisked like a woman on amphetamines. She didn't say a word as she poured them into a hot skillet. When the eggs were cooked, she dumped them on a plate and shoved it across the counter at me.

"I can't eat," I said, pushing the plate away.

"Eat the damn eggs!" she barked.

"Why are you yelling at me?" I barked back.

"'Cuz you a damn fool," she replied, clearly disgusted with me. "Now I know Jackson didn't just walk out of here without a little help from that mouth of yours. That man is crazy about you."

I picked up a fork and stuffed some eggs in my mouth.

"Apparently not," I said around the food that refused to go down my throat.

"Give me that plate." She yanked it out from under me and put it on the floor in front of Jet. He sniffed the pile of eggs and walk toward the living room. "What the hell's wrong with everyone around here?" She poured two cups of coffee and headed for the patio. "Come on. Let's go have us a talk."

I followed her outside and glanced at the chair where Jackson had been sitting the night before, probably for the last time. We sat in silence for a couple of minutes before I finally broke the ice. "I messed up, Sugar."

"Yeah, well, what else is new."

"Thanks. I feel so much better now."

"That boy ain't gone. He just needed a little break from whatever drama you've been giving him." She sipped her coffee and fanned the morning heat away from her face with a napkin. "Damn heat's about to eat me alive. One of these days I'm going to pack up and move my ass to San Francisco. None of this sticky mess out there."

The problem with Savannah was the humidity. Living on the coast with temperatures in the nineties was a recipe for disaster, if you liked to wear your hair straight or preferred anything but shorts and a tank top. Seemed criminal to expect a man to wear a suit and tie during the summer months.

"I know you didn't drop by this early just to cook me breakfast, so why are you here?"

She feigned offense and set her coffee cup on the table. "Since when do I need a reason to come over here and have a nice little cup of coffee with you?"

"You don't. But I know you, Sugar. Nothing gets you out of bed this early unless you're escaping something." I gave her a smirk. "Stopping by on your way home from somewhere or someone?"

"I wish," she said, picking up her cup. "No, baby, I'm here to get you locked and loaded for that invitation you fixin' to get."

"What are you talking about?" An uncomfortable feeling snaked its way through my body like quicksilver as I waited to hear about this mysterious invitation.

"You about to be summoned, girl. Lillian's got a house full of them council folks, and guess who's about to be the entertainment?"

Fin had estimated their arrival by today. I just didn't expect to be hearing about it this early in the morning, or from Sugar. "I'm afraid to ask what you mean by 'entertainment.'"

"Mama got a call from Lillian around three a.m., and she wasn't too happy about getting woke up. The council didn't waste no time trying to bring the hammer down on Esrial. Lillian had to think fast to keep them from taking Esrial back to whatever rock they crawled out from under, right then and there. Had to tell them about Mama's visions and the secret weapon." She finished her last drop of coffee and stood up. "Come on, girl. You got to get dressed. Everyone's waiting to see this secret weapon. That would be you."

I WASN'T TOO keen about being put on display for a bunch of uppity witches who thought the definition of justice was whatever struck their fancy at any particular moment. What happened to this tribunal they were supposedly coming to Savannah to conduct? Not to mention the fact that I couldn't get Jackson out of my mind, and they were wasting precious time that I could have been using to rectify our breakup.

Sugar and I pulled up to Lillian's house around eight thirty. Apparently, my immediate mission was to convince these "inquisitors" that I was uniquely qualified to fight this mysterious sorceress named Ijibah. I just needed to convince myself of that.

"Here we go, baby," Sugar said, freshening up her lipstick in the mirror before reaching for the car door handle.

"Really, Sugar? You're worried about how you look?"

"Got to have some confidence when heading into the lion's den," she replied. "We about to slay us some big ol' cats, so I got to feel fly before walking up them stairs." She nodded toward the house. "Let's do this."

I got out of the Eldorado and followed her up the steps, feeling substantially less confident and wishing I had some of that magic lipstick to light a fire in my own belly. Without knocking, Sugar opened the door and headed straight for the living room.

Expecting to be accosted by Lillian's housekeeper, I was surprised to have free access to the place as we walked into the vacant living room. Sugar whipped her head around the empty space, holding her hand up to shush me as I opened my mouth to speak. "Listen," she said, her eyes narrowing. Without a word, she made a beeline down the hall, stopping when she realized I was still standing back in the living room. "Come on." She waved for me to follow.

We stopped in front of the tall double doors that led to the grandest room in the house, the one I'd gotten a glimpse of the night of the Crossroads Society's annual ball. She turned around and fiddled with the hair framing my face.

I swatted her hands away. "What are you doing?"

"This is a job interview. We got to go in there and convince these folks that you can smack that witch right back to the grave."

Before I had a chance to reply, she swung both doors open and headed for the group of people gathered in the center of the room. I followed, trying to exude that same level of confidence

Sugar was projecting. Like she said, these were lions we were dealing with, and predators could smell fear from a mile away.

I stopped when I saw a set of violet eyes staring at me. The woman sitting in an elaborate chair at the far end of the room didn't look much older than me. Sitting in equally ostentatious chairs on either side of her were four other strangers.

"Sugar," Fin said from somewhere in the room.

I glanced at a man wearing a black suit. His dark hair shimmered like crude oil against his skull. Fin was standing next to him, shadowed by the man's considerable height.

The man's eyes traveled over Sugar's left shoulder and landed on me. "Is this the dragon?" he asked in an unimpressed voice.

Fin stood up. It was an automatic response when a woman walked into the room. A Southern thing engrained in his head. "Yes. This is Katie Bishop."

"Would you two like something to eat or drink before we get started," Lillian asked, drawing our attention to the buffet. "What's a breakfast meeting without a strong cup of coffee," she said, heading for the table loaded with everything from omelets to croissants. I even spotted stacks of waffles and pancakes. When hosting a group of people tasked with deciphering the guilt or innocence of a family member, you pulled out the big guns. Dressed to impress, so to speak. Esrial was family, and these five strangers sitting in front of us were here to decide her fate.

"I've had enough coffee," I said. "But thanks."

Sugar met Lillian at the table and poured herself a cup. "I ain't nearly as wired as I'd like to be." Then she twiddled her fingers over a platter of blueberry muffins. "Mind if I have one of these?"

"Help yourself."

Looking back at the unimpressed faces watching me, I surveyed each one of them. Besides the woman occupying the throne and the man in the stuffy suit, there were two more women and another man with hair as white as snow. One of the women extended the back of her hand toward me, like she expected me to walk over and kiss it. But before I could respond with a snarky remark to that ridiculous suggestion, Fin threw interference.

"Miss Bishop is an honorary member of the society. She's been an invaluable resource to us."

I glanced at Fin and waited for an introduction. Not that I was particularly eager to make their acquaintance, but I had a list of things to do on my day off. Finding Jackson, for one.

He took my visual cue and started with the man wearing the black suit. "Miss Bishop, may I present Godfrey Bellamy. He's with the international branch of the council, sent down here to represent the interests of the Southern members." He continued with the woman who had foolishly offered me the back of her hand. "Muriel Cane is with the local arm of the council."

Sugar shot me a look, and I prayed she didn't say something that might get us in hot water with these folks. My main objective for keeping the peace was for Esrial's benefit, not to make friends with the arrogant bitch with the god complex.

Fin bypassed the head honcho in the middle and continued with the robed minions on her other side, saving the best for last, I assumed. "Ingrid Walsh and Ian Davis are here as witnesses."

"Witnesses for what?"

"For the testimony," the queen bee sitting on the throne replied. "We're here to question the accused, and her responses to those questions must be recorded by impartial witnesses."

I met the mystery woman's intense stare. She had dark auburn hair somewhere between mahogany and copper, and her fair skin appeared almost translucent. Her violet eyes were windows to something I sensed was intelligence beyond the average human being, and it unnerved me to look at them for more than a few seconds. I became increasingly uncomfortable as she held my eyes in place with her gaze. Unless she was wearing some kind of designer contacts, I suspected there was a valid reason for my discomfort.

"*Impartial?*" Sugar scoffed. "Ain't nothing impartial about an inquisition."

Fin tensed, and I could see his fists squeeze tight. "You'll have to excuse Sugar," he said. "She has a very direct way about her. I'm sure she meant no offense, did you, Sugar?"

There was a warning in his voice that simmered her down. "Oh, I didn't mean to suggest you folks was unscrupulous or nothing like that," she said with a wide-eyed look. "I do apologize if I offended anyone." She turned her back to the strangers and surveyed the spread across the buffet, grabbing a waffle without bothering with a plate and fork. Then she turned back around and took a bite. The members of the council glared at her. The only one who showed no reaction to her insolence was the woman with the violet eyes.

Fin finally got around to introducing me to the woman in charge. "Katie Bishop, this is Raven."

"Just Raven?"

He nodded. "Just Raven."

I was about to move the conversation along and ask why I was summoned, when the doorbell rang.

"That would be our missing guest," Lillian said. Everyone in the room looked toward the double doors as Pearl May Mobley was escorted in by Davina McCabe. "Now we can get down to business."

16

"Mama? Why the hell didn't you tell me you was coming over here. I could have drove out there and got you."

May walked into the room and eyed the council. "How many times I got to tell you to watch that mouth," she said without taking her eyes off the strangers. "I got me a ride."

"I'm just surprised to see you here, that's all." Sugar glanced at Davina. "You taking her home, too?"

Ignoring Sugar, Davina headed for the coffee decanter on the table. "Sorry we're late. Some nutcase drove off the road, right into the river. Backed up traffic for miles. I don't know what the hell's going on in this town lately."

Fin offered May a chair but she refused. Advanced in age, May was still sharp as a tack. I'm sure she preferred the advantage of standing when confronted with a pack of wolves like the council.

Raven slowly turned her head to Lillian. "Where is the defendant?"

Fin quickly spoke up. "She's here, but the society would prefer to discuss the circumstances surrounding the case before we bring her in. Not that we don't think she'd be treated fairly, and in accordance with council law. But if you don't mind, we'd like to get a few things straight first, as insurance. With all due respect," he was quick to add.

"You were once married to the defendant. Is that right, Mr. Cooper?" Muriel Cane asked.

"Correct," Fin replied. "I won't deny my connection to the defendant, but I can assure you that what we have to say is relevant to the inquisition."

Raven gave him a cold smile. "We prefer to call it a conversation. But if hearing you out prior to bringing her before the council would ease your confidence in the process, then by all means, speak."

Fin wasted no time seizing the opportunity to speak in Esrial's defense. He approached the five council members and reached into his pocket, producing the piece of bone Davina had tossed on the table in front of me the other night. He held it out with the marks prominently displayed for each of them to see.

Godfrey's face went pale as his nose wrinkled. "Is that what it smells like?"

"Smells like?" I asked, confused.

Raven clarified. "Godfrey has a talent for identifying things that are evil in nature. His sense of smell is quite unique." She stood up for the first time and stepped toward Fin. Her height was considerable, at least six feet, and her limbs were as willowy as Emmaline's. But there wasn't a trace of meekness in her demeanor. She approached Fin and extended her hand with the grace of a gazelle, waiting for him to place it in her palm.

"The marks are from the grimoire," he said, handing her the bone. "It was left on Esrial's altar before the murder."

Raven examined the engraved marks on the bone before holding it up for Godfrey to get a good whiff. "Is it Adro's?" she asked, referring to the god whose bones were buried at the crossroads.

Godfrey nodded his head once.

"There is an intruder in our city," Fin continued. "We believe this sorceress is responsible for compelling Rita Cavanagh to kill her husband. Esrial was nothing but a convenient pawn." Fin nodded to the bone in Raven's hand. "That bone was used for the incantation, and Esrial was the conduit for the black magic, unbeknownst to her, of course. In fact, she wasn't even in the country at the time of the murder."

Raven handed the bone back to Fin. "Esrial was involved sexually with the dead man's wife, correct?"

"Yes, but—"

Raven halted him with a raise of her hand. "You are familiar with the theory of Occam's razor?" she asked. "The theory that the simplest explanation is usually the correct one." I knew where she was going with the question, and based on the look on Fin's face, so did he. "The simplest explanation is that Esrial resorted to black magic to kill her lover's husband. The spell may have been poorly executed, but the intent was as dark as the deed." She sat back down and gave Fin a cold stare. "I do despise those who break our laws, putting us all at risk of eradication."

Fin's expression hardened. "I can assure you that if Esrial was the architect of the spell that ultimately killed Harry Cavanagh, the timing would have been spot on. There wouldn't be any witnesses."

"I sympathize with your loyalty to your ex-wife," she continued. "But why should the council believe a much more convoluted explanation when there's such a simple one staring us in the face? Why shouldn't we chain her and take her with us right now to be dealt with in accordance with our laws?"

"Ijibah would like that." Everyone in the room turned to look at May, who was curiously examining the five council members presiding over the room. "You gonna give her exactly what she wants."

"Who are you, exactly?" Muriel asked with condescendence.

"*Exactly*," Sugar mocked, "this is my mama, Pearl May Mobley. She's about as powerful a conjure woman you ever gonna meet, so I suggest you show a little respect. Unless you want that wig flying off your head and catching fire," she added under her breath.

I stifled a laugh.

Obviously unaccustomed to being challenged, Muriel seemed startled from the force of Sugar's tone. "It was just a question," she said with a glare.

"Who is this Ijibah?" Raven asked.

May shook her head slowly, a slight grin edging up her face. "She's here for her land. Killed Harry Cavanagh to get it back."

"As I was saying," Fin said. "We have information."

Raven cocked her head thoughtfully and motioned for Fin to continue. "We'll hear you out before questioning the accused."

"We have reason to believe this intruder witch is responsible for the black magic used to enchant Mrs. Cavanagh, conveniently using Esrial as a conduit for the spell. You see, Cavanagh Holdings stole something that belongs to her. A piece of land. Ijibah's coming to get her revenge, and it looks like she's already started by killing the CEO."

"You expect us to believe that a single witch had the power to compel a murder from the other side of the crossroads?" she asked. "Through the will of one of our own?"

Fin was doing his best to remain respectful, but I could see the toll the questions were taking on his patience, in his own temple. "Did I mention the fact the Ijibah is dead? I'm sure you'd agree that death only elevates her expertise with the black arts."

Muriel's eyes widened. "Necromancy!" She seemed appalled by the suggestion that even more laws may have been broken.

"Not exactly," Fin said. "This one is coming back all on her own. She wasn't summoned, but she is getting her strength from a cone of power somewhere in the city. That power source will eventually bring her through the crossroads. If she's this powerful from the other side, imagine what we'll be dealing with when she breaks through."

Godfrey's brow furrowed. "Witches tend to be practical, Mr. Cooper. If this one is so powerful, why bother with Esrial at all? Why not just kill Cavanagh herself and be done with it?"

"Well, Mr. Bellamy, witches are also smart, and that would be a missed opportunity. What better way to take over our town than to bring down the reigning coven by framing one of their members for the high crime of practicing the dark arts." He paused, gauging their faces for acquiescence. "She gets her revenge and a new kingdom."

"Got to find the cone," May said. "Ijibah gettin' her power from somewhere in the city. You find that cone of power, then you got a chance to beat her. Otherwise we all be bowing down to that devil."

Godfrey gave May a bland look. "In my experience, intruders who think they can walk into the council's territory and break the rules are usually ignorant fools. We'll bring her in and have her kneel before the council, side by side with Esrial, and see which one breaks the fastest and confesses to the murder." He snorted arrogantly. "Shouldn't require more than a good dose of binding magic once she steps over the line of the crossroads."

"You stupid?" May said, making us all wince. "Ijibah got the fire! Ain't no binding spell going to work on a witch got the fire in her belly. Got to fight fire with fire. You can't see that, you the fool!"

His brow arched in amusement at May's audacity. "I suppose that explains Miss Bishop." His eyes focused on me. "I believe Fin referred to her as the perfect weapon to defeat the threat. That threat would be Ijibah, correct?"

I managed a saccharin smile for the dickhead who didn't have the courtesy to address me directly, like I was some heifer at a 4-H show.

Fin noticed the annoyance written all over my face and quickly intervened before I said something we might all regret. "Yes. As I've already explained, Miss Bishop is a dragon."

Godfrey looked at me with those same unimpressed eyes as when I first walk into the room. Then he raised his hand and motioned for me to turn around, to examine me from all angles.

"Forget it," I said, shaking my head. "You don't give me orders, *Godfrey*."

He nearly flew out of his chair but stopped cold when he heard the growl coming from my throat.

"I wouldn't do that if I were you," Fin warned. "Miss Bishop is not one of ours. She isn't governed by our laws, which puts you at significant risk if you choose to agitate the dragon." The slight grin on Fin's face suggested he'd taken pleasure in putting the man in his place, all within the respectful guise of keeping Godfrey safe from impending harm.

Raven seemed amused by the confrontation. She stood up and walked toward me, circling me to examine the tattoo peeking out from under my tank top. With her robe grazing the floor, it was difficult to determine if she was walking or gliding, but her gate was as smooth as a boat sailing over glass.

"You're a half-breed," she said. It wasn't a question.

I snorted without turning around to meet her eyes. "Yeah, well, if you want to split hairs. I prefer demi-dragon."

Her finger grazed my skin, and I turned to give her a cautionary look. "*Don't* touch me."

A smile formed on her face as she retracted her hand. "Show me," she demanded. My head cocked as I reconciled those two little words. "The dragon," she added in case I was too stupid to comprehend her order.

The room went dead quiet as everyone waited to see if I would comply. Even if I wanted to, it wasn't like I could just shift on command. The closest I ever came to having full control was when I unleashed the beast on the beach at night. Even then, it was more like the dragon compelling me to go there, waiting to set itself free over the discretion of the sea.

"Baby, you ain't thinking right," Sugar said to Raven, glancing at the others for reinforcements.

No one spoke up. I assumed they were all curious to see what would happen next, and I caught myself glancing at the high ceiling, wondering how much damage I would do to this beautiful room if I did shift. I shook off the thought and gave her a defiant glare. She glared back and waited to see if I'd back down and submit to her request. I'm sure she was accustomed to folks bending over backward to kiss her ass, but I wasn't one of them.

She turned and looked at Godfrey, giving him a silent order that sent a chill through me as he stood up and calmly walked across the room. He stopped at the buffet table and reached for a strawberry from the platter of fruit. Then he picked up a paring knife to trim away the stem before popping the whole thing into his mouth.

I glanced at Fin who seemed as nervous as I was.

Godfrey spun around and jabbed the paring knife into the side of Sugar's torso, wrapping his other arm securely around her chest to hold her still. A strangled gasp came from her mouth as her eyes flew wide from the shock.

Fin took a step forward but stopped when Raven shot him a glance. It was as if she'd thrown up a wall around him, holding him helplessly in place as he tried to move toward Sugar and Godfrey. None of us could move.

I looked at May, but even she was powerless against Raven's magic.

"The tip of that blade is just beneath her skin," Raven said to me. "A precarious position that if manipulated correctly, could pierce vital organs and end Miss Mobley's life. I suggest you cooperate, Miss Bishop, if you wish to spare your friend."

Sugar stood perfectly still as Godfrey threatened to plunge the knife deeper.

"I can't shift at will," I said, turning back to Raven. "The dragon has to want to come out." As soon as I said it, I regretted it.

"Well, then, let's give it a reason." Raven turned back to Godfrey and held his eyes for a few seconds. His hand twisted the knife slowly, and Sugar let out a howl that sent a collective gasp through the room. May was struggling against the magic that held her in place, but all she could do was mutter quietly as her arms and legs remained frozen by the invisible force controlling everyone in the room.

My eyes began to burn as Sugar's cries grew louder. The room brightened, and the sound resonating through the massive space amplified to a point where I had to cover my ears. Every breath taken, and every heartbeat coming from the people in the cavernous hall sounded like a war taking place between my ears. I glanced down at my hands and watched the talons emerge from the tips of my fingers. Rows of scales appeared across my arms with a quick clicking sound as they emerged from the pores of my skin.

Raven took a few steps back to give the dragon some space. For a moment, I thought I saw fear in her eyes, but it was quickly replaced with what must have been fascination. She reached for me, but before she could touch me, I opened my mouth and shot a river of flames at her feet.

Godfrey pulled the knife from Sugar's bleeding torso and

dropped it on the terrazzo floor, sending a clanking sound through the room as it hit the hard surface. Sugar clutched the open wound and nearly lost her balance. There were words coming out of her mouth, but they were nothing but distant muffled sounds I could no longer make out, as my sharp hearing muddied from the vibrations filling my head.

The room rocked from my wings hitting the walls on either side. Then everyone hit the floor as my powerful tail whipped around, sending the buffet table sideways and the trays of food flying into the air.

"Katie!" I heard Sugar call out. "Easy, Baby! You'll kill us all!"

I turned to look at her frightened face. Then I continued to scan the room until I spotted my target—Godfrey. The man scrambled backward toward the overturned buffet table, ducking behind it for cover.

"That table ain't gonna save you," Sugar sneered. "You low down son of a—"

One of my wings hit the wall again, sending a quake through the house. I was growing too fast, the back of my head already touching the high ceiling. A window smashed to my right as my other wing crashed through it. Before I could stop myself, I was heading straight for the small opening. The foundation shook as I slammed into the wall, freeing my head through the broken window. I reared back and slammed against it again, releasing a stream of flames that nearly set the whole place on fire.

"Stop!" Lillian screamed, as the spell that overtook the room seemed to fade and set everyone free. "You'll burn the house down!"

Something sharp stabbed me between the eyes, followed by a powerful ringing in my ears. I shook my head to clear the pain and prepared to break down the wall, but the pain intensified tenfold and nearly dropped me. I whipped my head around and saw Ingrid Walsh, one of the council witnesses, extending her arm in my direction. A ball of light came from the center of her palm, its bright rays beaming directly at me.

"Call off your witch!" Davina demanded, glaring at Raven. "If you kill that dragon, we're all screwed, you damn fool!"

The pain was excruciating, cutting straight down the center of my head and nearly blinding me. Without thinking, I opened my mouth and roared, shooting a bolt of flames at her feet. Ingrid screamed as the fire caught the hem of her robe and quickly spread up the fabric, engulfing her entire body. She danced around the room, arms flailing like a blazing bird trying to take flight.

As if he could stop the inferno, Ian Davis threw her to the ground, shooting wild looks at Raven as he frantically tried to extinguish the flames. It was a futile attempt to save her.

"What have you done!" he cried, rocking back and forth on the ground next to her charred remains, as the fire eventually died down. Ingrid Walsh was dead.

Raven seemed oblivious to the death of one of her own. Through it all, she remained perfectly still with a wicked gaze fixed on me. As Sugar said, I was the entertainment.

With a final glance at all the people running for the door, I swung my head back to the window and rammed the wall with every ounce of strength I had left. It breached, and I flew through the thick hole of drywall and brick, with dust filling the air from the explosive force.

I looked back down at Lillian Whitman's house as I ascended higher into the sky towards the baking sun. Raven was standing in the makeshift door I'd just created, grinning up at me as I flew out of sight.

17

I opened my eyes to the glare of the sun hitting me square in the face. Sand was sticking to my lips from the drool pooling around my mouth. It took me a minute to figure out where I was, but the grit between my teeth and the unmistakable smell of seawater told me I was lying on the beach.

"Are you dead?" someone asked.

With a heave, I propped myself up and looked at the boy. A Popsicle dripped from his hand as he hovered over me and licked it. He looked way too young to be on the beach by himself, but he appeared to be alone, near the potential drowning pool called the ocean that should have been any responsible parent's worst nightmare.

"I said, are you dead?" he repeated with a little more determination.

I wiped the sand from my lips and blinked the sun out of my eyes. "I don't think so." Based on the position of the sun, I figured it was late afternoon. "What are you doing out here by yourself? Where are your parents?" Despite the fact that he shouldn't have been wandering on the beach alone, I was actually relieved not to have an adult finding me passed out on the sand.

That would take a little more explaining. "Shouldn't you be in school or something?"

He shook his head. "School hasn't started yet."

A woman came running toward us—the missing mother, I assumed—and grabbed his arm when she reached him. "What did I say about disappearing like that, Jason?" Based on the way she was staring at me, I figured I must have looked pretty rough. "I'm sorry if he was bothering you," she said, turning to lead him back to where he'd wandered off from.

"Excuse me," I called out. "What time is it?"

She looked back at me cautiously. "It's almost five o'clock."

"Monday?" I asked, having no clue how long I'd been there.

Gripping her boy around the shoulders, she gave me a strange look. "It's Wednesday." Then she quickly steered him down the beach, trying to get away from the crazy woman who had no idea what day it was.

"Wednesday? Shit!" I looked around the beach, praying I'd spot a familiar landmark telling me I hadn't flown all the way to Florida. I considered yelling at the woman again to ask where I was, but I'd already pushed my luck, and the last thing I needed was for her to call the cops on the vagrant talking to small children on the beach.

I almost cried with relief when I spotted the Tybee Beach Pier about a quarter of a mile in the distance. I climbed to my feet and headed for the pavilion, trying to imagine what was happening back at the shop, with me MIA for nearly three days. Sugar and Sea Bass were probably having dual coronaries, but since Jackson and I were through, I doubted he even knew I was missing.

My pockets were empty when I reached inside, so I figured I'd be begging someone at the pavilion to use their phone. As I walked along the edge of the ocean, the events of Monday morning came rushing back—that giant hole in the side of

Lillian's house, Raven and her crooked council, Godfrey driving a knife into Sugar's side. But it was the image of Ingrid Walsh going up in flames that made me want to drop to my knees and throw up in the sand. She'd attacked me first, but I doubted the council would be very democratic in their delivery of my sentence. I didn't fall under their laws, but I had a strong feeling Raven had no intention of letting the act go unpunished. I'd made a new enemy.

I HANDED the phone back to the man on the pier and thanked him for letting me use it to call Sugar. It was less than forty minutes from my house to Tybee, which was where she'd been camped out since Monday, when I flew into the sky and disappeared for nearly three days.

Faint from hunger, I avoided the shops along the beach in favor of resting on the sand where I told Sugar to meet me. Even with all the insane events of Monday, I couldn't get Jackson out of my mind. What an ass I'd been. All he wanted to do was help me, and I made the colossal blunder of pushing him away, disguising my fear of letting him get too close with selfish independence.

The beach felt good as I plopped down on the sand and lay on my side in the fetal position. The memory of Jackson bringing me here on our first date, to see the miracle of the sea shifter turtles, was one I'd never forget. And our subsequent visits, with him waiting on the beach while my dragon got its fix of sailing through the night sky, were some of the best memories I'd ever have of our brief relationship.

I fought the urge to doze off. Sugar would make it out to the island in record time, I had no doubt. But fatigue finally won, and I slept until I felt the tip of a shoe nudge me in the side.

Sugar's tall frame was hovering over me, blocking out the warm sun when I opened my eyes.

"That was fast," I said, climbing to my feet. My eyes instinctively went to her waist. "Are you okay, Sugar?" I was a little surprised when she offered to drive out to get me, after having a knife twisted into her side a couple of days earlier. I assumed Godfrey was just trying to scare me into letting the beast out, not trying to inflict any real damage. But I figured she'd be recovering for a few days. Sea Bass or Abel could have picked me up.

She followed my eyes and lifted up her shirt to show me the bandage. "That little paring knife didn't do any real damage," she said. "Hurt like hell though. Mama put the juju on it and healed it up real fast. That piece of shit was just trying to make me squeal so you would shift." She rubbed the bandage and grimaced. "Itches like hell from that stuff Mama smeared on it."

"Well, it worked," I said, referring to Godfrey's attempt to provoke the dragon. "Thank God you're okay." My mind went back to that room where Godfrey threatened to filet her. "I don't know about the world that Blackthorn Grove lives in, but where I come from, the law doesn't commit felonies. Well, at least not in front of a room full of witnesses. Jesus, Sugar, Esrial is fucked."

Anxious to get home, I looked up and down the parking lot for the Eldorado. "Where's your car?"

Without answering, she stared at me with a questioning look. "Where the hell you been for the past three days?" The wooden heels of her platform shoes were beginning to sink into the sand as she waited for an answer. She glanced down at her feet. "These shoes is vintage, baby, and they're about to sink to China if you don't get to talking."

"Can it wait until we get inside the car?" I was eager to get home to take a shower and eat, and to make sure my poor cat had been tended to while I was gone. "Please tell me you've been taking care of Jet."

She bobbed her head and snorted in disgust. "I drive my ass all the way out here to get you, and all you got to say is *can it wait?*" Before I could respond, she wrapped her arms around me in a death grip. "Baby, I thought you was dead. I seen you break through that wall and fly away, and then Raven and the rest of them clowns took off after you. I thought they'd done killed you after what you did to that witness woman."

"I can't breathe," I mumbled against her chest.

She let go and smoothed my disheveled hair. "Sorry, baby. I'm just so happy you ain't dead. And Jet's fine. That cat's been eating like a king."

The image of Ingrid Walsh's charred and lifeless body filled my mind and made me a little queasy, but I'd acted in self-defense. I mean, what kind of fool uses dirty magic on a dragon and expects no retaliation? Even so, I had a feeling Raven and her henchmen weren't too pleased with me, and that god syndrome she appeared to have was about to come down on me like acid rain.

"I have a feeling I have a target on my back," I said.

"Well, I'm moving in for a while, with Jackson gone and all," she informed me. "I'll kill that skank-ass bitch myself if she tries anything. Give her a taste of Mama's juju."

Arguing with Sugar when she had an idea cemented in her head was usually futile, so I decided to wait until after we got home and had something to eat before setting her straight. No one was moving in with me. "Where are you parked?"

She flicked her head toward the entrance of the pier. The Eldorado was parked in a spot clearly marked with a sign that said No Parking, with its hazard lights flashing. "I ain't paying no two dollars to park for five minutes," she said, referring to Tybee's strict parking regulations. "Now let's get out of here before I get me a ticket."

We climbed into the car and headed back to Savannah. Sugar

was unusually quiet as we drove along the river. "I should call Fin," I said, figuring he'd probably already had the National Guard dispatched to look for me. And believe me, he had the connections to get it done.

She looked sideways at me. "Do I look stupid? I called that man the second I hung up the phone with you."

"Eyes on the road, Sugar," I said, getting a little nervous as she continued to stare at me. "I didn't dust one of Raven's witnesses, then sleep it off on the beach for days, just to die in a car accident."

"Don't you be no backseat driver. I was driving before you was even born." She pointed to the glove compartment. "Hand me them sunglasses in there."

I opened it and reached for the tortoiseshell frames. Next to the glasses was a pack of cigarettes—and a gun. "What is that, Sugar?"

She glanced at the glove compartment. "What the hell does it look like?"

"Since when do you own a gun?" I'd opened that glove compartment many times, but I'd never seen that gun before, which made me wonder if she usually carried it in her purse. Despite her dramatics, Sugar was basically levelheaded. But when she riled up, she could be a little unpredictable. "I hope you haven't brought that thing inside my shop. Do you even know how to use it?"

"Girl, I damn sure know how to use me a gun. Folks around her ain't as progressive as up there in New York City where you come from. Ain't no drunk little frat boys going to lay a hand on Sugar, unless I extend an invitation."

The look on her face told me she was speaking from experience. It never occurred to me that the fearless Sugar I knew could be a victim. "I'm just surprised to see it. Guns make me nervous."

"Good thing you ain't the one who has to use it." She held out her hand. "Give me one of them cigarettes, while you're at it."

Instead of reading her the riot act about abusing her lungs, I handed her one and pushed in the car lighter that miraculously still worked after decades. The Eldorado really was a feat of engineering, validating the old adage of, they don't make them like they used to.

"What happened to Esrial?" I asked. My stomach did a flip as I waited for bad news, that the council had done something drastic in retaliation for me incinerating one of their members.

Sugar took a drag of her cigarette and rolled her window all the way down to hang her elbow over the edge. "That's a good question. After you burned up the witness and flew out that hole you punched through Lillian's wall—shit, girl, that was badass— Raven ordered Fin to go fetch his ex-wife. Fin said *hell no*, but Lillian decided it was better to cooperate."

That surprised me. How could Lillian do that, turn over one of her own, knowing that the Southern Council of Witches had no intention of treating Esrial innocent until proven guilty? She was probably already dead or locked away in a place worse than a prison cell. The council wasn't here for justice. They were here to make an example out of Esrial, regardless of the evidence Fin presented, because it served an even bigger purpose—a warning to anyone who had ideas about challenging the council. The iron fist approach.

"That's a good question?" I repeated.

"Yep. Lillian went to fetch Esrial, but she was long gone. Looked all over that big ol' house. Even went down to the cottage where Emmaline stays. No sign of her there either." She had a smirk on her face. "Must have gotten cold feet about turning herself in."

"Must have," I said, knowing damn well they were hiding her. "Probably puts an even bigger target on my head though. That council obviously came here for blood, and they need someone to make an example out of."

Sugar dropped her cigarette butt into the coke can in the holder. "They have to get past me first. Anyway, I wouldn't worry about it too much. Esrial may not have had any witnesses to back up her innocence, but you got a whole room full of folks who saw that witch try to take you down. Self-defense, that's what I saw. So did everyone else."

That put me a little at ease, at least for now. All I wanted to do was take a shower and get some food in my stomach. Then I'd get back to worrying.

I gazed out the window and finally asked the question that had been at the back of my mind since waking up on that beach. "Have you heard from Jackson?" He had her number, so it was possible that he could have called her. My eyes squeezed shut as I waited for her to answer. When she didn't respond, I turned to look at her. She rested her hand on my shoulder, which wasn't a good sign. I shrugged it away and stared at her. "Sugar?"

"Baby, that man is gone," she said, ripping the Band-Aid off fast.

My throat went dry. "What do you mean he's gone?"

"Hopped on that bike of his and headed for the interstate. Last night," she added for clarification.

"How do you know?" I tried to keep my voice from cracking.

"Why don't we just get you home first. We can talk about all this over a big glass of whiskey." I slowly shook my head and waited for her to come clean. "I got eyes on him," she continued. "Been doing a little stalking while you was gone. Well, not me personally. Called in a favor and had someone find out what he's been up to." She glanced at me and then turned her eyes back to the road. "I love you, girl, but you got exactly what you asked for. You've been pushing that man away since the day he walked into that shop of yours."

She was right. I deserved to lose Jackson Hunter. He was the best man I'd ever met, and I was so wrapped up in trying to decide what was best for him that I lost sight of the fact that he didn't need me to make that decision for him. On the other hand, maybe I was just trying to leave him before he had the chance to leave me.

"My intel said he had a backpack about the size of all his worldly possessions flung over his shoulder. I-16 heads one way, right out of Savannah. That man was leaving town."

Atlanta, I thought. Jackson had come down from Atlanta a few weeks before I met him. Sugar was right about that backpack. Jackson wasn't about material things, and I imagined he could have easily fit everything important to him inside of a fairly small one.

"Then it's done," I said. "No use crying over it." I slid deeper into the seat and gazed out the window as we approached the city limits, feeling like I'd just been punched in the stomach.

18

"We better stop by MagicInk," I said, realizing I was being selfish by wanting to go straight home. It was barely seven o'clock, so the shop was still open.

"I already called Sea Bass," Sugar said. "He knows you're okay."

"That's not the point, Sugar. I need to show up and apologize to everyone for my disappearing act."

We took a right turn and headed for the shop. When we pulled into the back lot, I just sat there while Sugar got out of the car. My legs seemed to be frozen.

She bent down and looked at me through the driver's side window. "You planning to get out, or do I need to come around this car and carry your ass inside?"

I glanced at her and smiled weakly. "I don't scare very easily, Sugar, but I'm a little spooked right now." The dragon was getting stronger and more unpredictable. In less than a week, I'd either be Katie with the dragon on a leash, or I'd be the beast that occasionally took the girl out for a stroll. Of course, there was a third possibility. The ritual could go horribly wrong and

I'd be dead. Burned alive. "There's something I haven't told you."

Sugar wasn't stupid. Her uncanny intuition had her eyeing me like a hawk.

"Remember when I told you about my aunt showing up out of the blue?" She just stared and waited for me to get to the point. "She wasn't here for a family reunion." We were in the parking lot, so I gave her the condensed version of the conversation from that night, including the part about me having to die at midnight on my twenty-fifth birthday.

"Well, damn, girl!" She leaned into the open window. "Ain't there nothing easy about you? All the misfits in this town, and I go and pick me the one waving the biggest freak flag to be my best friend."

I smirked. "Takes one to know one."

"Yeah, you got that right. A couple of real winners." She got serious and gave me a look of concern, the kind I rarely saw on her face.

"That's why Jackson left." I fought back the cracking in my voice as I said his name. "God, sometimes I can be such an asshole."

"Naw," she said, shaking her head. "You a lot of things, but you ain't no asshole. Got you a big heart inside that chest, Katie B." She walked around to the passenger side and leaned against the car. "Besides, I wouldn't be caught dead driving down the street with some asshole in my ride. You know what they say about getting your ass out of the kitchen if you can't stand the heat. I guess that boy wasn't as tough as I thought."

I shook my head. "That's not it. He wanted to help. Kept telling me he wasn't going anywhere, so I cut him an escape hatch and shoved him right through it."

Sugar straightened back up and gave me an incredulous look. "What the hell's wrong with you, girl? You telling me that man knew about all this and still wanted to stick around? And you kicked his ass to the curb?"

"I—"

"I can't even listen to any more of this," she said, waving her hand dismissively in the air before heading toward the back door of the shop. When I didn't follow, she whipped around. "Well? You coming?"

I got out of the car and followed her through the door. The first thing we heard when we walked inside was the sound of Mouse wailing like a widow at a funeral.

"What's wrong?" I asked, glancing from Sea Bass to Abel. "What happened to Mouse?"

Sea Bass seemed surprised to see me. He stared blankly like he couldn't believe I was standing in front of him. Sensing the impending inquisition, I opened my mouth to explain that even I didn't know exactly where I'd been for the past few days. Instead of a question, he nearly broke my ribs hugging me.

"Where the hell have you been, Katie?" he asked as he let go and took a step back. "I've been worried sick about you!" He shut his eyes and tried to gather himself before continuing. I'd never seen him so frazzled, except for a couple of times when he and Maggie were on the outs. "Abel's been chomping at the bit to put his cop hat back on to find you."

I glanced at the client sitting in Mouse's chair, watching the whole spectacle with a curious look on his face. Fortunately, Mouse hadn't gotten past applying the stencil to his skin, so there was no ink on him yet. With the meltdown she was having, she was in no position to finish that tattoo. And even if she tried, one of us would have stopped her.

The man stood up and started to say something, but I beat him to it in order to save a client. "It's on the house," I said, nodding to his pectoral. "Come back tomorrow and Mouse will finish it up." I tried to give him the hint that it was time to leave, but he just stood there watching Mouse sob.

"Is she all right?" he asked.

"Come on, honey," Sugar said, escorting him to the door. "Mouse is going to be just fine. You come on back tomorrow to finish up that *free* tattoo, and Katie might even buy you lunch over at Lou's."

I shot her a warning look as she closed the door behind him. "Anything else you'd like to offer him? Maybe a lifetime of free tattoos?"

"Oh, I don't think that'll be necessary," she said with just as much sarcasm. "But I believe I did just save you a client with that nice little extra touch. I think you owe *me* a free tattoo," she added under her breath.

"Why is Mouse crying like a baby?" I asked anyone in the room who cared to explain.

Abel sighed and grabbed the broom leaning against the wall. "Damn place has been a nuthouse lately." He swept the floor and shook his head.

"That's putting it mildly," Sea Bass said, scratching his jaw. "That damn Agnes Freemont is the problem. She came over with that basket of muffins. Said it was a peace offering."

At the mention of Agnes, I automatically got an image of that cake at the picnic. I glanced around the room and spotted the basket next to the coffeemaker.

"I warned Mouse not to eat one. But did she listen? Hell no." Sea Bass walked over to the basket and picked it up, dangling it over the trash can. "I was going to toss the damn things, but I figured they might be evidence. Got to be some law against feeding people tainted food without them knowing about it."

Apparently, Agnes Freemont enjoyed tampering with people's minds, but she was crossing a line when she walked into my shop

175

and tampered with my employees, while they held sharp instruments and applied permanent ink to people's skin.

"Shut up!" Mouse yelled. We all turned to look at her when she stood up and glared in the direction of the shop window. Then she grabbed a bottle of black ink from a tray and hurled it across the room. The bottle sailed straight for the ceramic jug, but as it came within a few inches of the jug's face, it stopped in mid-air. A second later, it came sailing back, hitting Mouse in the forehead.

"Damn it, Mouse! What the hell did you do that for?" Sea Bass rushed to catch her as she started to fall. He glanced at the jug. "Did you do that, Harold?"

"Don't be ridiculous," I said, walking toward the basket of muffins.

Sea Bass looked shocked. "You aren't planning to eat one of them things, are you?"

"Of course not. Jeez, Sea Bass. Sometimes I wonder what's going on in that head of yours." I grabbed the basket by the handle and headed for the front door. "The bakery is still open." Abel and Sugar were suddenly behind me, following me out the door and down the sidewalk as I headed for Le Petit Gateau. "Follow me at your own risk, folks. Can't guarantee there won't be bloodshed."

"Whatever you do, boss, keep it legal," Abel warned. "We'll just tag along to referee."

"Shit," Sugar said. "I'll hold the bitch down so you can stuff them damn muffins into her mouth. Give her a little taste of her own nasty magic."

We reached the bakery, and I swung the door open with a little more force than necessary. An annoying version of "Für Elise" automatically triggered from the opening door, announcing our entrance. There was a single customer standing

176

near the register, scanning all the decadent confections displayed in the case that ran the length of the counter.

The woman glanced down at the basket of muffins swinging from my hand and furrowed her brow. "I hope you're not returning those," she said. "I'm picking up a birthday cake, and it better be good."

I smiled sincerely. "Well, that depends on whether you're looking for an orgasm, or a good cry."

Her jaw dropped.

Agnes came through a set of swinging doors carrying a white box. She hesitated for a second when she saw us. Seeing me was bad enough, but she'd made her distaste for Sugar clear, being the bigot that she was. She set the box down on the counter and opened the top to show the cake to her customer. "You're going to love the raspberry filling."

"I wouldn't eat that if I were you," Abel muttered.

"Mm-hmm," Sugar said. "She'll be loving something, all right."

Agnes shot them both a wicked glare, but the woman lost her concern the moment she looked inside the box. "It's perfect," she said, handing Agnes her credit card. Agnes returned with the receipt, and the woman picked up the box and headed for the door.

After her customer was gone, I could hear the lock on the front door engage on its own. She glanced at the muffins I was carrying, just before I grabbed one and threw it at her. Then I tossed the basket on the counter. "If you ever come into my shop again and try to feed my employees tainted goods, I'll burn this place to the ground."

Abel groaned.

She looked at the smashed muffin and huffed. "You heard that, Abel," she said without taking her eyes off me. "It's not very smart to threaten someone in front of an ex-cop."

177

"I didn't hear a thing," Abel said. He looked at Sugar. "You hear anything?"

She cocked her head. "I don't believe I did. Only thing I hear is them scrawny-ass knees shaking behind that counter."

Agnes smirked and then folded her arms in defiance. "What's the matter, Miss Bishop? Can't handle a little joke?"

I stared at her in disbelief. Then I grabbed another muffin from the basket on the counter and stalked up to where she was standing with that smug look on her face. "I'll tell you what. Why don't you come by the shop tomorrow for a complimentary tattoo." I shoved the muffin in her face. "I'll feed this to Mouse before she starts putting that little heart on your tailbone. What do you say, Agnes?"

"Amen, baby."

Agnes took a step back and glared at Sugar. Then she turned her eyes back to me, letting them wander around my face like she was seeing me for the first time. "You have no idea what's coming." A cocky grin slid up the side of her face.

I glanced down at her tightly clenched fist as a small line of blood trailed across her fingers. A drop hit the floor, and she relaxed the pressure and opened her hand, revealing gashes where her fingernails had punctured the thick skin of her palm.

"This bitch is crazy," Sugar muttered.

I gazed at the wound and couldn't help but wonder if Sugar was right. Maybe Agnes Freemont was a little off kilter. But then a more sinister thought crossed my mind. "Jesus, Agnes. Whose side are you on?"

Her cocky grin disappeared. "Whichever side is winning."

Not wanting to speculate or aggravate the situation further, I backed off and headed for the door. I was too damn tired for any more confrontation. Sugar and Abel followed me out.

"Ain't a tight screw in that woman's head," Sugar said as we headed back over to the shop. "Fin and Lillian need to have them a little come-to-Jesus with that witch."

Abel snickered. "No shit."

When we walked back into the shop, Mouse was just beginning to pull herself together and put a halt to the waterworks.

Sea Bass shook his head and let out an exaggerated sigh. "I don't know what the hell is going on around here." He picked up the bottle of ink Mouse had thrown at the jug earlier and set it on the counter. "So what happened over at the bakery? Did you kick her ass?" he said, throwing a couple of punches at the air.

"It ain't nice to beat up on the mentally disabled," Sugar said. "That Agnes Freemont is a little loose in the head."

I noticed a few more bottles of ink scattered on the floor, along with some of the tools from Sea Bass's tray. "What's all this?" I nodded to the mess.

He shrugged. "Just another thing proving how everyone in this town is losing their freakin' minds." He shook his head and laughed incredulously. "Carl Martin was in here earlier. I was tattooing his wife's name on his arm, and he suddenly bolted out of the chair and told me it was the wrong name. Now I've been knowing Carl and his wife for years, and I sure as hell know how to spell Cindy."

"He didn't eat one of those muffins by any chance, did he?"

"Nope, but he went ballistic and stomped out of here just before Mouse melted down. Didn't pay, either."

I went into the bathroom and grabbed a hand towel. After soaking it in cold water, I walked over to Mouse and lifted her chin to pat her swollen eyes. "Bad day, huh?"

She nodded and took the towel from my hand. "I'm sorry, Katie."

"Don't worry about it. We all have them. As a matter of fact, I just came off a marathon of shitty days."

Sea Bass looked at Mouse and snorted. "Big baby."

I shot him a condemning look. "You took one for the team, Mouse. I'm sure Sea Bass would have stuffed his face with Agnes's muffins if you hadn't been the canary in the coal mine."

"The what?" Sea Bass asked.

Before I could enlighten him, he changed the subject. "By the way, Fiona MacPherson has been trying to reach you. She called over here just before you showed up. Said you weren't answering your phone."

"That's because it's at home," I replied, glancing at Sugar. "Sugar didn't think it was necessary to bring it along when she picked me up this afternoon."

I headed for the counter and picked up the shop's landline. Sea Bass read me the number to MacPherson's Pub.

"Hey, Fiona," I said when she picked up. She must have recognized my voice, because I heard a sigh of relief on the other end of the line.

"I hear you stuck it to the council and went all dragon on them," she said without a greeting. "I'm glad you're alive."

I laughed at her very appropriate description of Monday's events. "Something like that. What's up?"

"We're long overdue for a gathering of the grove," she said.

"A what?"

"Girls' night. Tomorrow at the pub. I figured you could use one after this week."

As much as I needed a mind-numbing night of drinking with the ladies, her timing sucked. "I'd love to, but considering we have a rogue witch heading straight for town, and I'm pretty sure I have a bounty on my head, that's probably a bad idea."

"Au contraire, Miss Bishop," she said with a French hillbilly accent. "That's exactly why we need to have girls' night. You're about to meet the cavalry."

Something about her confidence in that statement made me

feel hopeful that there just might be light at the end of the tunnel. "Go on, Fiona. Convince me."

"Consider it a night of networking," she said, making her case. "You're going to need more character references than ever, now that you've killed one of the council members. In self-defense, of course. Come on, Katie. It'll be fun."

I agreed to show up at MacPherson's the next night. As I hung up the phone, Mouse started up again.

"Baby, you all right?" Sugar asked as Mouse began to whimper.

"For crying out loud," Sea Bass groaned. "What the hell is wrong now?"

Mouse pointed to the jug on the other side of the room, its beady little eyes looking right at her. "It's talking to me again!"

He rolled his eyes, but there was something in the distress on Mouse's face that made me uncomfortable. "I want that thing out of here," I said to him.

"Aw, come on, Katie."

"It better be gone when I walk in here tomorrow morning. If it's still here, I'll throw it in the dumpster myself."

19

I looked at the table by the window when I walked into the shop the next morning, praying I wouldn't see that face. The jug was gone as requested, and MagicInk was back to normal. No mess on the floor, and no wailing coming from any of my employees. Even Abel seemed to be in a particularly good mood as he swept the floor and hummed quietly.

The front door opened, and Mouse did her usual shuffle into the shop, like a sloth just waking up. Now that was slow.

"Morning, boss," she mumbled, following the smell of coffee in the back.

"Feeling better today?" I asked.

She nodded and poured herself a cup. As tiny as she was, she had the capacity of an oil tanker when it came to coffee, sometimes going back for three or four refills before ten a.m.

Sea Bass came walking through the back door a few minutes later and headed straight for his station, without his usual greeting. "Good morning to you too, Sea Bass," I said with false cheer. He kept rearranging his tray, moving things from left to right and then back again to their original position. "So you're giving me the silent treatment because I told you to get that jug out of here?"

He shook his head, still focusing on the tray. Then he abruptly turned around and planted one hand on his hip, while the other moved in an animated motion to punctuate his speech. "You know, Katie, sometimes you're just a little bit overbearing."

I let out a short laugh. "Overbearing? *I'm* overbearing?"

"That's right. You get in one of your moods and turn all bossy."

Abel listened in. "Well, she is the boss."

"Yeah," I said, raising my eyebrows. I wasn't particularly fond of throwing my weight around, and his attitude was exactly the reason why. It was much easier to take direction and let someone else deal with the daily drama, but my name was on the articles of incorporation for the business, so I was top dog in the room.

"Fine. Let's just start the day over." A wide, exaggerated smile crossed his face. "Mornin', Katie!"

My irritation diminished at the sight of his ridiculous grin, and I couldn't help but laugh. Sea Bass was one of my best friends, and I wasn't about to let an argument over a ceramic jug get in the way of that. I picked up a pencil and threw it at him. "Get to work, or you're fired."

With the drama under control, I got back to work and checked to see how many scheduled customers we had coming in that day. A good bit of MagicInk's business came from walk-ins, but I could usually tell by the number of booked clients if we could cover our daily expenses. Since I owned the building we were standing in, at least the burden of rent was no longer an issue.

Fin walked through the front door. As usual, he took his time crossing the room. He had a swagger about him that matched his genteel Southern demeanor, patient and deliberate. But I knew the formidable creature he was capable of becoming if provoked, or if his charter with the Crossroads Society was threatened in any way. I had to respect him for his loyalty, even if it meant he could turn on me if I ever became a liability to the society and their mission. I had no intention of ever testing that loyalty.

"Good morning, Fin."

He ran his eyes over my face and raised his brow. "You seem to attract calamity wherever you go, Miss Bishop."

"Oh yeah?" I shrugged off the comment. "Are you still entertaining Raven and her corrupt posse over at Lillian's house?" I tried to sound casual, but inside I was shaking like a leaf. Either he was here to tell me everything was fine and Raven and her gang had flown off to investigate the next big case, or I was about to be summoned again, this time as a defendant accused of murder.

"Fortunately, Miss Bishop, the council has taken an interest in your talents and has decided not to prosecute. You're much more valuable as a free woman, as long as you agree to help us defeat this intruder." His smile barely reached his cheeks. "Of course, a room full of witnesses who will corroborate your use of self-defense does help."

"Lucky me." He just stood there, not offering any reason for the personal visit. "You could have just picked up the phone, Fin."

"Yes, I suppose. But after that little display of demolition the other day, I guess I just wanted to see you for myself. To make sure you're in one piece. As they say, seeing is believing."

A vision of Lillian's beautiful house—after I destroyed the ballroom—popped into my head. "I guess I'll be mortgaging this fine building you just gave me to pay for the damages."

"That won't be necessary."

I found that hard to believe. "Really?"

"If you haven't noticed, Lillian is filthy rich. And she has good insurance. We'll just call it an expense of doing business."

That business involved catching a fire witch who was about to break through the crossroads and storm the city if we didn't find that cone of power and shut it down. Besides, I was provoked. If anyone was responsible for the repairs to Lillian's house, it was the Council of Southern Witches. And incidentally, they owed me for pain and suffering.

"I appreciate you coming by, Fin, but if you don't have any other business to discuss, I have work to do." I glanced at the door, hoping he'd take the hint and leave.

He gazed at me for a few more seconds, and then he reached for my hand and kissed it. "I'm glad you're safe, Miss Bishop."

I'd always felt that Fin had a little crush on me—the allure of the dragon and all—but what made me so uncomfortable was the way his lips on my skin sent a tiny flapping of butterfly wings circling my stomach. Not like the way Jackson made me feel, but a fluttering, nonetheless. After all, he was an attractive man.

I pulled my hand back and quickly reached for something to fumble with to hide my ridiculous nerves. The phone rang a second later, interrupting the awkward moment. I picked it up and turned to the computer to schedule an appointment for the client on the other end of the line. By the time I hung up, Fin was gone.

I DON'T KNOW what I expected when I walked through the front door of MacPherson's, but it wasn't this. The women sitting at the bar, slugging back shots of liquor, didn't look like witches at all.

"Katie!" Fiona yelled from behind the bar. "Get your ass over here!"

There was a vacant stool that they'd obviously saved for me, smack dab in the middle of the bar. The blonde sitting to the left of it turned around to greet me as I sat down.

"Well, look who decided to fly in," Temperance LeBlanc said. "Savannah's own little dragonfly."

I smiled politely, that same overwhelming impression smacking me in the head as her aura careened into mine. She was wearing a floral pattern like the one she had on at the picnic, but the skirt barely made it to her knees and wrapped tightly around her thighs, like cellophane.

"You remember Temperance?" Fiona asked.

Temperance LeBlanc wasn't the type of woman you easily forgot. "Of course," I said. "Nice to see you again."

Fiona glanced around the room. "You didn't invite Sugar?"

I ain't wasting my time in a room full of cocky-ass witches, she'd said when I asked her if she wanted to come. Then she did that thing with her face that looked like she'd just bitten into a lemon. The discussion ended pretty quickly.

"She had other plans." I lied, deciding it was best not to start someone else's feud.

Emmaline was sitting to my right. "Hey, there," I said, bending sideways to give her a gentle hug, mindful of how sensitive she was about being touched. She actually hugged me back, which gave me hope that our friendship was on the upswing.

"Are you all right?" she whispered in my ear before pulling back.

"I'm fine. I woke up on Tybee Island and slept it off on the beach."

She looked concerned. "I heard Ingrid Walsh tried to get inside your head with dark magic."

"Is that what she was trying to do? I thought dark magic was off limits. Isn't that why they're trying to railroad Esrial?"

Someone scoffed behind me. "Yeah, it's off limits, all right. As long as the council members aren't the ones using it."

A woman with short black hair and blue eyes was standing behind me with her foot propped up on the bottom rail of my stool. I gave her a warning look because she was dangerously close to invading my personal space.

"Oh, sorry. Bad habit." She took her foot off my stool. "Penelope Kingfisher, but I'll kill you if you call me that." She stared at me with a neutral expression and extended her hand.

I reluctantly took it.

Fiona slapped a glass of scotch down on the bar between us. "Penny can be a real asshole sometimes," she said. "But she's the first asshole I'd call if I needed someone to watch my back." She leaned onto the bar with her elbows, displaying her ample breasts front and center. I wondered if it was for the benefit of the masculine yet attractive woman shaking my hand.

"So . . . I should call you *Penny*? Or is it the Kingfisher part you don't like?"

"Penny would be preferable. Kingfisher doesn't bother me in the slightest." She squeezed my hand a little tighter than I was comfortable with.

"Penny is a welder by trade," Fiona said. "Satisfies all the welding needs of the coven. So if you ever need an iron fence mended, she's your girl." She locked eyes with the woman, and it occurred to me that Penny might be Fiona's current muse.

"Are you two . . ."

Fiona looked at me oddly for a second, and then they both started to laugh. "Please," Fiona said. "I have better taste than *that*."

Penny snorted. "Yeah, I don't think my husband would appreciate me dating such an ugly woman." She grinned at Fiona and looked down at my glass. "Where's mine?"

The embarrassment must have been written all over my face, because they both reassured me that Penny got that a lot, being a welder and what some people would stereotype as slightly masculine.

After downing my drink, I felt less like an ass and waited for

Fiona to introduce the rest of the witches sitting at the bar. There was Cat, the tiny woman with the black hair who ran a candy shop down by the river, and Desiree Brown who developed computer software by day and read tarot cards for tourists at night. I recalled meeting Cat at the picnic.

"Desiree is the brains of the coven," Cat said. "Went to MIT."

I raised my eyebrows. "Wow. That's a mighty fancy pedigree."

Fiona decided to chime in with a little information about me. "Katie got her degree from Columbia. What was your major again?"

"Environmental engineering," I reluctantly replied. It always sparked a conversation about why I threw it all away to open a tattoo shop. Of course, I was a business owner, so my education came in handy and didn't exactly go to waste.

Instead of the usual questions, Madge Miller, the older witch I recognized from the night I interrupted the ritual at Lillian's house, spoke up. "Columbia? Do you know Thomas Hillside?"

Hillside had been one of my professors. "How do you know Professor Hillside?"

"We went to grad school together."

She looked to be in her mid to late sixties, which was around the same age as my old professor.

"Madge used to teach at MIT," Emmaline said. "Desiree was one of her students."

Carmen Santos, the witch who'd helped herself to my boyfriend at the picnic, walked to the back of the bar and wrapped her arm around Fiona's waist. "We've got us a real Mensa gathering tonight, don't we?" She winked at me. "Smart women make me horny." She started at Fiona's cheek and worked her mouth down to her lips. Apparently she liked everybody.

Her Mensa comment was kind of funny, because I was actually a member. But that was something I preferred not to advertise. I'd tested and reluctantly joined at my adoptive father's request. A little insurance for my college applications.

"Now this one," Fiona said, pointing to Carmen, "is my type."

So was I, but Fiona had finally let that ship sail a while ago.

I gave Carmen a catty look. "We met at the picnic. Well, sort of. You were a little too busy with my boyfriend to notice me."

She cocked her head. It must have been difficult to keep them all straight. Eventually she flashed me a wicked grin. "The tall guy with the bike?"

"That's the one. I think he had a little too much of that cake."

The front door swung open, and two women made their grand entrance. "The party can start now, bitches!" the redhead announced while the blonde pumped the air with her fist.

A couple of guys at the pool table started catcalling as the women headed for the bar.

"Easy, boys," Fiona warned. "You know the rules. You can stay if you behave yourselves and shut up. But I'll kick your asses to the curb if you disturb girls' night." Being the owner's daughter and Lillian Whitman's granddaughter had its perks, including the privilege of kicking out anyone she damn well pleased.

"The one with the loud mouth is Sharma Murphy," Fiona said.

"She's a brilliant artist," Emmaline blurted out.

Sharma responded with a slight Irish accent. "I wouldn't say brilliant. Provocative, maybe." Her eyes landed on mine. "I hear you're a real beast." She crossed her arms and looked me over. "A dragon?"

"Hush, woman!" Madge said, eyeing the men who were within earshot. They seemed oblivious to the comment and continued with their game of pool.

"The blonde is Taylor Swift," Fiona continued.

I waited for the punchline, but the other women looked completely unfazed by the name. "Taylor *Swift*?" I repeated, careful not to offend anyone in case it wasn't a joke.

Someone snickered, and before I knew it, the humor spread across the bar to everyone except Taylor, who suddenly went from cocky to irritated. I detected a suffocating feel in the air, like a vacuum. The oxygen in the room felt like it was getting thinner.

Cat rolled her eyes. "Calm down, Taylor. You should be used to it by now."

"Yeah, well I had it first, damn it!" Taylor shoved between Cat and Desiree to get to the bar. "Give me some Fireball," she demanded. "Hurry up before I break something."

Fiona answered my unspoken question. "In case you're wondering, that's her real name. But she did have it first." She handed Taylor a glass of the cinnamon liquor. "Drink it fast, and then stop fucking with my bar."

"Taylor is a psychic vampire. And unpredictable," Penny added. "She'll suck the whole room dry if she doesn't get that temper of hers under control. Alcohol usually calms her down before she does any real damage though." She let out a heavy sigh and shook her head. "A nickname would probably help, at least when she's introducing herself, but she refuses to use one."

"Why the hell should I?" she spat. Fiona served her a second shot, and the oxygen in the room stabilized as she calmed down.

Taylor and Sharma took the last two vacant stools, and Fiona lined up a row of shot glasses in front of us, setting an extra one down for herself. Then she filled them with a clear liquid that looked like water. "Johnnie!" she hollered to the kitchen. "Take over for me. Girls' night has officially commenced."

Johnnie was the pub's cook. He also served as mediator of bar fights, seeing how he was bigger than most men and had Irish fighter blood in his line. Fiona had told me that his father was some boxing legend back in Belfast. He knew how to pour a drink too.

Fiona pulled a stool out from under the bar and carried it to the other side, wedging it between me and Temperance. "Okay, ladies. Drink up."

We all downed the clear liquid in our shot glasses, and I nearly choked. "What the hell was that?"

"Poitín," she said with a grin. "Don't worry. You only get one shot."

"Jesus, Fiona! Is that Irish for gasoline?"

She laughed and ran her tongue along the inside edge of her shot glass. "Something like that."

"It's kind of like moonshine," Emmaline explained, setting her empty glass back down on the bar.

Fiona snorted, "it *is* moonshine."

Apparently, I was the only poitín virgin at the bar. "I think I'll stick to scotch."

Johnnie poured me a glass of Guinness, and I started to ease into the effects of the alcohol. A night of mindless drinking was just what I needed.

"How's Jackson?" Fiona asked.

There went my peace, right out the window at the mention of his name. "I don't know. I haven't seen him for a while."

Her face sobered. "You two broke up?"

"Something like that. I guess I pushed my luck one time too many. Sent him running for the hills."

"Well, shit. I thought you two would end up at the altar, bound and handfasted."

I scoffed and took another swig of beer, eyeing her awkwardly as the image of Jackson in a tux began to swirl around in my head. "Getting a little ahead of me there, Fiona."

"I agree with Fiona," Emmaline said. "I thought I saw it in the cards."

Fiona shot Emmaline a look, but I caught it.

I set my beer down. "You know, you guys have got to stop tiptoeing around me. I'm a fucking dragon. I think your secrets are safe with me. And you," I said to Emmaline. "I know what you're capable of. You're nothing but a reluctant badass."

"Well—" Emmaline began in that tiny voice of hers.

"And what about the rest of you?" I said, cutting Emmaline off. "Got any more witchy secrets you'd like to hide from me?"

Fiona stood up and reached for a bottle of whiskey behind the bar. "Okay, folks. Time to get real." She offered me another drink, but I decided to stick with beer for the rest of the night. Then she turned to the men at the pool table and pointed to the door. One of them grumbled in protest, but the others weren't interested in dealing with Johnnie if they didn't take their asses outside.

After the pub cleared out, she began to divulge the talents of every witch sitting at the bar.

"You already know what Taylor and Emmaline can do," she said. "So let's see." She looked up and down the bar and nodded to Madge and Desiree. "Those two have some pretty freaky skills with animals, as in the ability to talk to them. I mean, *really* talk to them. Dead ones too," she added. "Madge has a particularly strong connection to dogs and horses, and Desiree can charm a hawk right out of the sky." She leaned in and discreetly expanded on those abilities. "I've been told that they can actually get inside the mind of their subject and see through the animal's eyes. But they don't like to talk about that part."

"Do you have any pets, Katie?" Madge asked.

"I have a cat. His name is Jet."

"If you ever want to know what's on his mind, I'd be happy to come over and have a little talk with him. Although cats can be a little difficult to get inside of."

I wouldn't mind knowing where Jet came from, and why he

showed up on my doorstep right after I moved to Savannah. "I'll keep that in mind, Madge."

"Cat is kind of like Agnes Freemont," Fiona said, moving down the bar. "Only she likes to condense her magic into bottles of oil and distilled alcohol. Flying ointment is her specialty, but I wouldn't advise eating any of that candy she sells in her shop down by the river."

By the smirk on Fiona's face, I had a feeling there were a lot of unsuspecting tourists down by River Street getting a little something extra in their bags of pralines and fudge.

"Let's see," Fiona continued. She glanced at Temperance, but moved on to Penny. "That woman right there is freakishly strong. Kind of like Jackson. And Sharma is psychic. She can read minds, but not everyone's."

"That's right," Sharma said from the other end of the bar. "You're safe though. I can't see a thing inside of that head of yours, Katie."

"What's her talent?" I asked, nodding toward Carmen.

Fiona gave me a blank look. "Well, look at her. She's an expert in the art of persuasion. If you ever need to make someone stupid to get them talking, especially a man, you call Carmen."

I glanced at the beautiful Latin woman and remembered seeing her all over Jackson. I was sure it was just Agnes Freemont's cake spell that had him receptive to her advances at the picnic, but I couldn't deny the warm and fuzzy feeling I got just looking at her. It was like she exuded some kind of pheromones.

That only left two women at the bar with unrevealed talents. I stared at Temperance for a moment, but Fiona discreetly shook her head. "Temperance's secrets aren't mine to tell," she whispered.

"What about you?" I said. "What's your hidden talent?"

Fiona cocked her brow. "Mine? I pour a damn good drink,

and my grandmother is the high priestess of Blackthorn Grove. It does have its benefits." She polished off her whiskey and fiddled with the empty glass. "Look, Katie, we all have something to offer, whether it's flying on a broomstick or just predicting an earthquake. But the real power of the women sitting at this bar is our collective mind and the shitstorm we can create when we pull it all together. Believe me, you don't want to be on the receiving end when we do a working."

"I'll take your word for it," I said. "But I'm a little curious. Covens generally don't advertise, and other than a few of you being grandfathered in by your relatives, I can't see a single common thread between any of you. How did all of you end up finding Blackthorn Grove?"

Madge took the liberty of answering the question. "We didn't. The coven found us. Just like it found you."

Just as I was starting to have a revelation about that, I caught a glimpse of something on the muted TV above the bar. It was the eleven o'clock local news, and Chase Stone's picture was plastered across the screen.

"Johnnie," I said. "Turn up the volume."

20

I thought my head was going to explode when I tried to lift it off the pillow, and I actually saw stars behind my eyelids. I was pretty clearheaded when I left MacPherson's the night before, so it wasn't the amount of alcohol I drank that made me feel like I'd been run over by a truck. I suspected the Irish moonshine was the culprit, quietly wreaking havoc in my brain while I nursed my beer.

The night had ended prematurely when I saw the news headline that a local businessman had been murdered. Chase Stone's lifeless body was discovered near the Savannah River, nearly decapitated by a deep slash to the throat. Since the society had connections at the coroner's office, I'd called Fin on my way home to find out what he knew about the murder that wasn't being made public. But all he could tell me was that the death was suspicious, since a large amount of cash in his wallet and a pricy Rolex hadn't been touched. The remote location where the body was found—near the oil terminals—didn't make it any less suspicious.

Jet jumped on the bed and let out a determined meow. "Jesus, Jet! Stop screaming at me!" Poor guy. All he wanted was a bowl of food. But that little voice of his sounded more like the roar of a lion to my pounding ears.

I managed to swing my legs over the side of the bed and stand up without hurling all over the floor. Then I dragged myself to the kitchen for a tall glass of ice water and a couple of ibuprofens.

"Coffee," I mumbled to Jet. "Coffee first, then food."

With the coffee started, I filled Jet's bowl and opened the refrigerator to grab a piece of cold pizza—the best medicine on the planet for a hangover. I'd read somewhere that Japanese pickled plums were good for hangovers too, but since I didn't have any and didn't have the slightest idea where to find them, pizza was my best option. Fortunately, it was Friday, one of the slower days at the shop. People were too busy partying on Fridays, so they usually waited until Saturday to get their tattoos. It was one of the better days to go into work feeling like shit.

I had a cup of coffee with my pizza while I replayed the previous night over in my head. I'd met some interesting characters over the years, and the women at MacPherson's the night before were no exception. How many times in your life do you meet someone who can literally suffocate a room just from being in a shitty mood?

The sound of my phone ringing startled me out of the thought. Fin's name popped up on the screen. I picked it up and got a weird feeling. "Since you never call me this early in the morning and we just spoke last night, I assume you aren't calling just to chat," I said without a greeting.

"You sound pleasant this morning, Miss Bishop. Fiona must be getting soft."

I snickered under my breath. "I didn't feel this good thirty minutes ago. Coffee does wonders." I decided to cut to the chase so I could get ready for work. "What is it, Fin?"

Hesitation was never a good response when you asked

someone that question. Particularly when dealing with purveyors of bad news.

"Looks like we'll be attending two funerals," he eventually said.

As my brain reconciled what he'd just said, my imagination went wild with terrifying thoughts of who the other deceased was. "Are you about to break my heart, Fin?" Images of Sea Bass and Sugar crept into my head. And then Jackson. My heart began to race, and suddenly I couldn't breathe.

"You don't really think I'm that cold, do you, Miss Bishop?" I said nothing and waited for him to continue. "Rita Cavanagh died this morning. She was found dead in her cell around two a.m."

I nearly dropped the phone when I slumped with relief. "What happened? Did she kill herself?" It wasn't unusual for inmates to find a way to off themselves in prison, especially when faced with an unbearable future. Shooting your husband dead in front of a room full of witnesses, and having no memory of the act, certainly put her in the category of a person with an unbearable outlook for her remaining days on this earth. Not to mention the guilt she must have felt.

"Asphyxiation is the presumed cause of death, pending a full autopsy, of course." Fin had carte blanche access to the coroner's office, which had come in handy lately. "We believe she was murdered."

"Murdered?"

"The guards found a plate of peach pie on the floor next to her bed. One of the inmates in the next cell said she could hear the plate hit the ground just before Rita started gurgling and throwing up violently. We believe she was killed with black magic. The kind Ijibah would use."

My head was spinning with thoughts. People choked on hotdogs and other types of food every day. A piece of pie could have easily gotten lodged in her throat. "Don't you think murder is a little far-fetched, Fin? Maybe she just choked on the pie."

I could hear him inhale sharply on the other end of the line, like he was irritated by me questioning his theory. "She vomited blood. Not just a little bit of blood, Miss Bishop, all of it. Every drop. By the time the guards made it to her cell, she'd bled out. Now I'm not a doctor, but there are few maladies plaguing mankind that involve bleeding a body completely dry." He let that sink in for a moment before continuing. "In the realm of dark magic, it's as simple as collecting strands of hair from your victim's comb. That's the kind of stuff a dark witch cuts her teeth on."

The thought of Rita Cavanagh spewing blood all over the floor of her cell made me wince. No one deserved to die like that, and it made me want to defeat Ijibah even more.

"There's something else," he said.

I huffed. "There always is."

Ignoring my sarcasm, he continued. "One of the guards found a piece of bone on the floor, next to the broken plate."

"I guess that's what she choked on," I said, knowing damn well bone wasn't an ingredient in peach pie. "Whoever baked it fucked up royally."

"If it wasn't for the kiddie pool of blood on the cell floor, that might be a remote possibility, Miss Bishop. But as I said, there's more."

I was losing patience. "Jesus, Fin, would you just get to it. And by the way, what the hell was Rita Cavanagh doing with a piece of pie in her cell in the middle of the night? What did she do, order room service from the prison commissary at two a.m?"

He did as I asked and got to the point. "A piece of bone was also found in the breast pocket of Chase Stone's shirt. My sources down at the coroner's office said the two bones appear to match."

A lump formed in the back of my throat as I listened to him

connect the dots, adding a whole new level of complexity to the situation. "Are you telling me that the bone found in Rita Cavanagh's cell came from the same animal—well, I assume it's an animal—as the one found in Chase Stone's pocket?"

"I'm telling you that it was a single bone broken into two pieces. And as for your question about how she got her hands on a plate of peach pie, records show that she had a visitor that evening—Agnes Freemont."

"*Fuck*," I hissed into the phone.

"Now I don't have to tell you what Agnes Freemont is capable of doing to an unsuspecting consumer of her baked goods, do I?"

That sneaky bitch. I remembered her comment when we paid her a visit Wednesday night to return that basket of contaminated muffins. *You have no idea what's coming*, she'd said.

Fin continued with the condemning evidence. "We looked at the security footage. Agnes passed a small box to a guard on her way out—right after that same guard enjoyed one of her complementary éclairs. Her bakery is famous for them. I'm sure he was more than happy to accept that box of pie for Rita Cavanagh, after eating that tainted éclair with a spell compelling him to make sure she got it."

"You don't think Agnes slit Chase Stone's throat, do you?"

Fin sneered. "What do you think, Miss Bishop?"

Agnes Freemont didn't have the brains to orchestrate such an elaborate double murder. Slipping a piece of pie to a prison guard was one thing, but slitting a man's throat required a level of evil of which even Agnes wasn't capable. Either Ijibah had found another conduit as powerful as Esrial, or she kill Chase Stone herself.

"If Ijibah did this, Fin, she must have made it through the crossroads already."

"Maybe," he replied. "Unfortunately, the only person who can give us answers is Agnes. We found her this morning, nearly catatonic and mumbling like a child in the kitchen of Le Petit Gateau. She was tracing symbols of the elements in a pile of flour on the floor."

Even with everything she'd done, I couldn't enjoy the image of Agnes doodling like a child on the floor. She was probably just another one of Ijibah's pawns, like Esrial. But this time there was clear evidence of guilt. I had to wonder if Agnes knew exactly what she was doing when she delivered that bone to Rita Cavanagh. But karma is a bitch. Whatever deal she made with the devil came right back around to bite her in the ass.

"You mentioned something about going to the funerals," I said. "Other than meeting Chase Stone last week, I don't even know these people, Fin."

"Rita Cavanagh won't be buried for a while, pending notification of kin outside the country. Chase Stone will be cremated. There's a memorial service this Sunday. Understandably, his widow is distraught and plans to stay with family in Charleston for a while, hence the rushed memorial service."

"I don't need to be there, Fin. You were in business with the man, not me." It didn't feel right to show up at Chase Stone's memorial service without having any personal connections to the family. I'd just be an interloper witnessing the grief of a young widow.

Fin went silent for a moment on the other end of the line. "If there is one thing you can always bet on," he finally said, "it's the arrogance of a psychopath. You see, Miss Bishop, a killer will almost always show up for the publicity. It's an ego thing. A validation of their superiority and ability to outsmart everyone in the room. If Ijibah has broken through the crossroads, I suspect she'll be there, in one form or another."

"I wouldn't call a dead sorceress a psychopath, Fin."

"No?" he replied. "And if you're wrong?"

He was right to push me. If Ijibah did show up at Chase

Stone's memorial service and I wasn't there to go all dragon on her, I might have a room full of dead bodies on my conscience.

"Okay," I said. "I'll go."

———

"Damn! You trying to kill my ass?" Sugar snapped at Sea Bass as I was walking through the back door of the shop. "I know you got to put that needle to my skin, but have a little mercy, baby, and warn me before you hit the bone."

"I ain't hitting no bone," he replied. "It's just not a real fun place to get a tattoo."

I snickered as she lay back down on the table to endure the rest of the session. Sea Bass was putting a tattoo on the back of her knee, a notoriously painful spot.

"Well, look what the dog dragged in," she said, glancing at me with a cocky grin. "I see Fiona didn't kill you."

My hangover had subsided substantially. The conversation with Fin did the trick, making me wonder if half the misery of a hangover was psychological. "Anyone heard the news?" I asked.

"You mean about Chase Stone getting himself offed down by the river?" Sugar said.

"That, for one."

Sea Bass looked up from Sugar's leg. "What do you mean *for one*?"

"Rita Cavanagh is dead too. They found her in her jail cell early this morning, lying in a pool of blood. *All* of her blood, apparently," I added, visualizing the mess all that blood must have created.

Sugar tightened her lips and glanced at Sea Bass over her shoulder. "You need to finish up so I can get off this table and find out why the hell I'm the last one to know about all this." She grumbled unintelligibly as he turned off the machine and wiped the excess ink off her skin. "I'm getting real tired of being treated like some second-class member who ain't got no interest in what the hell's going on over there at the society."

"Maybe that's because you usually don't," I said. "You avoid the society like the plague." Her wild-eyed glare nixed my candid remark. She was clearly not receptive to reality this morning. "I'm sure your phone will be ringing any minute now with the news."

She climbed off the table and dug through her purse. "I better call Mama. She's probably already sensing something's going on. I swear that woman can smell an earthquake coming from a thousand miles away."

Before she got the chance to make that call to May, Dickie Winslow walked through the door and got everyone's attention. He was a regular who never bothered to make an appointment, preferring to take his chances that Mouse would be available whenever he showed up for a tattoo. Propping the door open with his heavily tattooed arm, he stood halfway over the threshold and glanced at something on the sidewalk. A second later, he continued inside and headed over to Mouse, who was sitting at the desk in the back with her face buried in a book. "What's that book you got there?" he asked.

Mouse snapped the book shut and stuffed it under a stack of papers. "Nothing you'd be interested in." She liked to read racy romance novels, but she didn't like to announce it to clients. It kind of ruined her image.

"I guess if you've got time to read a book, you've got time to give me a tattoo," he said with a little attitude, taking the liberty of sitting down at her station.

She gave him an eat-shit-and-die look and slowly dragged herself up from the chair. Mouse was always happy to accommodate a client, but she resented the cocky regulars who thought they had some kind of frequent flyer privileges in the shop.

Sugar raised her brow. "I'd be careful with that mouth if I was you. Two kinds of people you don't want to piss off—the person cooking your food, and the person about to put ink on your ass."

Mouse snickered, picking up a tattoo gun and tossing it back and forth from one hand to the other. "That's right." Her grin went flat as the fun ended and she got down to business. "What do you want, Dickie?"

He pointed to the one remaining bare spot on his arm. "I was thinking maybe you could weave something in there to connect it all together. Just cover up the hole." Dickie had a lot of oddball art on his body, like cartoon figures and caricatures of famous people. His face suddenly brightened like a light bulb had gone off in his head. "Like that thing out there." He nodded toward the front window.

Everyone in the room looked at him for clarification. "What are you talking about?" Mouse asked.

Dickie suddenly looked confused. "Hey, why is it sitting out there anyway? Someone's just going to walk off with it."

A little anger hit me as I headed for the front door to see what he was talking about, but I already knew. I looked down at the sidewalk and lost it. "Sea Bass!" I yelled, trying to keep my temper in check. "I told you to get that thing out of here!"

When I looked back at him, he was standing there with his arms stretched out and a what-the-fuck look on his face. "What are you talking about, Katie?"

"That!" I nodded toward the face with the chipped nose staring back at me. It was the creepy jug I'd ordered him to remove from my shop.

He met me at the door and looked down. I thought he was going to pass out, as his face blanched and his hands began to shake. "You messin' with me, Katie?" he asked, taking a step back.

"Am *I* messing with *you*?" I shoved past him and headed for the drawer at the desk where I kept a few handy tools—including a hammer. "You've got five seconds to pick that thing up off the sidewalk and get rid of it, or I'm swinging." There was something wrong about that jug that made my skin crawl.

Sea Bass shook his head. "I didn't put it there. I swear. I rode my bike this morning. How the hell would I get it on the back of my Triumph?"

"I don't know," I said. "Maybe you dropped it off with your car and went back home to get your bike."

He furrowed his brow and planted his hands on his hips. "Are you listening to yourself? Why would I bring it back here knowing you'd probably do something like that," he said, pointing to the hammer in my hand.

"Lord, Jesus!" Sugar said. "What the hell kinda crazy is going on around here with you two? She walked over to the door and looked outside at the center of all the controversy. "I see," she said, looking a little less irritated than a moment earlier. "Now that is a little bit odd." She bent down and wedged her hands under the heavy jug. "Well?" she said to Sea Bass. "Help me carry it inside."

I stopped her. "I don't want it in the shop."

"Well, we can't leave it out here."

"Why not?"

She grumbled something under her breath. "Just help me pick the ugly thing up, Sea Bass."

They brought it inside, and Mouse's eyes bugged out. "I came in through the front door this morning, and that thing wasn't out there. Sea Bass was already here too," she said, confirming his innocence. "I think I would have noticed it."

Dickie, who had been listening to the conversation, spoke up. "I'll take it if no one wants it."

"I don't think you want to do that," Sugar said. 'Unless you like having evil spirits in your house."

Sea Bass scoffed. "What are you talking about, Sugar?"

She circled the jug, examining it from every angle. "Where'd you say you got this thing?"

"A yard sale. Over there near Liberty Street. Well, it was more like a sidewalk sale."

Sugar reached out. "Give me that hammer."

I thought Sea Bass was going to have a coronary. But before he could stop her, Sugar swung like Thor. The head of the hammer hit the center of Harold's ceramic eyes, creating a terrible sound but barely moving the jug. You'd expect a blow like that to shatter the thing, but it just wobbled slightly, with its undamaged eyes daring us to do it again. She did, only harder. Still, it refused to break or even crack.

Sea Bass was suddenly over his infatuation with it, getting on board with the rest of us. "Let me try." He gave it a hell of a blow, but the damn thing seemed to be made of titanium.

"Maybe Abel can break it," Mouse said. "He'll be here any minute now, and he's a lot stronger than Sea Bass."

Sea Bass gave her a dirty look, but Sugar intervened before the rivalry could escalate. "Now that's enough, you two. That thing ain't going to break without a little extra mojo to send its ugly ass straight back to hell. We need to get it to Mama's house."

21

I cancelled my two appointments that day, and we loaded Harold into the trunk of the Eldorado and headed out to May's house. We needed to talk to her about the two murders anyway, so we were killing two birds with one stone.

The jug bounced around the cavernous trunk violently as we hit the rough road heading into May's neck of the woods, smashing against the metal jack and the spare tire every time we took a turn.

"Let's see how strong you are, you no good, dirty-ass piece of clay!" she yelled over the back seat, hitting the accelerator and then braking hard.

"Damn it, Sugar! I don't know about that jug, but you're definitely giving *me* whiplash."

She swung her arm over the top of the seat and patted my shoulder. "Don't you worry, baby. Anything I break, Mama can fix." She pointed to her stash in the glove compartment. "Give me one of them cigarettes."

"Why don't you just keep them on the dashboard in front of you? You ask me to hand you one every time we get in the car. You can't reach them if you're driving alone."

"Exactly. Keeps me from smoking too much. Got to think about my lungs, girl."

I shook my head and handed her one. "Chase Stone is being cremated. Fin and I are going to the memorial service on Sunday."

"Sunday?" she repeated. "The man ain't even cold yet. How the hell's all his people going to get here in time for the service?" The lighter popped out and she lit her cigarette from the hot coil, mumbling around the butt. "Need time to line up them nurses."

"Nurses?"

She took a drag and responded through the exhaled cloud of smoke. "Yeah, you know. For the grieving folks. The throwers." She glanced at me oddly like I was missing something obvious. "Oh, I see," she said. "I guess them lily-white funerals your people have don't think about stuff like that." She took another drag and sent the smoke exhaling out the side of her mouth. "Well, I guess nurses are more useful at a funeral, anyway. When you got an actual body for folks to wail over."

I grinned at her. "Half of your folks are lily-white, Sugar."

"Well now, that is true. But like the song says, papa was a rolling stone. I ain't never met none of my white kin on daddy's side. Hell, you and me might be related. We do kind of look alike." She gave me a glance and grinned. "Girl, you're almost as pretty as me."

"And you're going to get us killed if you don't keep your eyes on the road."

We approached May's driveway, and Sugar made a point of taking the turn extra sharp, sending the jug careening through the trunk one last time before we turned it over to May for a little hoodoo ass whipping.

Sugar popped the trunk and took a step back when she saw the mess. "Sweet baby Jesus!" she said, examining the ripped carpet and the dents the jug had left in the exposed metal. "If I wasn't such a sensible person, I'd roll that damn thing into the street and run it over."

"You'd probably bust your tires and bend the grill trying. I'm beginning to think that thing is indestructible."

"Let's just get it up on the porch." She reached inside to grab it by the handles. Together we managed to lift it out of the trunk and carry it to the steps. "Watch where you're going, and don't step on that trick board. Mama will have a conniption if we break it. She's already going to whoop my ass when she sees me bringing this thing into her house."

I stopped halfway up the steps. "You didn't call her and tell her? Does she even know we're coming?"

"I was going to, but I figured it was best not to give her a chance to say *hell* no." Her eyes widened as she shook her head. "We got to get rid of this thing, girl."

Before we reached the porch, May opened the front door and swung a shotgun up to eye level and pointed it at us. "Mama!" Sugar yelled. "Put that damn gun down!"

May looked at the massive jug we were hauling up the steps. "Get that abomination off my porch!" she growled. I'd never heard May use that voice before. The small woman with the perpetual smile sounded downright demonic. "Take it around back." She went back inside and slammed the door behind her.

Sugar and I looked at each other. "What was that all about?" I asked, wondering if we'd made a huge mistake bringing the jug out here without May's consent.

"Mama's fine. Probably just smelled the devil inside this thing and thought she had a couple of demons about to knock on her door. Ain't the first time."

We carried it back down the steps and dragged it around the side of the house, careful not to step on any of May's vegetables and herbs. Her mood was bad enough. Trampling on her garden might get us killed.

May was waiting for us near the pile of earth she was always digging through. She'd shaped it into a mound about a foot tall and four feet wide. I don't know what was so special about that dirt, but I bet it had some powerful properties infused into it, the way she always worked it with her hands.

"Bring it over and drop it right there." She took a tree branch fashioned into a walking stick and pointed to the center of the mound. "That thing smells like rotten flesh."

I caught myself sniffing the air, but all I could smell was a tea olive bush in bloom somewhere in the vicinity of the house.

"Sea Bass picked it up at some yard sale in the city," Sugar said.

"I know where it came from!" May shot back. "Came from the devil herself. Ijibah got spies everywhere."

May was suggesting that the jug was planted. She was also suggesting something even creepier. "Are you saying what I think you are?"

Sugar looked at her mama, and we both waited for May to confirm that the jug was alive.

May's eyes flashed. "That thing is possessed. Got some Ijibah inside."

I took another look at it, sitting lopsided on top of that dirt pile in the glare of the sun. It looked harmless, but then I remembered all the strange things that had been going on in the shop, especially the incident with Beth Hendricks attacking me, and somehow knowing about the dragon. And then there was the incident with Mouse, saying it was talking to her the night Agnes Freemont fed her those funny muffins. At the time, I just assumed she was high on Agnes's magic—which she was—but now I realized she was getting bombarded from both ends.

"I told Sea Bass to get it out of my shop, but it came back on its own this morning. How do we get rid of it for good?"

May smacked it with the stick and waited to see if it moved.

"Got to destroy it. That thing ain't never gonna stop coming back."

"We tried that," I said. "We even took a hammer to it, but not a single crack."

She laughed. "That ain't how you do it." She pointed to the chip missing from its nose. "See that? Right there's were the demon entered. Got to get broke before you can be unbreakable."

"I don't understand."

"I think what Mama is trying to say is, breaking off a piece of that nose made it indestructible. Kind of like stressing a bone to make it stronger. It gave the demon a doorway, and that ugly thing ain't never going to break again. Ain't that right, Mama?"

"Something like that." May studied me for a few seconds, somehow reading the rest of what was on my mind, "I know what that witch did to Rita Cavanagh over at the jail. Killed Chase Stone too."

"Fin told you?"

She just smiled and then walked back toward the house. "Don't go near that thing," she warned without turning around.

"No problem," I muttered. But Sugar couldn't help it. She inched closer to the mound of earth where the jug was barely stabilized. A good wind would probably send it tumbling on its side. "Didn't you hear what your mama just said?"

She swatted her hand at me. "Hush!"

The wind suddenly picked up, and I swear that jug shifted its eyes in her direction when she bent down to look at it. The dirt under the jug swirled into a tornado around her, flying at her like tiny little birdshot being blasted from a gun. She screamed as the swarm of dust pelted her eyes, throwing her back against the ground as she clawed at her face.

I growled at the possessed jug, my eyes blazing green as I felt the dragon tearing at my skin. The sensation was shocking and nearly paralyzed me with fear. I'd never felt pain before when the dragon came out, but this time it felt like it was about to rip the skin right off my back.

May came barreling through the kitchen door with a mason jar in her hand, distracting the beast and sending it back inside of me. "Back to the ground!" she ordered, dipping her fingers into the jar and flicking something that looked like red wine at the earth. The tornado ceased, and the particles of dirt circled the jug three times before settling back down to the mound.

May dropped to her knees, pulling Sugar's bloody hands away from her eyes.

"Mama? I can't see!"

"We're gonna fix it," she said, smiling at Sugar.

I nearly lost it when I bent down next to Sugar and saw the damage. "What can I do, May?"

"Go inside." She nodded toward the house. "Fetch me that jar of seeds on the kitchen counter."

I ran inside and spotted the jar. There was a piece of masking tape across the front that said KUDZU. On top of the seeds inside was a small bag made out of something that looked like cheese-cloth. I ran back outside and handed the jar to May.

"Now, you watch my boy while I deal with that devil." She spoke in the same scary voice she'd used when she met us at the front door with that shotgun. She climbed to her feet and straightened her dress. "Hand me that blood."

Glancing at the mason jar on the ground, I swallowed hard. "Blood?" I guessed it wasn't red wine after all. I handed her the warm jar, wondering if she'd heated it up, or if it was freshly extracted from something inside the house. I pushed it out of my mind and cradled Sugar while May got down to business.

She approached the dirt mound, the jar of blood in one hand and the seeds in the other. With a banshee-like cry, she hurled the blood at the jug. The jar shattered in an explosion of color that reminded me of red cellophane confetti glistening in the light from the blazing sun. The blood dripped down the ceramic sides, entering the earth at the base of the jug. Then she took the jar of seeds and twisted the lid off. She reached inside and extracted the cheesecloth bag, tossing it to the ground before sprinkling the seeds over the dirt.

The jug lurched. "Don't you dare!" May hissed. She took a step back to grab the bag she'd tossed on the ground. Then she carried it over to a nearby bush and opened it, shaking the contents on the ground out of view. Whatever it was, it was definitely moving. It scurried into the bush. "You done your job," I heard her whisper. "Go on, now. You're free."

A minute later, I felt the ground rumble. "What's going on, May?"

She pointed to the jug. "Gettin' sent back to where it belongs."

Through the mound of earth, I could see something poking out. Tiny green leaves began to emerge in a tight circle around the base of the jug. They grew swiftly and reached upward, anchoring to the ceramic sides like ivy covering a brick wall.

By the time I looked down to check on Sugar and then back up, the vines had completely engulfed the jug. "What is that, May?"

With that familiar twinkle in her eyes, she grinned. "Kudzu. The dangerous kind. Been fed real good."

We watched in silence as the vines spun around the jug like a spider encasing an insect, covering it completely until it looked like a little bush planted in the middle of the mound. Then it slowly started to sink. Inch by inch it disappeared, until all that was left was a funnel in the dirt where the jug, vines, and blood had been swallowed up.

All I could do was shake my head. May had once again astonished me with her magic.

I glanced at Sugar when she stirred in my lap. When I looked up at May, she was heading inside the house. A few seconds later, I heard a loud whack, followed by the sound of a blender pulsing ice. When she finally came back outside, she was carrying a towel and a small bowl.

"What is that?" I asked. It looked like pomegranate ice chips.

Without answering me, she got down on her aging knees and lifted Sugar's head. She held the towel under Sugar's chin and told her to open wide. Then she popped a large piece of the ice into her mouth. "Suck on it."

Sugar tried to spit it out. "I can't, Mama! You know how I feel about vamp blood!"

I groaned as I watched her suck on… vampire blood? "You have got to be kidding me?" I said to May. "Is that what you threw at that jug?"

She shook her head and gave me a toothy grin. "That was the blood of—"

"Uh-uh. I don't even want to know."

She looked down at the bowl. "Kept it in the freezer for an emergency. Had a debt owed to me. Ain't nothing more powerful than the blood of a night crawler for fixin' what usually can't be fixed."

Sugar kept struggling until May had finally had enough. "Be still!" she ordered. "You want to see through them eyes again?"

Sugar finally relented and sucked on the frozen blood, with obvious displeasure. We sat on the ground with her for a good thirty minutes while the blood worked its magic, slowly healing the small but devastating lacerations to her eyes. When she finally sucked and swallowed the last piece, May got up to get more.

"No, Mama. I'm good." She nearly fell over when she tried to stand up, and it was apparent who'd be driving the Eldorado back to the city. I dreaded the thought of steering that relic through the streets of Savannah. For the second time in a week. Once was enough.

We went inside so Sugar could clean up. May prepared an herbal solution to gently clear away any remaining dirt trapped under her lids. Then she fed us. I didn't realize how hungry I was until I smelled her chicken and dumplings cooking on the stove. Sugar ate like a beast. May said it was a side effect of the superior blood running through her veins, assuring her that her ravenous appetite would pass in a day or two.

"Ijibah will try again," May warned as we were leaving. "If I was you, Katie, I wouldn't be picking up any strays until we get her dealt with."

"I wasn't planning to, May."

When we reached the car, Sugar went straight for the driver's side. "What do you think you're doing?" I grabbed the handle before she could open the door.

"Well, if you'd get your hand off my door, I'll be driving us home. I need a shower and a damn toothbrush."

I shoved her aside with my hip. "No, you're not. I'm driving." Still a little woozy, it took her a second to regain her balance. In the meantime, I swung the door open and ducked inside, hitting the lock for insurance.

"Girl, get your ass outta my driver's seat." I ignored her, and she eventually walked around to the other side. "I ain't never rode in the passenger seat of my own car."

"First time for everything," I said. "Now give me the keys." She tossed them at me, and I cranked the engine before she changed her mind. Thankfully, it only took two attempts before the car started up. Any more than that, and I'm sure we would have been going at it again.

We were barely out of the driveway before she started back-seat driving—too many lane changes, driving too fast, riding the brakes like a grandma.

"Look, we're almost at the shop," I said. "Just let me drive!"

She let out a huge sigh. "Just remember—you break it, you buy it."

We ignored each other until we pulled into the lot behind MagicInk. "I know you don't have a long drive, Sugar, but I should probably take you home. Those eyes aren't fully recovered yet."

She got out and slapped her hand down on the Eldorado's hood. "This baby ain't sitting in no one's parking lot overnight. Vandals are just waiting to jack up a classic like Hazel." She wisely decided to put on her sunglasses for the drive home. "What time are we heading over to the memorial service on Sunday?"

"You want to go?" It surprised me.

"Hell, yeah. If that bitch decides to show up at the service, I want to get a good look at her with my own two eyes. Then you can kill her."

22

Sugar showed up at my house on Sunday about an hour before Fin's driver was scheduled to arrive to take us to Chase Stone's memorial service. I'd made it through Saturday without incident, but I did vet every person who walked into the shop like they were trying to get past the security checkpoint at the airport.

She was wearing a black jumpsuit that flared into bell-bottoms just below the knees, with matching sleeves that did the same at the elbows. With her shiny black wig smoothed straight down over her shoulders, she looked like a black panther. The only thing that broke it up was a rainbow scarf tied around her neck.

"Let's have us a drink before that fancy car shows up," she said, setting a brown paper bag down on the counter. Inside was a bottle of tequila and a couple of limes. "You got any ice?"

I reconsidered my own outfit, a conservative navy dress hanging on the closet door in my bedroom. Buying a black dress for the sole purpose of attending the service wasn't in my budget, but I did have a black skirt and a couple of colorful blouses to choose from.

216

"Is it inappropriate to wear a navy dress?"

"No, baby," she said, eyeing my robe. "Navy is about as boring and mournful as it gets. You go on and get dressed while I make us a couple of margaritas."

"We are not getting buzzed on tequila before the service, Sugar."

"Buzzed?" She stared at me with a cocky smirk on her face. "One little drink will barely take the edge off."

"I need my edge," I replied. "Are you forgetting why we're going?" Fin was expected to pay his respects to his dead business partner, but I barely knew the man. Chase Stone's memorial service was my ticket to a possible glimpse at the sorceress we were hunting, and if we were lucky we might be able to track her back to the cone of power where she was probably hunkering down for the big showdown that was coming.

I headed for the bedroom to slip on that dress I was second-guessing. With a pair of black pumps, it looked respectful enough. I arranged my hair over my shoulders but decided to pull it back into a more conservative ponytail.

Sugar greeted me back in the kitchen with a margarita. "I made it a little weak so you wouldn't get all giddy," she said. I took a sip, and I had to admit it did calm my nerves a little. She eyeballed my outfit, twirling her index finger for me to turn around. "A little boring, but you look good and mournful." Then she glanced down at my feet. "I do like them shoes though. What size are they?"

"Never mind my shoes, Sugar. Fin's driver is going to be here in a few minutes, so let's get to the plan."

"We got us a plan?"

"No, but we should. All we're doing tonight is looking for anything suspicious."

Her eyes bugged with mock ignorance. "You mean like the deceased getting his throat slashed from ear to ear?"

I took a therapeutic breath and considered my words carefully. Tonight could end very badly, and if Sugar was going to waltz into that service all cocky and unprepared, it might be best if she didn't go at all.

Before I could bring up the touchy subject, my phone rang. Fin's driver had arrived ten minutes early. "The car is here." I dumped my drink in the sink and grabbed my purse.

Sugar downed the rest of her margarita and followed me out. "Well, well," she said, spotting the car parked out front. "Fin sent the big guns tonight."

"He always does." Fin was a wealthy man, and while he rarely drove it himself, he always sent the Bentley to pick me up.

Joseph held the door open for us. He glanced at Sugar and nodded with a discreet grin, and I got the feeling it wasn't the first time they'd met. I knew from past comments that Fin was no stranger to the Blue Light Club, so I assumed she'd met him on one of Fin's visits.

We climbed in, and Sugar immediately went for the hidden bar between the seats and eyed the champagne bottle. "A little bubbly?" She pulled out one of the glasses and waved it back and forth in front of me. Then she leaned forward to speak to Joseph. "Is this bottle for us, baby?"

He glanced at her through the mirror and nodded. "Make yourselves at home, ladies."

"Well, ain't that nice of Fin," she said, settling back in her seat before reaching for the bottle.

"Put it back, Sugar. We'll be there in ten minutes."

The service was being held at the Chase residence. While it was common to hold a memorial service in a funeral facility, Chase Stone and his wife had a beautiful home in the middle of town, just as large and grand as any funeral chapel in Savannah.

Reluctantly, she put the delicate glass back in the holder of the mini bar. "You need to loosen up, girl. Ain't every day you get handed a free bottle of Cristal."

"Yeah, well, it's not every day that you might get yourself killed by a sorceress at a memorial service for one of her victims," I shot back. "I prefer to take my chances sober and alert."

Fin was waiting on the sidewalk when we pulled up to the house. He opened the door for me to climb out and looked slightly annoyed when he spotted Sugar getting out on the other side. "Lovely as ever, Miss Bishop." He took my hand and helped me out of the car. "I don't think I've seen you this bright and polished since the society ball. Not that you don't look lovely every day."

Sugar walked around the car. "What about me, Fin? You like what you see?" she turned sideways and struck a pose.

"Always, Sugar. You are one of a kind."

"Don't you know it."

He leaned in to whisper. "You didn't mention you were bringing a guest."

"You didn't ask. You have a problem with that?"

"Not at all." He glanced at the line of people walking up the steps. There we even more coming down the sidewalk in their black mourning attire. "Looks like a full house. Let's hope it doesn't turn into a war zone."

"Now that would be a memorable memorial service," Sugar said. "When I die, I want the society to throw me a big ol' party and then toss my ashes into the Savannah River. Don't be putting me in no ground."

"Noted," he replied. "We'll make sure to have a real celebration before feeding you to the fish."

The three of us climbed the steps and entered the crowded house. There must have been twenty people in addition to us crammed into the foyer, trying to get to one of the much larger rooms. In the living room, I spotted a tripod with an enlarged photo of Chase Stone framed with a bunch of bright orange lilies.

"Tiger lilies," I said. "Symbols of wealth and pride. How appropriate."

"Are you a gardener, Miss Bishop?" Fin asked.

I laughed at the thought of all the house plants I'd killed over the years. "I have a black thumb when it comes to plants, but I put a lot of lilies on people's skin. It helps to know the meaning of a particular kind of flower to do it justice with ink."

Sugar pushed through the crowd, making a path for me and Fin to follow. We made our way into the living room and took up the space in the corner by the front window, surveying the crowd for anyone who looked suspicious. I wasn't sure what we were looking for, maybe a woman peacocking around the room who no one—including the widow—recognized, or someone taking an unhealthy interest in the widow herself. Anyone out of the ordinary was a target to be questioned.

I spotted a couple of men standing in the opposite corner. One of them looked familiar. As I looked closer, I realized it was Detective Ryan, the Chatham County detective who'd questioned me about Christopher Sullivan's murder earlier that summer. I was brought down to the police station based on an anonymous tip that turned out to be a hoax, but I could tell by the way he looked at me that day that he thought I was guilty—which I was, self-defense or not.

Not interested in a reunion, I turned my back to the two men, hoping the detective wouldn't spot me from the other side of the room. A minute later, I heard a voice behind me.

"Miss Bishop?"

I casually turned around and tried to act surprised, hesitating as I pretended to place his face. "Detective Ryan, right?"

"Seems like every time we run into each other, there's a murder involved." He had a cocky smirk on his face.

"Oh?" I replied. "Does that mean you've found Christopher Sullivan's body?" To my knowledge, they'd never recovered the remains Fin and his "cleaners" managed to get rid of. No body meant no murder. At least for now.

Fin tensed when I glanced at him, suddenly making the connection between me and the detective, I assumed.

"Not yet," Ryan said. "But it's only a matter of time. A body always surfaces eventually." He took a swig of his drink and stared me down. "I wonder what we'll find when it does."

I glanced at his exposed badge and the glass in his hand. "Looks like you're here on official business. Do you drink often while you're on the clock?"

He jiggled the ice cubes floating around the golden liquid. "Tea. You can taste it if you'd like." He shifted his eyes to Fin. "How do you know Mr. Cooper here?"

"I don't think that's any of your business, Detective," Fin said before I could answer. The look in his eyes gave away the malice he felt for Ryan. It was pretty clear the two men had a history, and I was just adding to their obvious dislike for each other.

The detective finished his tea, and then he turned and walked back to his buddy on the other side of the room. He exchanged words with the man who I assumed was his partner.

"Is that him?" Sugar asked. She knew all about my trip down to the precinct that day. "I guess them boys are here looking for the killer too. If only they knew what they was getting themselves into."

Fin finally pulled his eyes away from Detective Ryan. "Promise me you'll call if that bastard ever bothers you again, Miss Bishop. It would be my pleasure to make him regret it." A second later, he spotted the bar. Savannah sobered up for nothing and no one, not even to memorialize the dead. "What are you ladies drinking?"

I decided to go easy on the alcohol. "I'll have a glass of red wine, please."

Sugar contemplated what she wanted to drink. The widow had hired a bartender, so the options were endless. "You know, I think I'll have me a vodka martini. Just make sure that boy behind the bar uses the good stuff. Three olives and a little dirty."

While Fin went to fetch our drinks, Sugar and I surveyed the crowd. I noticed a beautiful young woman sitting on a sofa that had been moved back against the far wall, making room for folding chairs for the eulogy we'd all have to suffer through.

"I'll make you a deal, Sugar. I'll personally make sure you get that party and then get dumped into the river, if you promise to ban any eulogies at my memorial service."

"Deal, baby."

The woman on the sofa seemed a little too distraught, like she was about to crumble under the weight of her emotions and burst into tears. She kept staring at the photo of the deceased, dabbing her eyes with a napkin and taking shuddering breaths.

"That one over there," Sugar said, nodding toward the woman I was watching. "She's the mistress."

"Why do you say that? Maybe she's family."

Sugar shook her head. "She ain't no family. See how she's playing with that fancy little necklace she's wearing? I bet he gave it to her. That widow's going to smell her out the second they're in the same room together."

Fin returned, balancing three drinks in his hands. "You ladies see anything interesting while I was gone?"

"Just your run-of-the-mill mourners," I said.

Sugar took a sip of her martini and continued to scan the crowd over the rim of her glass. Her eyes flashed as she recognized a familiar face entering the room. He was an attractive man about Fin's age, wearing a sharp suit. His hand rested on a woman's waist as he steered her into the living room. Sugar raised her hand to shoulder level, twiddling her fingers at him as she mouthed *hey, baby*. He spotted her and looked away, quickly moving back into the foyer with his companion, who I assumed was his wife or girlfriend.

Fin followed her eyes. "You know Phillip Lennox?"

"Oh, I know Phillip real well. He comes into the Blue Light sometimes. Through the back door," she added with a sly grin.

"Mr. Lennox owns a couple of Savannah's finer eating establishments," Fin said. "Are you familiar with The Montreal, Miss Bishop?"

The Montreal was one of those places where you could easily drop half a month's rent on a meal for two. "Sure, I'm familiar with it. I must have walked right past it half a dozen times, but I can't say I've ever been inside."

Sugar stretched her neck out to see where he'd gone, but I had a feeling Mr. Lennox had already steered his companion back out the front door, with Sugar not being very discreet about their acquaintance.

The room suddenly became animated as Marla Chase entered and took her seat next to the blown-up photograph of her dead husband. Wearing a black mourning dress and a conservative pair of low pumps, she had her eyes fixed on her lap.

"Well, would you look at that," Sugar said. "You didn't tell me he had a taste for chocolate."

One look at Marla Chase told you she was the product of mixed parentage, just like Sugar, with light brown skin and lovely pale eyes.

"You're the last person I thought would make a comment like that," I said.

She kept her eyes on Marla, the wheels in her head actively working. "I just think it's real interesting that a rich white man like Chase Stone didn't find him some lily-white debutante to marry. Can always keep a pretty little thing like that on the side. Men like Chase Stone usually do."

For the next forty-five minutes, we listened to the steady stream of people give their speeches about what a great man Chase Stone was, and how tragic it was to see his life ended in such a brutal way. But people naturally found only the good things to say about someone at a memorial service. In fact, I'd never once heard anyone on the local news talk about a murder victim as being a real son of a bitch, even if he or she was. But despite all the kind words about Chase Stone tonight, the man I'd only met once had clearly revealed who he really was—an abusive asshole with a fat bank account.

When the service was over, Fin went to pay his respects to the grieving widow. He took her hand gently in his as they conversed. Then she looked down at the empty glass in his other hand and reached for it. Despite his protest, which was visible from across the room, she walked over to the bar and proceeded to refresh his drink. Odd I thought, for a woman who'd just lost her husband a few days earlier to some maniac with a knife. Grieving family members were the ones usually being fussed over, not the other way around. Maybe it was just her way of coping, tending to other people's needs.

When the next group of people approached to express their condolences, Fin politely moved on and walked back over to us.

"How's she doing?" I asked.

"Well, how do you think she's doing?" Sugar said. "Her sugar daddy's dead." She polished off her second martini, spearing the last olive with a fancy stainless-steel cocktail pick. "I wonder if these little picks are party favors."

I shook my head. "Cold, Sugar."

"Hell, y'all were thinking the same thing. But you know what? Now that he's dead, I guess she gets everything." She cocked her head in thought and furrowed her brow. "You don't think she had anything to do with it, do you?"

I ignored her insensitive question and looked over at Marla Stone to see if the line of people had cleared out. She was alone, standing next to the fireplace and staring down at the Persian rug. "My turn to pay my respects," I said, setting my wine glass on the table before making my way across the room. As I approached her, I thought about how beautiful she was, even in mourning without a stitch of makeup on her face.

"I'm so sorry for your loss, Marla." I offered my hand as she continued to stare at the floor. A moment later, her eyes flicked up. Without raising her head, she gazed at me through her long sable lashes, ignoring my outstretched hand. The crooked smile on her face sent a rush of chills up my spine, causing my beast to stir.

"Miss Bishop," she said in a much deeper voice than I remembered.

Without realizing I'd done it, I took a step back. She took a step forward to close the distance I'd just created between us. Then she reached out to touch my hand, which was now retracted and pressed against my stomach. It was like a mild electrical current had run up my arm when she pressed her palm against my skin.

I glanced down and noticed a bracelet around her wrist. Ivory or vintage Bakelite, I thought. But as I looked closer, I realized it was a chain of thin, curved bones, strung together by links of gold or brass. She briefly exposed the underside of her hand as she pulled it away, allowing me a glimpse of the strange mark embedded over the bright blue veins of her wrist.

My breath caught as I took another step back and looked at her face. Her smile turned condescending, as she casually pulled her long black sleeve over the mark I knew I'd seen before.

I looked across the room at Fin and Sugar. From the startled look on my face, they must have known something was wrong, because they were suddenly walking toward me. When I looked back at Marla, she was disappearing through a door on the other side of the room.

"We're leaving" I said when they reached me. "We need to go see May."

23

"Are you planning to tell us why you dragged us out of that house without even saying goodbye to the grieving widow?" Fin asked as the three of us climbed into the Bentley and drove out of town toward Pearl May Mobley's house.

"Yeah," Sugar said. "I need to call Mama to let her know we're coming. Mama don't like surprises, and she ain't going to appreciate us crashing her Sunday evening business without a damn good reason."

A damn good reason indeed. Those bones around Marla Stone's wrist were enough to make me question who and what she was, but it was that mark on the underside of her wrist that sent a shudder through me. By the look on her face. I think she wanted me to see it.

"The grieving widow has some explaining to do," I said.

"I knew it!" Sugar dropped her phone before she could dial May's number. "Something wasn't right about that woman."

Fin stared at me cautiously when I started to explain. "There's a mark on her wrist, right under that bracelet of bones she was wearing."

"Bones?" Fin said, growing noticeably more concerned by the second. "Are you sure about that?"

"At first I thought it was just a piece of vintage jewelry, but when I got a good look at it, there was no doubt they were bones strung around her wrist." I'd seen more bones over the past couple of months than I cared to, making me somewhat of an expert at spotting them. But it was that incriminating mark that made me realize that we'd been looking for something that was right under our noses all along. "That mark on her wrist is the same symbol we saw in the eggshells May read to us."

Sugar turned to look me in the eye. "Are you shittin' me?"

"No, ma'am."

Fin seemed confused. "One of you two want to tell me what's going on?"

"Katie and me went out to see Mama a while back. She was deep in the dirt, rustling up some mojo when we got there. Pulled her an egg out of the earth and read the shells."

I explained. "There was some dirt stuck to the inside membrane of the shell when it cracked open. It kind of looked like a rune, and it was definitely the same mark I just saw on Marla Stone's wrist. And then there was that damn fly."

Fin cocked his head. "Fly?"

"Thousands of them came flying out of the mound of dirt when May smashed that egg into it like Nolan Ryan. One of them got stuck to the shell. May said it was the devil." I sat back in the plush leather seat and focused on the back of Joseph's perfectly coiffed head as we drove deeper into the outskirts of town, with that symbol stuck in my mind clear as day. "If anyone needs to tell us what's going on around here, it's May."

"Mama don't do nothing without a good reason," Sugar said.

Fin sighed. "Sugar's right about that. I guess we're about to find out."

May's house was dark when we pulled up. Sugar never did

make that call, I supposed because she didn't know how to explain why we were coming. It was either a fact-finding mission or a confrontation.

We climbed the steps cautiously. The last time we showed up unannounced, we found ourselves staring at the barrel of a shotgun. It was best to approach quietly to give Sugar a chance to warn May.

"Don't step on that one," I whispered to Fin, pointing to the discolored board at the top of the stairs.

"He knows about that," Sugar said. "The man's known Mama for decades."

"What the hell kind of car is that?" someone said. "You got you a chauffeur in there?"

Fin turned to May, who was sitting in the dark corner. "Now, you know Joseph," he said. "He's fetched you enough times over the years."

May struck a match and lit the pipe in her hand, sending a sweet and spicy smell floating through the air.

"Mama, you told me you quit smoking that thing."

"Told you a lot of things that ain't true."

The look on Sugar's face was priceless. "You been lying to me my whole life?"

"Settle down," May said. "I ain't never lied about anything important." She stood up and took a few more puffs before tapping the contents of the pipe into a small bowl on the railing. Then she walked past us and opened the front door. "Come on inside. Y'all want anything to drink?" Fin and I both declined, preferring to move things along as quickly as possible.

"I'll take some of that ginger beer, if you got a batch ready." Sugar practically beamed. "Mama makes it herself. Better than any of that stuff they sell over at the grocery store. Got a nice kick too."

May walked back in the room and handed Sugar a glass of

something that looked more like lemonade, but the smell of ginger was unmistakable.

There was no time to waste. "We're here about that mark you showed us in those eggshells." She took a seat and settled back, looking at me like she was waiting to hear an actual question, or something a little more substantial to jog her memory. "You know what I'm talking about, May. That dirt symbol stuck inside the shell. Right next to that fly you were so interested in."

"I know why you're here," she said. "That mark's been beating at my head all day. Same as you."

"Me?"

May nodded once. "Everything's just about to come together. You seen that mark. You about to be in the fight of your life, girl. But don't you worry, May done put in a good word for you at the crossroads."

I didn't want to offend her, but we were in a hurry. Fin had know May for decades, so I glanced at him for a little backup in moving the conversation along. He leaned forward in his chair and prompted May to get to the point. "Tell us what the mark means, May."

For the first time since I'd met her, May looked weary, like she was tired of trying to fight whatever was coming. The perpetual twinkle in her eyes was gone, and her brow furrowed tightly as she released a shuddering breath. "It's a birthmark," she said. "That land belongs to the original queen of Savannah. She was here before any of us. Don't no one want to mess with that kind of power. That mark belongs to the rightful heir to that land you done stole, Fin. The queen's daughter."

"Now, hold on," he said. "I didn't know about any of that. All I did was fund the project."

"Don't matter," she continued. "You was putting that building up on Ijibah's land. You the enemy." Then she turned her gaze on me and her eyes softened a bit. "She knows what you are, girl. You the biggest threat of all, with all that fire inside of you. Ain't no one a match for Ijibah, except for you."

Sugar, who had remained quietly enthralled by the conversation, finally spoke up. "Will someone tell me what any of this got to do with the widow? Did I miss something?"

We all looked at May because Sugar raised a good point. What did any of this have to do with Marla Stone? "I don't understand," I said. "Why does Chase Stone's widow have that mark on her wrist?"

May looked at me like I was speaking French, or some other language she wasn't familiar with. "Girl, what are you talkin' about?"

"The mark," I said. "I saw it on Chase Stone's widow tonight. It was on the underside of her wrist."

May shook her head. "Can't be."

"No offense, May, but I know what I saw."

She was pretty adamant about it. "That birthmark is for the daughter of the land."

The room went quiet as everyone mulled over the facts. I was the first to state the obvious question on everyone's mind. "You don't think that Marla Stone is Ijibah? Is that even possible?"

May gave it some consideration. "Ijibah ain't come through the crossroads yet. I'da known it if she did."

"You sure about that Mama?" Sugar asked.

"Sure as I'll ever be. If Ijibah done broke through the crossroads, them shells would've told me."

"Then why did I see that mark on Marla Stone's skin?" Before anyone could answer, an unsettling thought entered my mind. "Uh… folks, is it possible that the 'queen' had more than one daughter?"

A light bulb seemed to turn on in the room as everyone appeared to catch on to what I'd just said. May stood up faster than I thought possible for a woman of her age. She headed straight for the kitchen, and I heard the back door open. The rest of us followed and watched as she made a beeline for that pile of dirt she liked to play in so much, with the moon nearly full glowing overhead.

"Mama?" Sugar said as May dropped to her knees and dug her fingers into the dirt, sifting through it like she was feeling for something specific.

"Shells don't lie," she kept saying over and over in a steady mantra, until she finally hit something with her hand. When she pulled it from the mound, she was holding another one of those mysterious eggs that seemed to live in the earth. Without standing up, she wasted no time crushing the egg against a large stone at the edge of the pile. The black yolk covered her palms as she gathered up the broken shells. A smaller swarm of flies spun up around her, but she seemed oblivious to them as she examined each of the shells, eventually finding the one she was looking for. "See that?" she said, holding it up for all of us to see.

We couldn't see the shell in the dark, so Sugar walked toward her.

"Stay back!" she warned. "I'll read it to you." She moved something around with her index finger, nodding as she seemed to get the message in the shells loud and clear. Then she proceeded to tell us what I already suspected. "Two flies," she said. "Sisters."

"I told you!" Sugar said, "That grieving widow just wasn't right."

We all looked back at May, who was feeling through the dirt again. She found what she was looking for and pulled her hand back out, only this time the egg she was holding was larger than any chicken egg I'd ever seen.

"What do you got there, Mama?"

"Shhh!" May hissed. She smashed the egg, but instead of a black yolk oozing out, the shell split into two pieces and fell away from whatever was growing inside. May stumbled back as the small chick began to screech and flap its tiny wings.

The dragon stirred on my back, sensing the birth of something evil in that pile of dirt. Before I knew what was happening, my eyes were on fire and I was staring down at the claws breaking through the tips of my fingers. I took a few steps back from Fin and Sugar, hoping the beast would settle down and disappear before they turned around and saw what was happening behind them.

The chick began to grow. A set of gray and white feathers emerged from its naked wings, followed by a sharp beak and a set of golden eyes that turned toward us with a keen gaze.

"Lord," May muttered as it stood up and towered over her, taking on the form of something between a raptor and a human. "Ijibah be knocking on the gate."

Sugar whipped around to look at me. "That's an owlman!" she blurted at the same time she noticed the bright green glow of my irises. The excitement on her face faded as her eyes traveled down my arms, and then to my hands that were suddenly more talons then fingers. "Now hold on, Katie." Her face blanched as she moved back to make room for my growing wings. "Just take a couple of deep breaths, girl."

Fin turned around when he heard the growl coming from my throat and ducked out of the way with Sugar.

The owl let out a deafening screech and spread its enormous wings, nearly knocking May backward with the powerful gust of wind they stirred up. A second later, it took flight, veering sharply east as it headed in the direction of the city.

"Ain't no owlman," May said, transfixed by its silhouette against the bright moon, oblivious to the dragon being born behind her. "That's an owl*woman*, heading for the cone of power. She 'bout to escort Ijibah through the crossroads."

Suddenly hearing the commotion behind her, or maybe it

was the sight of dirt dusting the sky from my expanding wings, May spun around. A wide grin spread across her face, and her eyes flashed with excitement. Then she got down to business and jerked her head in the direction of that bird disappearing in the distance. "Go on, girl. That owl will lead you straight to the cone of power."

I raised my wings into the air and brought them down with a single powerful stroke, setting off into the sky, knowing that the next time I touched down I'd come face-to-face with Ijibah.

24

I soared over the city lights, leaving enough distance between me and the owl to avoid a midair confrontation. But she knew I was behind her. I suspected that was her plan, to lead me to the cone of power. If it was energy Ijibah needed to come through the crossroads, what better source than a dragon?

The owlwoman headed straight for the Cavanagh Holdings construction site, which was exactly where I suspected we were going. But as she descended and approach the sinking building, she sailed right over it and continued east.

As if she'd simply dropped out of the sky, the owl suddenly disappeared over the cemetery. The lights in the park had gone out, and all I could see were the trees and the tops of tombs scattered around the acres housing the dead.

As I touched down in the cemetery, the wind from my wings sent a spray of rocks and coins flying through the air, homage left on top of headstones by those visiting the dead. My wings folded and disappeared, but to my horror, the transition back to flesh and bone had stopped somewhere between the woman and the beast. Though my wings were gone, my limbs were still covered in tiny emerald shields, with the sharp points of my talons still protruding from my fingertips. I could still feel the heat radiating from my eyes.

The date suddenly popped into my head. My twenty-fifth birthday was the day after tomorrow, and I'd done nothing to prepare for it, hoping my predicted destiny was just the ramblings of a crazy long-lost aunt. And then there was the fact that my boyfriend had left me, and I'd been kind of busy dealing with a dead sorceress who was about to take over the city. But now I knew my fate if I did nothing because I was showing signs of becoming the beast permanently.

A voice in the darkness distracted me. It was coming from the south end of the park, where the graves supposedly ended but were rumored to extend well past the cemetery boundaries. I cocked my head to listen, and then I followed it.

At the far end of the park, I spotted a bright light. I moved closer and realized it was a hole in the ground with a beam shooting out of it like a giant spotlight aimed at the sky. The light was intense, and had I not been in half-dragon mode, I probably would have been blinded by looking directly at the rays. Marla Stone was standing at the edge, unaffected by the light as she conversed with a tall woman with gray hair. The woman was naked. When she turned around and looked at me, her sharp golden eyes gave her away. It was the owlwoman, waiting for Ijibah to come through the doorway they'd opened.

The woman gave me a hard look before turning back to Marla. She nodded to signal the start of what I assumed would be the grand finale. Marla reached into her pocket and pulled out a small sack. She shook it to release its contents into the air. It looked like black powder floating in the wind, but a second later, that powder began to swarm into a funnel, manifesting into a cloud of flies like the one I'd seen at May's house. It was heading straight for me. There was no time to react before the swarm was around me, encasing me in a cocoon of flies that filled my mouth, nose, and eyes. The buzzing sound was deafening as they invaded my ears, and I frantically tried to breathe through the cloud of insects threatening to travel down my throat and fill my lungs.

As I panicked and fell to the ground, an instinct as old and powerful as the line of dragons I descended from kicked in. I rolled on my back and opened my mouth to beckon the swarm inside. A second later, fire came pouring out of me, setting the black tornado into a blaze of whirling flames, filling my mouth with the taste of charred insects.

I spat the disgusting carnage out of my mouth and stood up. The women had lost interest in me. Either they assumed I was dead, or their window of opportunity was about to close forever. I suspected that window was closing, so they had to work fast and make do with the power they had.

The owlwoman circled the ring of light, chanting in a language I didn't recognize. Marla threw something into the hole that sent a spark shooting into the sky and then joined in on the chanting. They circled faster, and the light began to wave and shimmer, as if the heat coming off it had created a moving mirage between them.

The dragon suddenly took over again and started to lift me into the air. But striking was a very bad idea. Ijibah needed to be sent back to the grave permanently, but how do you kill something that's already dead? The only way to do that was to let her come through the crossroads so someone skilled at banishing could send her into oblivion for eternity. She needed to come through and be detained until I could figure out how the hell to drain her power, or hold her to face the council.

I managed to take control and descend back to the ground. They were too preoccupied with their circling to notice me step behind a tomb.

The light suddenly intensified tenfold. It exploded, sending a million glowing embers into the sky, turning the gaping hole into a cauldron of fire. Even from a distance, the energy was incredible.

"*Fuck,*" I hissed quietly.

"Ijibah!" Marla screamed, her face turning rabid from the spell that seemed to possess her. She kept repeating her sister's name in a mantra, staring at the hole until the fire started to change shape. The flames twisted and swirled around the blue center, forming the figure of a woman at its core. I was beginning to regret passing up the opportunity to stop them. Anything that could withstand that kind of heat would probably laugh at a dragon's breath. When the owlwoman took something from Marla Stone's hand and stepped over the edge of the hole, hovering in the center of the flames, I *really* started to regret that decision.

For the next few minutes, the owlwoman faded in and out like a hologram, between a bird and a human figure. Then the flames became an inferno, sending a wave of heat through the park that blew the trees sideways and seared their leaves. I flew backward and hit a headstone, the force knocking me out. When I came to, Ijibah was standing about ten feet away.

"Little dragon," she said with a cocky sneer. "Ijibah got her a little dragon."

She was shorter than I expected, but the aura that surrounded her was ten feet tall. If the eyes were indeed the windows to the soul, her hazel irises, circled by rings of fire, were terrifying enough to crush any doubt that she was the devil. There wasn't an ounce of kindness in them.

The dragon responded. My wings sprouted again, and I flew toward the sky. I made it about twenty feet up before something wrapped around my neck and pulled me back to the ground.

"What the fuck?" I yanked at the manacle around my throat.

Marla appeared and circled her arm around Ijibah's waist. She kissed her sister on the cheek and took a step closer to get a better look at me. "I thought you'd put up more of a fight." Amusement seeped through the mock perplexity on her face. "Oh... you don't know, do you?"

I glanced back and forth between them, trying to hide my shock. "Know what?"

She fiddled with the bracelet around her wrist, and I noticed that a couple of the bones were missing, replaced with a length of gold chain. "Even a dragon isn't immune to the power of Adro," she said. Ijibah opened her hand. She was holding one of the missing bones from the bracelet, along with the other end of the chain attached to the manacle around my neck. "The chain conducts the bone's power," Marla continued, slowly shaking her head. "You shouldn't have closed your eyes, Katie. Not even for a second." She must have put it around my neck when I hit that headstone and passed out. That same wicked smile she'd given me at the memorial service appeared on her face when she saw the revelation in my eyes.

I was no stranger to the power of Adro's bones. I'd hunted down a rogue god named Legvu when I first went to work with the Crossroads Society, but not before he stunned me with those same bones and tried to kill me. Adro was an entity of pure evil, and his bones were my kryptonite. Those bones were *everyone's* kryptonite. Legvu buried them at the crossroads, which I assumed was right under our feet. Until now, the location of the crossroads was a mystery, and those bones had never been found. They were presumed to still be buried—except for the ones now circling Marla Stone's wrist.

"So you're the one who's been feeding Ijibah her power. Or was it that owl?"

She let out a curt laugh. "The power came from me, but the owl was a necessary sacrifice to deliver the bone and escort her through the portal. We would have brought her through sooner, but I had some cleaning up to do first."

"You mean by killing everyone who stood to inherit that land?"

"Of course. And now that my husband is dead, it all comes to me. Well, it *was* mine in the first place before it was stolen from my family." Ijibah gave her sister a warning look. "Ours, I mean," Marla quickly added.

Doing my best to hide my fear, I snorted and tried to come off cocky. "Then I guess you're just as guilty as your big sister here. You might have me in a tough spot right now, but the council will kill you when they find out you're the one who handed Ijibah that bone ticket to come through the crossroads." I gave her a smug smile and tried to steady my trembling hands. "Give up Ijibah, and maybe the council will strike a deal and let you live."

The laugh that came out of Marla Stone's mouth this time made me shudder. She took a step closer and wiped the smirk off my face. "You can't kill what's already dead." The glamour vanished, and her flawless skin sagged as the underlying flesh began to drip off of her bones. Her lovely bluish-green eyes turned into cloudy wells of spoiled egg whites. Even her hair appeared to be rotten, as the smell of death filled the air.

Realizing how fucked I was, I lunged and slashed my claws at Ijibah's throat. She yanked the chain, and a surge of magic jolted me back to the ground. The shock traveled from my neck down to my legs, knocking me out again.

Ijibah was hovering over me when my eyes opened. "I think I like you better this way. As a hybrid. Keeps you small enough."

"Small enough for what?" I asked, wishing I hadn't.

"Small enough to chain you next to my throne. Or maybe I'll put you in a cage in the middle of Oglethorpe Square, as a warning to anyone who thinks they can challenge me. Either way,

I'll enjoy feeding off of you. You'll be my own personal battery."
She bent down closer and stroked a lock of my hair. "But don't
worry. I won't take enough to kill you. Dragons are prized pets."

As I swallowed what little saliva was left in my mouth and let
the image of that cage sink in, I heard voices coming from every
corner of the cemetery. Neither Marla nor Ijibah blinked when
the voices got louder. My dragon's auditory senses were excep-
tional, and it was obvious I was the only one who could hear it.
More rustling sounds followed, and I got a glimpse of something
flash past the south fence at a pretty remarkable speed.

They noticed my eyes darting around the cemetery and
turned around to see what was so compelling. Satisfied that there
was nothing there, they proceeded with their plan.

"Up!" Ijibah barked. "We have a city to take back."

I climbed to my feet and glanced discreetly around the
tombs. We weren't alone, and I was praying whoever it was would
get on with it before Ijibah dragged me out of the cemetery to
some secret lair where she'd keep me imprisoned with those
bones.

"I wouldn't leave just yet." Madge Miller stepped out from
the shadows. "Katie isn't your pet, so kindly drop that chain."

The look on Ijibah's face was priceless—and a little scary. She
glared at the intruder, but her wicked smile flattened when she
saw the gray-haired woman standing under a tree. She sniffed the
air as if a scent had floated past her nose. "You're going to regret
stepping into the crossroads, witch."

Madge tilted her head and contemplated the threat. "No,"
she countered with a shake of her head. "I don't believe I'll be the
one regretting that."

Her attitude didn't sit well with Ijibah. Not wanting to let go
of my chain to deal with Madge herself, she whipped her head
around and gave her sister a silent order. Marla flew into the air
and headed for Madge, screeching like a banshee as she rose

higher. She was a few yards away from Madge when a second voice rang out from the north. It seemed to interfere with Marla's levitation, because she stopped in midair and dropped to the ground.

"All right," Penelope Kingfisher said, stepping into view to my right. "This is getting a little boring, and *Game of Thrones* is coming on soon." She glanced at her watch. "Shit! I'm missing it!" She looked at me and paused. "Damn, Katie. You look a little stuck in the in-between."

A second later, Fiona showed up, followed by Cat and Carmen. Desiree and Temperance stepped out next. The cavalry had arrived.

Ijibah opened her mouth to speak, but before she could get a word out, Penelope dropped to her knee and slammed her fist down on the ground, sending a mild earthquake through the cemetery. I braced myself as the ground shook and continued to reverberate.

Marla gasped and stared at something on the ground. She froze as bones began to peek through the dirt around her. Ijibah seemed just as stunned, but the end of that chain was still gripped tightly in her hand.

Penelope delivered another blow. The bones kept surfacing, sifted from their grave by the continuous vibrations disturbing the earth beneath the cemetery.

Ijibah let out a wail. "Adro!"

I stared at the protruding bones and realized what they were. We were surrounded not only by the remains of Savannah's departed citizens, but by the bones of Adro.

Right on cue, Sharma and Taylor appeared on opposite sides of the two intruder witches. "Hey, Sharma," Taylor said. "You take the one who looks like she's about to liquefy. I'll take her ugly big sister."

Ijibah turned to Taylor. Her hand opened, and a spark

appeared in the center of her palm. In an instant, it grew into a revolving sphere of fire the size of a bowling ball, reminding us all that Ijibah was a fire witch who could burn the city down to the ground if it suited her. It was also one of the reasons I'd been summoned by the society, to fight fire with fire. Unfortunately, I was incapacitated by that bone in her hand.

"Incoming!" Sharma yelled.

Taylor hit the ground as the flames hurled at her like a torpedo. She rolled behind one of the tombs, just as the fireball grazed the edge of her leg. She let out a few choice expletives and climbed back to her feet, fixing her eyes on Ijibah.

Whatever Taylor was doing must have worked, because Ijibah dropped her hand before she could ignite another fire bomb. Seeing her sister in distress, Marla took a step toward her, abruptly stopping as Sharma stared her down and somehow held her in place.

"You've got about ten seconds before these bitches break free from my psyche-out," Taylor said to me. "Make them count, or we're all dead."

I took her cue and yanked the chain as hard as I could. It barely budged from Ijibah's hand.

"Let me try," Someone said.

I turned around and saw Emmaline standing behind me. Her voice was so birdlike that I forgot she was capable of stirring up a hurricane with her mind. I'd never seen it with my own two eyes, but I'd been told.

Emmaline stepped next to me and set her eyes on Ijibah. I waited for something pretty amazing to happen, but all I saw was her seemingly quiet gaze focus on her target. Then I realized what she was doing. Ijibah stood still as a stone, but I noticed a barely detectable tremor rattling her head. It got more noticeable as her skin started to turn red, and her eyes began to bulge. A strange sound was coming from her mouth, and I realized she was trying to scream. Emmaline was nuking her.

"You should be able to free yourself now," Sharma said. "Emmaline is damn good at that. But that dead thing over there is pretty unpredictable, so you better hurry."

I yanked as hard as I could, and the chain slipped from Ijibah's hand as if the bone's engine had simply run out of gas. But I knew it was the microwaves Emmaline was sending to Ijibah's head.

The bone flew through the air, landing at Sharma's feet. "Damn thing better not mess me up," she said as she reluctantly snatched it off the ground and shoved it in her pocket.

Madge took her cue next, rushing Marla to snatch the bracelet off her wrist while Sharma held her in place with more of that mind mojo. Then she dug into Ijibah's pocket and found the other bone the owlwoman had given her to make it through the crossroads. It was probably used up, but better safe than sorry.

Everyone stepped back as the dragon fully manifested. Then Taylor and Sharma fell to the ground, spent of their energy as the spell broke.

Ijibah regained her senses and darted her eyes to her empty hand. Then she turned to her sister standing next to her, who looked dumbstruck and deader than ever.

The two witches backed up as I hovered over them. A fierce beast with a bone to pick, so to speak. With a mighty roar, I opened my jaws and sent a river of fire down on Ijibah. I knew the fire couldn't kill a fire witch any more than it could kill me, but it would damn sure incapacitate her long enough for the witches of Blackthorn Grove to take her into custody. Then it would be up to the council to decide her fate.

As soon as she saw the fire rain down on her sister, Marla leapt for the hole in the earth that was growing weaker and dimmer by the second. She dove in and disappeared seconds before it closed, back to the world of the dead where she belonged.

"We have to hurry," Madge said.

The witches gathered the unearthed bones and placed them around Ijibah's stunned form. The bones of Adro were arranged end to end in a pentagram. The pentagram was probably overkill, but when dealing with a sorceress as powerful as Ijibah, it was stupid not to use every trick in the book.

Once she was caged in the pentagram of bones, the witches got busy stringing together a necklace of smaller ones, including the bones from the bracelet her sister had worn. The bones served whoever possessed them, and right now the witches of Blackthorn Grove were their keepers.

When the necklace was complete, Esrial emerged from the shadows. She took it from Madge's hand and stepped over the pentagram. She smiled with false benevolence at the sorceress who'd killed her lover and tried to ruin her life. Then she slipped the necklace over Ijibah's head, rendering her helpless with the very power she thought was hers for eternity.

"I guess you're not that powerful after all," I said to Ijibah, staring at the pathetic witch who'd had me in chains minutes earlier, threatening to put me on display like a sideshow attraction. "You know, it's funny," I continued, looking her squarely in the eye. "I should hate you for what you've done, but all I feel is pity. You're a sad witch with nothing left. Even your own sister abandoned you." I turned to walk away but stopped to get in one more dig. "And you're dead!"

25

It was around midnight when I heard a knock on my front door. The moment I got home from the cemetery, I headed straight for the bathroom and sat on the floor, staring at the half-formed scales that started at my ankles and covered most of my body, leaving only the skin on my feet and part of my hands looking normal. The mirror had confirmed that while my face was still recognizable and I still had my hair, my skin was somewhere between pale white and emerald green. At least I still looked human.

I ignored the second knock. A few minutes later, I heard footsteps outside the bedroom door.

"I'm coming in there if you ain't out here in ten seconds," Sugar warned. "So you better not be doing your business in there."

"I don't think that's such a good idea, Sugar. Go home."

A woman of her word, she waited the ten seconds before barreling through the unlocked door. "Can't be that bad—" She stopped cold when she got a good look at me. "Sweet baby Jesus!"

"I warned you." I climbed off the floor and headed for the

kitchen, glancing at the open patio door. "I should just make you a key."

"'Bout time."

I swung the cabinet door open and grabbed the bottle of scotch, filling a glass more than halfway full. "You want one?" She grabbed the bottle from my hand and then downed the glass I'd poured for myself in a single swig, wincing from the burn. "What the hell are you doing, Sugar? Give me that damn bottle!"

She held it out of my reach. "I don't think it's such a good idea to be mixing alcohol with . . . all that," she said, waving her hand up and down my freakish body. "I ain't no doctor or scientist, but I ain't stupid either."

"Dear Lord!" I wailed, sitting down on one of the kitchen stools. "What's happening to me?"

She looked at me like I was plumb crazy. "You know what day it is, girl?"

I glanced at the kitchen clock and watched the hand tick past midnight, declaring it officially Monday. "It's the day before my birthday," I said with a cheesy grin.

"Mm-hmm." Her eyes darted around the room. "Where the hell is that damn phone of yours?"

"Why?"

"Because you got a call to make."

I shook my head. "It'll pass."

"Are you out of your ever-lovin' mind? Have you *looked* in the mirror?" She spotted my purse and made a beeline across the room. After rooting through it, she pulled out my phone and handed it to me. "Baby, you in denial. Now either you call that aunt of yours, or I will."

She was wrong about me being in denial. I knew exactly what was coming, and that's what scared the hell out of me. Becoming the dragon permanently was bad enough, but what scared me more was the idea of lighting that match and burning myself alive in some ritual that only had a fifty-fifty survival rate. I didn't think I could do it.

I shuddered as I took the phone and pulled up the number Marianna had given me the night we sat in that booth at Lou's Diner. For all I knew, she lived in another state and wouldn't have time to get here anyway. I was sure by now she figured I'd resigned myself to living in the Slovenian Alps with dear old dad, since I hadn't called her to prepare for what had to be a complicated ritual. You didn't just pull the trigger twenty-four hours prior to something like this and say, let's do it.

I dialed the number and waited nervously to see if she'd even pick up. After all, it was past midnight on a Sunday night. She answered before the second ring.

"It's me," I said, trying to ignore the knot in my stomach threatening to make me throw up all over the kitchen floor. We talked for all of two minutes, most of it consisting of her asking me questions, and me responding with *yes* or *no*.

Sugar stared at me impatiently as I hung up the phone and set it on the counter. "Well? What did she say?"

I exhaled the breath I was holding and reached for that bottle she was still gripping in her hand. "She'll be here in the morning." I finally poured myself that drink and took a sip, looking down at Jet as he rubbed against my ankles. "Sugar?" I said with a heavy sigh.

"Yeah, baby, what do you need?"

"If I die tonight—"

She shook her head briskly. "We ain't having this conversation again."

The gravity in my eyes must have been startling, because for once she shut up and let me continue. "Just promise me you'll take care of Jet if something goes wrong. I can't bear the thought of him being homeless."

She hesitated and then shrugged. "I guess I got room for a cat. But it ain't going to be necessary," she quickly added.

We sat at the kitchen counter for the next few minutes, sharing a drink in silence. Then she got up and headed for the front door to go home and get a little sleep before the fireworks began. Jet followed at her heels, like he knew he was about to walk out that door with her permanently.

I WOKE up to sounds coming from the living room. The bright sun glaring through the shades told me it was midmorning, which meant I'd overslept by a good two hours.

"Shit." I swung my legs over the side of the bed and searched for my robe. I found it thrown over the chair and quickly put it on to see who'd broken into my house this time. I needed to be more diligent about putting that metal bar in the patio door track.

As I crept down the hallway, I recognized Sugar's voice. I turned the corner just in time to hear the two women burst into laughter as Sugar flipped some pancakes.

"Good morning, Katie," Marianna said as she heard me walk into the kitchen. When she looked at me, her eyes grew wide. "Oh, dear!"

Sugar glanced at me and shuddered with mock fright. "Katie's having a little trouble shifting back from the beast."

"Obviously," she said over the rim of her cup. "But that's to be expected. It's frustrating for the dragon too, not being able to go back to sleep."

I poured myself a cup of coffee. "I see you've met my burglar friend."

"Didn't want to disturb your beauty rest," Sugar said. "You'll be needing it tonight."

"I wish you would have. I'm late for work."

Sugar rolled her eyes. "Girl, it's Monday."

"Thank God," I muttered, remembering what day it was. The shop was closed on Mondays. I wouldn't have been able to work anyway, with that birthday ritual looming over my head. "What are you two laughing about in here?"

Marianna grinned and took a sip of her coffee. "Sugar was just telling me a little bit about your shop. This Sea Bass character sounds amusing. I'd like to meet him once we get past this ritual business. Mouse and Abel too."

"You're mighty optimistic. I should probably start packing my bags for Slovenia."

She set her cup on the counter and lost her pleasant smile. "If you've already given up, Katie, I might as well leave." Then she stood up and glared at me. "Or should I call you Katarina?"

Well that stung, but I deserved it. With my need to self-deprecate my fear away, it never occurred to me that this could be a devastating night for her as well. If the ritual wasn't timed perfectly, she'd have to helplessly watch as I burned to death. Of course, I could do nothing and become Katarina as the clock struck midnight tonight, but that wasn't an option I was willing to accept. I'd rather choose death.

"It's Katie," I replied firmly.

"Amen and *damn* straight," Sugar said, flipping a pancake onto my plate.

Aunt Marianna smiled slyly. "All right then. Let's tame the beast."

I tried to force myself to eat as we discussed our strategy for the ritual, but each bite was like chewing leather that refused to slide down my throat. I finally pushed my plate away.

"You'll need to eat something before the ritual, or you'll be too weak," Marianna began. "And the potion I'll be giving you an hour before we start will make you sick if you take it on an empty stomach. Understood?"

"What is it? Eye of newt?" I couldn't resist.

"Eye of something," she replied.

Sugar's face turned sour. "Girl, I might have to take my chances with the pain, if I was you." She stuck her tongue out. "Couldn't make me drink none of that eyeball shit."

Marianna laughed. "It's not that bad. Believe me, the alternative is far worse."

Trying to get past the image of a pot of simmering eyeballs, I changed the subject. "What happened to Ijibah after I left last night," I asked Sugar.

For obvious reasons, I'd gone straight home after capturing her, to hide myself in the bathroom before any locals or tourists spotted me. The commotion in the park was enough to bring the news helicopters circling, and by the time we had Ijibah chained with bones, people were already starting to gather. Fortunately, the strange and outlandish wasn't unusual in Savannah, and the eyewitness accounts of a dragon and a bunch of witches in the middle of Colonial Park Cemetery was just another day in one of the most haunted cities in America. But still, I thought it wise to stay out of sight in case people started to break out their cell phones and take pictures.

"I didn't stick around to find out," she said. "All I know is when you took off after that owlwoman, Fin called Lillian to let her know we was coming over. When we got to her place, the whole damn coven was there. When they all took off, so did I."

"I don't know how they found us in the cemetery, but I'm sure glad they did." I shuddered at the thought of what would have happened if the witches of the grove hadn't shown up to save my ass. "Do you know what Ijibah planned to do with me?" I asked, still irked at the thought. "She threatened to keep me chained up like a pet. Then she said she might put me on display in a cage in the middle of one of the squares. My birthday would have come and gone, and I'd be some sideshow attraction for—" It suddenly occurred to me that I had no idea how long a dragon lived.

"For eternity," Aunt Marianna said, completing my thought. "A zmaj dragon rarely dies. Although it is possible to kill one, a full-blooded zmaj will never die of natural causes. Which is another reason why I chose to alter my own destiny when I was your age." She took a bite of her breakfast. "I like pancakes, and I have no desire to live for eternity. When my time comes, I plan to welcome the afterlife with open arms."

"Amen to that," Sugar said, snapping her fingers. "You ever read any of them stories about people dying and coming back to life? It's so nice on the other side, they just want to stay dead." She took a bite of her pancakes and contemplated the idea a little more. "Shoot. If I'm still alive at a hundred, I'm pushing my wheelchair off the bridge into the river."

"But how did the coven know where to find us?"

"Mama told Fin that the cone of power had to be somewhere near all them bodies they been digging up over at the construction site. Didn't take no rocket scientist to figure out that the cemetery next door was overflowing with Ijibah's dead relatives. Well, the ones buried around the outskirts of that fancy iron fence they put up around it. Besides, when they got to the construction site, they saw that light beaming into the sky. Either them ghosts were having them a disco party, or the grieving widow was about to raise Cain."

"I wonder what they'll do to Ijibah?" I figured the council would either let her rot forever in some dungeon with those bones around her neck, or they'd sentence her to death—permanently this time.

Sugar shrugged. "I guess they'll have one of them tribunals they like so much."

I scoffed. "Yeah, like the council has ethics."

I was sure Fin would be having a conversation with me soon. Killing a fire witch was no easy task, especially when she'd just keep coming back if she wasn't dealt with properly. If they did sentence her to death, it would involve dark magic to do it, and I knew part of that dark magic would involve me raining down on her like a fire storm. I hoped there was another way, without me being the ultimate executioner. Self-defense was one thing, but aiming a hurricane of fire at a caged target was something I wasn't sure I could do.

"Katie? *Katie?*" Aunt Marianna pulled me back from the horrible thoughts running through my head. "We have to prepare for tonight."

I nodded. "Yes. I guess so."

"Let's see," she began, running the ritual steps through her mind. "There's the potion you'll need to take an hour before we begin. It will lessen the pain, if there is any. Before the ritual begins, I'll have you change into a special robe that's designed to burn swiftly with a natural accelerant. Without it, you won't meet the precise timing of your death."

"Damn!" Sugar said. "Katie told me all about this burning alive shit, but I don't know if I can handle all this detail."

"It's okay if you can't be there, Sugar." I tried to give her an out clause for having to witness her best friend go up in flames and possibly burn to death. "I'll understand. Hell, I don't know if I could watch it myself."

Her face turned indignant, like I'd suggested she boycott my wedding. "Oh, I'm gonna be there. I'm just a little nervous about everything."

You're nervous?

I made a mental note to give her permission to abort one last time before we started the ritual tonight, right after I drank that stuff that was supposed to dull the pain.

"I guess we won't be doing it in here," I said, looking around my living room. "Wouldn't want to set the house on fire, would we?" It was a poor attempt at humor, but no one was laughing. I pointed toward the patio door. "Out there, maybe?"

Marianna smiled sympathetically. "We'll perform it at my house. I have a space suited for this type of ritual."

"Your house?" Sugar and I both said in unison.

"Where the hell is that?" Sugar asked. "I ain't traveling, and I ain't leaving my best friend to face that damn dragon alone either. No offense, but you ain't nothing but a distant relative."

"I would expect no less of you, Sugar. I hope it's not too much of an inconvenience to drive just outside of town."

My head cocked as I tried to understand what she was saying. "Wait a minute. Are you telling me you live here? In Savannah?"

The look on her face was a mixture of amusement and surprise. "Yes, of course. I live where you live. At least until after your birthday." She looked back and forth at our shocked faces. "Where did you think I lived?"

She seemed so genuinely perplexed by my reaction, that I had a hard time being angry with the fact that all this time she was just a short drive away. I could have gotten to know her better.

"Why didn't you tell me?"

She shrugged. "I guess I assumed you knew. I didn't think you cared where I lived."

I looked her in the eye. "All I ask of people is that they never lie to me, inadvertently or not. Don't ever do it again."

"I promise," she said. "Now, the clock is ticking. Let's get down to business."

26

A fter Sugar and my aunt left that morning, I spent the day doing busy work around the house. I must have scrubbed my kitchen so spotless, it would have come up clean under a microscope. Then I sat down with Jet and explained that he might be going to live with Sugar. I also told him he needed to like that idea and behave so he didn't end up on the street again. I even compiled a list of his favorite foods and his eating schedule.

Sugar showed up around nine p.m., and Aunt Marianna arrived a few minutes later to take us to her house. It took less than forty minutes to reach it, tucked away behind a veil of mature oak trees about a quarter of a mile off the road that led us deep into the country. She'd explained that she preferred animals over people, and she'd chosen a property that would isolate her from the latter, only requiring her to come into town to stock up on groceries and other necessities.

"This is nice," I said when we arrived at the house.

A set of headlights pulled up behind us. Sugar climbed out of the Eldorado and looked around the property. "Kind of spooky living out here all by yourself. Ain't you worried about some crazy maniac breaking in?"

She laughed and headed for the front door. "You're forgetting what I am." She was referring to the fact that while she looked like your average fortyish woman who wouldn't stand a chance against a band of marauding home invaders, she was actually just like me. Anyone attempting to do her harm would regret it the moment she sprouted her wings and unleashed her dragon.

"Oh, that's right," Sugar said. "I guess that means there ain't going to be some big ol' guard dog behind that door, since you don't need one for protection."

Marianna opened the door, and out came a beast who made a beeline straight for Sugar. The black Great Dane jumped up and attempted to put its front paws on her shoulders, sending her tumbling backward against a large bush.

"Wolfgang, off!" Marianna ordered.

The giant dog sniffed Sugar, running its soft jowls over her face before heeling at his master's side. "Sorry about that. He's very friendly, unless you give him a reason not to be."

Sugar straightened back up and adjusted her wig. "I guess so. Now let's get inside so I can wash this dog off my face." I snickered as she walked past me. "Yeah, that's real funny, girl. Don't be calling me for help if that thing takes a shine to your leg."

My nerves settled a little when we walked inside. The house was beautiful. A sprawling mid-century ranch, it had a cavernous sunken living room that led to a giant wall of windows framing the back of the house. It was huge, with unusually high ceilings that reached up to a loft area on the right side of the room. Beyond the windows was a paved patio that must have been as long and wide as the living room, with a fire pit at the far end and a large fountain that fed into a small pond adjacent to it.

"We'll perform the ritual on the patio," Marianna said.

Seemed like an appropriate spot to set someone on fire. The

fact that we didn't see a single house for miles as we drove out would guarantee our privacy.

She threw her bag on the entryway table and headed toward the hallway. "Make yourselves at home. I'll be right back."

Sugar wasted no time nosing around the place. She stepped down into the sunken living room and dragged her finger along the back of the sofa on her way to get a better look at the backyard. "This stuff ain't cheap," she commented, picking up a figurine on the table to examine the mark on the bottom. "What did you say she does for a living?"

"I didn't. Good question though." I had no idea where my aunt got her money. For all I knew, she robbed banks.

Marianna returned a few minutes later and set a tray of food and drinks on the coffee table. "I hope you like cheese. I wasn't sure if either of you were meat eaters, and cheese seems to satisfy both carnivores and vegetarians. We'll have to play it by ear if either of you are vegan."

Sugar twirled her index finger over the dazzling array of cheeses. "You just whipped this up? You've been in that kitchen less than five minutes."

Marianna smiled. "I threw it together before driving over to pick you up this evening."

"Well, I'm a carnivore," Sugar said. "But I do like me some fine cheese." She reached across the platter and spread some Roquefort on a cracker. "The stinkier the better." She devoured it in a single bite.

Marianna glanced at the clock on the fireplace mantel and synced her wrist watch down to the second. "It's almost eleven, and I bet you haven't eaten since breakfast."

Knowing I had to drink something foul that required food in my stomach, I forced myself to eat a few crackers topped with cheese. After swallowing the third one, Marianna got up and went to get my pain reducing cocktail. She returned with a glass containing a dark brown liquid.

I looked at the glass and took a deep breath. "The simmered eyeballs?"

She chuckled and handed it to me. "It's really not that bad, and you *must* drink it all." Without hesitating long enough to change my mind, I turned up the glass and downed every drop. The flavor reminded me of roasted peppers with a hint of honey.

"Good girl. Now Remember, the goal is to begin at the exact moment when you're between the woman and the dragon. You'll be halfway into your transition, so your human skin will be tough enough to fend off the flames. But the dragon's skin will be just starting to form, making it weak enough to burn."

"What about this?" I nodded toward my green skin. I was already lingering somewhere in between, which meant I was ahead of schedule. I figured I was already where I needed to be when I lit that match.

She began to reiterate all the things that could go wrong. "If you start too soon, your skin won't be strong enough to withstand the fire. But by the looks of you, that won't be a problem. I hope," she muttered under her breath. She hesitated before continuing. "You'll have to rely on your instincts, Katie. You'll know when the time is right."

Well, that really helped. If I lit that match too soon, I'd burn to death. So would the dragon. "Remind me of what happens if I start too late."

"Then the dragon wins. It's the same outcome as if we did nothing at all. The beast will wake up permanently and become the master." She ran her hand over my rough hybrid skin. "Unfortunately, your current predicament also gives the dragon a head start. We won't have a second to waste. In fact, I think we should start a minute early before this dragon skin becomes impenetrable. I could hold a match to your skin right now, and you might not feel a thing." Then she looked at my hands and feet which were barely green. "You'll have to tuck these under your arms and legs to minimize any damage."

She suddenly went quiet. The look of concern on her face did nothing for my confidence. "I'll do it," she said. "I'll light the fire when the time is right."

I stared at her in disbelief. "I thought I had to set myself on fire?"

She shook her head. "Most of us are alone when we do this, so it's usually not an option. And there are few volunteers," she added. "But I've done this enough to know exactly when the time is right." She glanced at my green skin. "And since your circumstances are a bit unusual, I think it's best."

In other words, I'd fuck it up. "Thank you," I said, feeling tremendous relief.

She smiled at me. "Of course. You're my family."

"What about my hair?" I suddenly realized I might be borrowing wigs from Sugar for a while—if I survived.

She grinned and took one of my black locks between her fingers. "There isn't a fire in the universe strong enough to burn the hair of a dragon. It holds a great deal of your power." She cocked her head curiously. "Haven't you ever wondered why you rarely cut it? When you do, it grows back quickly, doesn't it? Practically overnight."

It was true. I couldn't remember the last time I had it cut. It was a waste of money.

Sugar was listening intently to the conversation. "Well, I hope to hell you know what you're doing, lady."

Marianna looked at her and sighed. "I've assisted with this ritual more times than I care to remember. Keep in mind that I've been through it myself. But there are no guarantees." Then she turned back to me. "You have until 11:59 p.m. to change your mind. We either start, or you end up with your father at Mount Triglav by dawn."

"No." I shook my head firmly. "We're doing this."

She nodded once and got up to leave again. When she returned, she was carrying the ritual robe over her arm. "You can change in there," she said, pointing to a door on the other side of the living room.

I came back in a few minutes later wearing the plain black robe that smelled of something bitter—the accelerant I assumed. "Now what?" I glanced nervously at the fire pit that was suddenly ablaze on the patio.

"Whatever you'd like," she said. "You should try to relax, if you can."

As I sat down on the sofa, a warm feeling rushed through me, like a shot of whiskey sliding down my throat. It must have been the potion kicking in. I sank deeper into the cushions and let it lull me into a hazy state of semi-sleep.

"She okay?" I heard Sugar ask from what sounded like the far end of a tunnel.

I could have sworn only a few minutes had passed before I felt Marianna's hand leading me out to the center of the patio. I turned back to see Sugar standing in the doorway.

"It's safer for her to stay inside," Marianna's distant voice said. "Now, remember to tuck your hands and feet."

I nodded.

"Are you ready, my darling?" she whispered.

I knelt down on my calves, covering as much of my feet as possible. Then I tucked my hands under my arms and closed my eyes before nodding my head.

As the second hand on her watch reached a minute before midnight, she lowered a torch into the fire pit. She touched it to my sleeve and set it ablaze. The accelerant sent the fire racing up my robe and across my shoulders, quickly engulfing me. I fought to keep my eyes sealed shut as the robe disintegrated and the flames licked at my skin, fearing I'd see my flesh melting away from my bones, triggering the pain to break through the veil of drugs shielding me from agony. My ears were filled with the sound of crackling flames, and then the world went silent as the strangest sensation came over me. I felt like I was splitting in two.

Taking a leap of faith, I slowly opened my eyes and gazed through the blue flames that were now silent and soothing against my skin. I was no longer looking at Sugar and Aunt Marianna with my own eyes, but the dragon's.

A flicker of movement appeared in my peripheral vision, but it quickly disappeared as my eyes tracked across the darkness and the silhouette of the trees. A second later, my senses flared from a familiar smell hitting my nose. But before I could place the scent, a pressure began to build in my gut, twisting and fighting against my stomach and ribcage with such force that I thought something was about to burst through the walls of my chest. I nearly doubled over from the pain, but then the battle inside of me went eerily still like a switch had been flipped. And then I opened my mouth and screamed, releasing a tsunami of fire from the pit of my stomach, through the pathway of my solar plexus.

Sugar gasped in horror, glancing at the flowing fountain feeding water to and from the pond.

"Don't even think about it!" Marianna hissed. "If you can't handle this, leave!"

Sugar heeded her warning and stared back at me helplessly, anguished by the scene that would probably give her nightmares for years.

I pulled my eyes away from hers and looked down at my arms, trying to pinpoint where an unsettling smell was coming from. The fire was out, but my skin was black and charred, incinerated by the flames. "No," I whispered, trying to stand up. Something went wrong. My skin was supposed to be strong enough to withstand the fire, but it was literally burnt to a crisp and beginning to fall away from my muscles. Thank God I was numb and felt nothing but a flood of emotions. Aunt Marianna had miscalculated. We'd started too soon, before my skin was ready. But at least I would never become the dragon's slave, because I figured we were both about to die.

Something stabbed me deep in my chest, and my lungs filled with heat. I couldn't breathe. I fell backward and the stars came into view.

"Help me pick her up!" I heard someone say. "We have to get her inside!"

And then there was nothing.

THE STEADY TICK of a clock filled my ears as I floated in darkness. If this was death, it was a lot nicer than I expected. I saw no light pulling me toward it and no grim reaper beckoning me toward the gates of hell. I was surrounded by a quiet and peaceful nothing.

A second later, my eyes popped open as I gasped violently for air, catapulting myself off the floor.

"Take it easy, baby," I heard Sugar say. "You've been out for a while, but everything's going to be fine."

"Katie?" Marianna said, touching my arm. I looked down at my sunburned skin beneath her hand.

"We did it?" I asked.

She shook her head. "You did it."

"But I saw my skin. It was black and charred."

"You saw the dragon's skin," she corrected. "We were right to start early. If we had waited another minute, it would have been too late."

I reached for my face and felt my tender but intact skin. Then

I checked the hair cascading over my shoulders. I also counted my fingers and toes and realized I was naked. Aunt Marianna grabbed a blanket from the chair and draped it over me.

A laugh burst from my mouth. "So it's over? I'm normal?"

"Ain't nothing normal about you, girl," Sugar said. She had me in a death grip a moment later. "I was so scared when I saw you out there looking like a human torch. I almost threw your ass in that fountain." She nodded to it through the window, and then fought back a cracking sound in her voice. I'd never seen Sugar cry, and for some reason, it felt wrong. "But Marianna gave me the stank eye before I could do it," she continued. "That woman is downright scary."

Feeling a little unsteady, I headed for the sofa. I must have turned around too fast, because I got a little lightheaded and saw a flash of fire in my eyes. It was enough to halt me in my tracks.

"You okay, baby?" Sugar asked.

Instead of answering, I turned around to look at them. Sugar gasped so loud she lost her footing and landed on the floor. Aunt Marianna reached down to help her up—and to move her back a few feet to make room.

"Take a deep breath and control yourself, Katie." Aunt Marianna's voice was firm. "You're in charge now."

Something was wrong. The dragon had never emerged so quickly, and with so much haywire energy, making me feel like an over-caffeinated bull in a china shop. It was like putting on roller skates for the first time, awkwardly trying to get my bearings.

My wings exploded from my sides, flapping wildly from one end of the expansive living room to the other. Marianna winced as a bookcase full of delicate trinkets toppled over, sending porcelain and glass smashing in every direction. The house shook as my back repeatedly slammed against the high ceiling. But as much as I wanted to crash through the wall of glass windows and fly off into the night, I was stuck floating in place.

"What the hell is happening!" Sugar yelled, taking an involuntary—and foolish—step toward me.

Marianna grabbed her by the arm and moved her back against the wall. "Apparently the dragon is having a hard time taking orders," she said. "It's awake, but it hasn't quite realized that it's not in charge anymore. It feels chained. Hence, its inability to move from its place."

"Well, do something!" Sugar said.

"Katie!" I heard someone say behind me.

Sugar and Aunt Marianna glanced past me. They looked surprised, and a fleeting smile crossed Sugar's face.

Another bookcase came crashing down when I whipped around. Jackson caught the tip of my wing before it could slice through his chest, and my heart skipped a beat. I planted my talons back down on the floor and let out a roar, sending a stream of fire in his direction. He dodged it just in time and looked at the spot where it singed the door. Then he turned back to me and furrowed his brow.

"I guess you're the boyfriend," Marianna said as he glared at me in disbelief. "Don't be offended by her attempt to skewer you and toast you alive. She can't help it. Her mind is saying one thing, but the dragon isn't listening. She needs to calm down and realize she's the boss now."

"*Ex*-boyfriend," Sugar corrected. "But since he showed up, I guess we'll give him a little bit of credit."

"You didn't think I'd let her go through this alone, did you?" he said.

"Well, you sure as hell rode out of town awful fast." Sugar snorted and bobbed her head. "Hell, I'm surprised you even bothered to listened to that message I left you last night."

"What message?" he shot back.

"Enough!" Marianna said. "The two of you can continue your feud after we've talked the dragon down."

Jackson gave Sugar a fierce glare and then turned back to me. I was stunned, frozen in place as my dragon waned in and out of its stupor. He stepped closer and reached for me, but the dragon refused to let him near, and I knew why. Our connection was too powerful. Confused or not, the beast knew the one thing that could turn the power in my favor was the man standing across the room.

I let out a warning growl that shook the house.

"For fuck's sake!" Jackson hissed, lunging forward to grab the edge of my wing. He yanked it with his freakish strength and brought me tumbling toward him. I slid and hit the wall, bringing the pictures crashing down in a shower of glass. The next thing I knew, he was straddling me, running his hands over my scaled face, bringing me back from that place where the dragon and I were both trapped.

"You better remember who the fuck you are," he growled back at me. "You're Katie Bishop, and you're coming home with me."

I could feel the beast fading and my strength growing. Within a couple of minutes, Jackson was stroking my sunburned but human skin.

Sugar cautiously approached us, but Aunt Marianna grabbed her wrist and shook her head. "Give it a minute. We need to make sure the dragon knows its place, and that man is doing a damn good job of fortifying her authority over the beast."

A few minutes later, Jackson stood up and extended his hand to pull me off the floor. I got to my feet and took a few steps back to put some distance between us. "Where the hell have you been for the past week?" Before he could answer, I brushed my disheveled hair out of my face and grabbed the closest object within reach—a small figurine on the coffee table—and hurled it at him. "You're an asshole! I love you!"

He caught it with one hand and stepped forward, reaching

for my waist to pull me against him. After a thorough kiss, he took my hand and led me toward the door, where I suspected his Harley was parked just outside.

"Uh, Katie," Sugar said as we were about to leave.

I smiled back at her, making a mental note to call her in the morning to thank her for being such an amazing friend. "What, Sugar?"

She gave me her signature smirk. "Baby, you naked as a jaybird."

27

Jackson walked into MagicInk around noon. I'd promised him a burger over at Lou's if he could manage to forgive me for being such an inconsiderate ass the day I practically shoved him out of my life. The cat was out of the bag. I'd used the *L* word the night before, and a couple more times after we got home and spent the night making up for lost time.

God knows what would have happened if he hadn't shown up at my aunt's house when he did. When I asked him how he knew where the ritual was taking place, he told me that he'd had his eye on me. And then there was the fact that Sugar had called him and left a message, but he hadn't gotten around to listening to it. He didn't need to, since he'd been stalking me that day. Not in a creepy way, but in a concerned way. He said he was prepared to respect my wishes if I still wanted him gone after the ritual.

"Good morning, Superman," I said as he walked over and bent down to see what Sea Bass was tattooing on my thigh. It was a Harley with the letter *J* worked into the center.

He gave me a curious look, knowing how out of character it was for me to do something so impulsive. I was always commenting about what a bad idea it was to put someone's name on your skin, especially a permanent reminder of your future ex.

"I figured I can always think of the *J* as homage to my cat if you decide to leave me," I said, referring to the other man in my life—Jet.

"And the bike?" he asked.

"Well, Harleys are always cool."

Sea Bass turned off the machine and wiped the excess ink off my skin. "All done." He glanced at Jackson. "Don't make her regret it."

The door opened, and in walked Fin sporting a grin. "I can't tell you how pleased I am to see you in one piece, Miss Bishop." He acknowledged Jackson with a nod. Then he glanced at my new tattoo. "I suppose this means you'll be sticking around, Mr. Hunter?"

"You got a problem with that?" Jackson replied, knowing that Fin Cooper had an affection for me that sometimes blurred the lines of professionalism. It was harmless, and I wasn't convinced it was anything more than curiosity.

Fin gave him a polite smile but didn't respond to the remark. He took a seat and crossed his ankle over his knee. "I thought you might like an update on Ijibah."

"You could have just called."

"Well, yes, but then I wouldn't have the pleasure of your company." It was one of Fin's standard lines whenever he decided to deliver news to me in person. I could almost recite it as it came out of his mouth. "Ijibah was brought before the council last night."

I held my breath and waited to hear her fate. A death sentence would require me to decide whether to comply with the council's orders or leave them to find an alternate means of sending her back to the grave. "And?" I said when he paused.

"The Southern Council of Witches has sentenced Ijibah to an eternity of servitude."

"What does that mean?"

"It means she'll be indentured to the council until they tire of her. If and when that happens, they'll send her back to the grave for the last time." Seeing the concern on my face, he clarified. "Don't worry, Miss Bishop. She'll serve her time far away from Savannah. If and when they decide to destroy her, you and I will be having another conversation. However, I don't anticipate that happening for a very long time."

I was relieved that the business of catching Ijibah was over, but there was still another matter. "Go on, Fin. Spit it out."

"If you're referring to the death of Ingrid Walsh, you can relax. Due to the nature of the incident—"

"You mean how she attacked me first."

Fin sighed and continued. "In light of your participation in the capture of a dangerous criminal, the council has absolved you of any wrongdoing."

Sea Bass snickered. "Well, ain't that nice of them."

I suspected Fin felt the same way, that the council was an intrusion that he was glad to see go. He stood up and headed for the door. "You're a free woman," he said without looking back.

As he left, I wondered how long it would be before he walked back into my life with the next calamity. But right now, I was just happy to be done with the current one.

"You ready for lunch?" Jackson asked.

I examined the tattoo in the mirror. "Looks good, Sea Bass."

He folded his arms and looked at his handiwork. "Damn straight it does."

"We're heading over to Lou's for lunch," I said, heading for the door. "Hold down the fort."

Jackson and I walked across the street and ordered at the counter before grabbing our usual booth. A couple of minutes later, I heard my name yelled across the room. As Jackson got up to retrieve our food, I thought about how lucky I was to have someone like him. You could go your entire life without ever finding that one person who fit you like a missing puzzle piece. I was pretty sure I'd found mine. I also knew him well enough to know when something was bothering him.

"You know, Jackson," I began as I swallowed a bite of my grilled cheese. "It's been a while since you and I have had the luxury of sitting down to enjoy a good greasy meal in peace. The only thing that could possibly make this moment better would be for you to tell me what the hell is wrong."

He set his burger down on the plate and finished chewing his mouthful of food. After swallowing, he reached around to scratch the back of his neck, which was one of those little habits I'd learned to recognize when something was eating at him. "Yeah. I guess we need to have a talk."

"Okay, now you're making me nervous." We'd been back together for less than twenty-four hours, and he was telling me we needed to have a talk?

He cut to the chase. "I got a call from Cairo a few days ago." Cairo and his clan were old friends of Jackson's. They also happened to be something called Dimensionals, shifters with the unique ability to take on the form of inanimate objects, like walls and doors. Even something as massive as a bridge. "Kaleb is on his way to Savannah. The whole damn pack is coming."

"The Sapanths?" I suddenly lost my appetite. The Sapanths were a pack of shifters out of Atlanta that he used to ride with. He'd told me about Kaleb and his daughter—who he'd had a brief affair with—right after we met. "Is Kara coming with them?"

He let out a short laugh that had no humor in it. "She's the reason they're coming."

"Jackson? What are you trying to tell me?"

Kaleb was the leader of the Sapanths, and he was not pleased when he found out that Jackson had slept with his daughter and took off not long after, deserting the club for fear that he had a bounty on his head.

"I'm trying to tell you that Kaleb wants his daughter married off, and I'm the lucky guy."

"Because you slept with her?" I couldn't believe Kaleb thought he could force Jackson to marry Kara. "This is the twenty-first century, Jackson."

"Ever hear of a shotgun wedding?"

"That's not funny." I forced myself to take another bite of my grilled cheese. "Damn it, Jackson. I thought we might actually have a little normalcy around here for a while. At least until Fin shows up again," I muttered under my breath.

He reached over the table and squeezed my hand. "Don't worry, I'll handle it. I just wanted to warn you. I wouldn't put it past him to show up at the shop to check out his daughter's competition."

"I dare him," I said, not intimidated in the slightest about meeting the dangerous shifter who thought he owned Jackson.

He let go of my hand and leaned back into the booth. "That son of a bitch couldn't care less about finding an appropriate husband for his daughter. He just wants the money."

"Money?" I said, swallowing my mouthful of food. "What money?"

———

READ KATIE BISHOP'S BACKSTORY TODAY!

Want to know more about Katie? Read THE FITHEACH TRILOGY and find out where it all began.

THANK YOU TO MY READERS

A book means nothing without someone to read it. Thank you for that. I hope you'll consider taking a few minutes to leave a brief review, even if it's just a sentence or two. Feedback is always appreciated and vital for authors.

ALSO BY LUANNE BENNETT

THE FITHEACH TRILOGY

The Amulet Thief (Book 1)

The Blood Thief (Book 2)

The Destiny Thief (Book 3)

THE KATIE BISHOP SERIES

Crossroads of Bones (Book 1)

Blackthorn Grove (Book 2)

Shifter's Moon (Book 3)

Dark Nightingale (Book 4)

Bayou Kings (Book 5)

Conjure Queen (Book 6)

Dirt Witch (Book 7)

Daddy Darkest (Book 8)

HOUSE OF WINTERBORNE SERIES

Dark Legacy (Book 1)

Savage Sons (Book 2)

King's Reckoning (Book 3)

THE CHRONICLES OF JESSE AMES

Red Widow (Book 1)

Gods & Savages (Book 2)

Sign up for news and updates about future releases!

LuanneBennett.com

ACKNOWLEDGMENTS

As always, I owe so much to the Katie Bishop Beta Reader Group for reading the book and providing priceless feedback—on the shortest notice ever!

Thank you to my clan: Sonja, Joshua, David, and Gina for donating your precious time and talent. Thank you, Jen, for tirelessly combing through the manuscript for all those imperfections we writers blow right past without seeing.

And of course, Sharon—you know why.

ABOUT THE AUTHOR

LUANNE BENNETT is an author of fantasy and the supernatural. Born in Chicago, she lives in Georgia these days where she writes full time and doesn't miss a thing about the cubicles and conference rooms of her old life. When she isn't writing or dreaming up new stories, she's usually cooking or tending a herd of felines.

I love to hear from readers. Contact me at:
www.luannebennett.com
books@luannebennett.com
facebook.com/LuanneBennettBooks

Printed in Great Britain
by Amazon